COURT
OF
WINTER

KRISTA STREET'S SUPERNATURAL WORLD

Links to all of Krista's books may be found on her website:
www.kristastreet.com

COURT
OF
WINTER

fae fantasy romance
FAE OF SNOW & ICE
BOOK 1

KRISTA STREET

WELCOME TO THE FAE LANDS

Court of Winter is book one in the four-book *Fae of Snow & Ice* series, which is a slow-burn, enemies-to-lovers, fae fantasy romance.

This book takes place in the fae lands of Krista Street's *Supernatural World*. Although Krista's other paranormal romance books also feature the fae lands, the *Fae of Snow & Ice* series is entirely separate so may be read before or after her previous series.

Solis Continent

Brashier Sea

Ice Caves
Pentlebim

Kroravee

Isalee

Solisarium

Floating
Meadows

Prinavee

Gielis

Highsteer
Castle

Osaravee

Duval

Murlands

Harrivee

Suxbee

Bay
of
Korl

Barvilu

Tala Sea

Glassen
Barrier
Islands

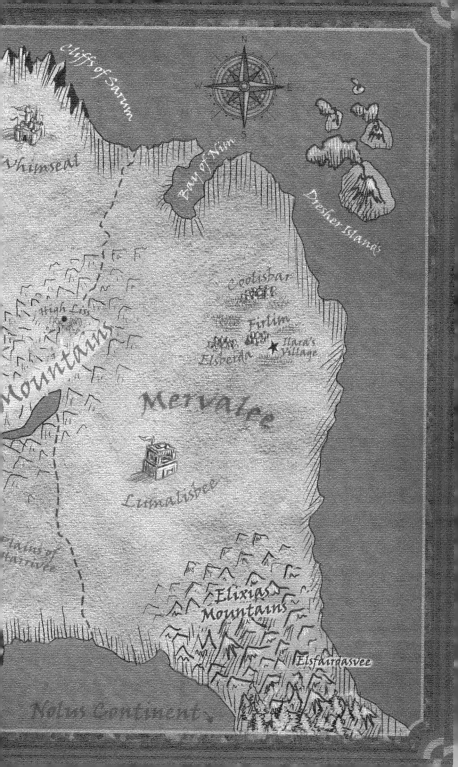

GLOSSARY

<u>Territories of the Solis Continent</u>

Harrivee – the middle southern territory, coastal cities often fighting with the Lochen fae. Territory color is yellow.

Isalee – the northernmost territory, Cliffs of Sarum on its northern peak. Territory color is white.

Kroravee – the northwestern territory, most reclusive territory, very unwelcoming even to other Solis fae. Territory color is purple.

Mervalee – the easternmost territory, richly blessed with *orem,* borders the Nolus continent. Territory color is green.

Osaravee – the southwestern territory, coastal cities often fighting with the Lochen fae. Territory color is red.

Prinavee – the central territory, where Solisarium, the capital of the Solis continent, resides. Territory color is the royal palate: blue, black, and silver.

✳

Seas of the fae lands

Adriastic Sea – the ocean to the west of the Nolus continent.

Brashier Sea – the most northern sea in the fae lands, large icebergs often present.

Tala Sea – the ocean to the south of the Solis continent.

Terms

Affinity – the magical ability that each Solis fae develops at maturing age. Maturing age happens around thirteen years of age in the hundreds-year-long life span of a Solis fairy. A Solis fairy's affinity can be common or quite rare, weak or very strong. Most Solis fae only have one affinity. Very powerful Solis fae have more than one.

Archon – a fairy that holds power over a village, city, territory, or land. There are tiers of archons, and the more land that an archon manages, the more politically powerful that archon is. The most powerful archon on the Solis continent is King Novakin.

Blessed Mother – a magical life force of the fae lands that nurtures growth and life among the fae. The Blessed Mother is not a goddess but a force from nature that is similar in strength and power to the gods. The Blessed Mother is believed to reside deep within the land at the heart of the planet. This belief is unique to the Solis fae.

Defective – a Solis fae who is magicless and never develops an affinity.

Full season – the equivalent of one year.

Millee – the Solis fae unit of measurement, the equivalent of one mile.

Orem – the magic that infuses the Solis continent, allowing plants and crops to grow in freezing temperatures. *Orem* is replenished by celestial events and comes from the gods.

Solls – a term Solis fae use when they clink glasses to celebrate, like Cheers.

Fae races

Solis fae – the Solis fae reside on the icy, most northern continent of the fae lands planet. Solis fae have silvery white hair, crystalline blue eyes, and wings. They typically live for thousands of years.

Nolus fae – the Nolus fae reside on the central continent. They often have various shades of colorful hair, pointy teeth, glowing skin, and otherworldly strength. They typically live three hundred years, but royal Nolus fae live for thousands of years.

Lochen fae – the Lochen fae reside on a southern continent, islands, and in the seas throughout the fae lands. They can morph into fish-like creatures, similar to mermaids, but they can also walk on two legs and live on land. There are subspecies of Lochen fae that live in fresh-water rivers, lakes, and ponds. The Lochen fae typically have green eyes and varying skin shades and hair colors.

Silten fae – the Silten fae reside on a separate continent across the Adriastic Sea, west of the Nolus continent. They have animalistic features: horns, scales, hooves, and tails, and they are the most varied in how they appear. Most live in underground dens, hollow logs, or wooded forests, but Silten fae with more human-like bodies reside in cities.

Fae plants and food

Acorlis – a root vegetable, sweet flavor with an orange skin, similar to a sweet potato.

Cottonum – a plant similar to cotton.

Leminai – a bright-green alcoholic drink common throughout the fae lands.

Salopas – a fairy version of a bar with no serving staff. There are magically enchanted trays that serve patrons.

Fae animals

Colantha – a large cat that resides in jungles.

Domal – an animal similar to a horse but more intelligent.

Ice bear – a large bear with a naturally white furry coat and six-inch claws, which stands eight feet tall on two legs. An ice bear's coat can change color to match its surroundings.

Snowgum – the most feared ice creature whose magical ability allows it to become invisible for short spans. Snowgums resemble a large feline.

Trisilee – a tiny bird with wings that flap hundreds of miles per hour, like a hummingbird.

PRONUNCIATION GUIDE

Names

Ilara Seary – Ill-are-uh Seer-ee

Norivun Achul – Nor-ih-vun Ah-cool

Cailis – Kay-liss

Krisil – Kris-ill

Evis – Eve-iss

Sandus – Sand-us

Balbus – Bell-bus

Patrice – Pah-treese

Haisley – Hay-slee

Nuwin – New-win

Daiseeum – Day-zee-um

Novakin – Naw-vah-kin

Lissandra – Li-sahn-druh

Drachu – Draw-koo

Michas – My-kiss

Sirus – Seer-us

Meegana – Mee-gah-nuh

Georgyanna – George-ee-ah-nuh

<u>Fae Races & Territories</u>
Solis – Saw-liss

Nolus – Naw-luss

Lochen – Lock-uhn

Silten – Sill-tun

Mervalee – Merr-vuh-lee

Isalee – Iss-ah-lee

Prinavee – Prin-uh-vee

Harrivee – Hair-uh-vee

Osaravee – Oh-sar-uh-vee

Kroravee – Quor-uh-vee

CHAPTER 1

"This is a good one, don't you think, Ilara?" My sister, Cailis, held out a bread loaf for me to inspect.

The crust was firm and the loaf probably several days old. A few specks of mold discolored the bottom, but a sharp knife would cut it off, and the rest of the loaf looked edible.

I nodded. "Yes. Let's take it."

Cailis placed the bread in our basket as we carefully picked through the second-hand goods in Firlim's outdoor harvest market.

A light dusting of crystalline snow drifted in the air. The dazzling snowflakes covered the vendors' canopies in a fine layer of white lace as my sister and I shopped.

Today's selection was meager, as seemed to be the case lately, but if we picked the right items, we would have enough ingredients to add a variety to our meals this week.

My stomach growled. *Mother Below,* I was looking forward to supper. We hadn't eaten yet today.

Since the discounted portions of the market sat in sacks and buckets on the ground, we kept bending over, and as I neared the edge of the vendor's table, a female's cloak from the neighboring stall brushed against my face. She probably didn't even know I was there.

"They're dying, all of them," the female hissed to her friend. "They say all of their fields are filled with black stalks and gray dirt."

I cocked my head but stayed crouched.

"Oh, pish posh, you listen to too many rumors." The female's friend grabbed a warm shawl off the vendor's table as translucent snowflakes continued to fall from the sky.

"It's true." The first female tried on a hat as a few flecks of snow fell onto the wide rim, which hid the tips of her pointed ears. "All of their crops are dead. I heard the entirety of Isalee Territory is worried about starving this winter."

The other female sniffed. "It's all rumors. Never you mind. The celestial events ensure the land stays fertile."

"It's *not* a rumor. It's true!" Her friend huffed. She planted her hands on her hips, and her wings flexed with her annoyance. "Neither the Safrinite comet nor the alignment replenished our continent's magic. We were scorned, and because of it, our crops are dying. Just watch. We're all going to starve."

I straightened so quickly that my cloak's hood fell off my head. I tried to pull it back up, but both females froze when they saw my hair.

"What have you heard about Isalee?" I asked urgently, ignoring their shocked expressions as they assessed my unique hair color.

Both eyed my wingless back, then studied my hair again. The first female backed up, then pulled her friend with her.

"Please," I said in a softer tone, taking a step toward them. "Tell me."

I opened my mouth to ask more, to see what further they knew, but they both shook their heads and made the sign of the Blessed Mother before scurrying away.

A pit formed in my stomach and not from their dislike of my defective state. My brother, Tormesh, had told us the same thing about the crops last summer when he'd returned home following his march with the Solis Guard. He'd been adamant that the crops were dying in Isalee Territory because our land's *orem* hadn't been replenished during the last celestial event.

I squeezed my eyes shut at the memory of my brother's face as a familiar pained ache clenched my chest.

A finger poked my side, and I whirled around, holding onto my cloak's hood this time.

"Were they talking about dead crops?" Cailis said under her breath.

"Yes, it's the same as what Tormesh claimed."

A troubled look came over her face, but then she nodded at my cloak. "I keep telling you to secure it with clips."

I shrugged. "I was in a hurry this morning. Besides, I can't help that I'm different and defective, and if some fae are going to judge me for it, what can I do?"

Granted, even defectives had wings. Why the Mother hadn't blessed me with those, I didn't know, but no Solis fae had black hair. Everyone else's hair was white or silver, like a normal Solis, not black as pitch like mine.

I shuffled closer to my sister. "Are we done? I'm not sure we'll have enough rulibs to cover all of this." I held out our full basket.

Cailis frowned as she surveyed our choices. "That bread loaf should last us at least a week if we don't have more than one slice each morning. And the preserves are old, but they still appear good."

"What about meat? Do we have enough for a cut?"

Cailis pulled out the coins from her pocket and counted them carefully. "At today's market value, we can afford half a cut. Should we indulge?"

I nodded. "We could have it with the radishes I pulled last week, and I'm guessing the potatoes will be just as plump. If we boil them and add a few of the greens, it'll be a filling meal."

"Thank the Mother your garden is doing so well. If that continues, we should be able to survive winter as long as we're frugal."

"It'll continue." I nodded toward the meat hanging from the vendor's canopy. "Are we buying it then?"

Cailis grinned, then pointed to one of the thick roasts and asked the vendor to cut off half a portion.

The vendor shook his head. "'Tis already sold. I have nothing available to sell to you."

My sister scowled. "That's a lie."

The vendor's lips parted as annoyance flashed across his face.

"My sister's affinity is truth," I explained quickly. "Perhaps you misunderstood her question. We would like to buy a cut of meat."

But the vendor's bushy eyebrows pulled together even more, and he crossed his arms. He studied my wingless frame next, then turned away. "We don't serve defectives here."

Oh. My jaw dropped as a flush worked up my neck.

Cailis's cheeks reddened. "Is there a good reason you don't? We have rulibs." She held out a palm of coins.

The vendor's disdainful expression grew. "On your way. I'm not selling to the likes of *her*."

Warmth bloomed across my chest as I struggled to keep my chin up.

Cailis dropped our full basket on his table, and the contents spilled everywhere. "Fine. We don't want to give the likes of *you* business anyway."

She grabbed my arm and hurried us away, but he was the third vendor in the market to deny us this season. Even though Firlim was vastly bigger than our village, I'd grown careless. I needed to ensure my cloak always stayed up so the locals here didn't begin to recognize our faces.

"I'm sorry," I said quietly to my sister as she marched us out of the market.

"Don't be. He's an ignorant dung-head. You've done nothing wrong, and not everyone's like him. Some are more sympathetic about your state."

But despite her reassurances, the sound of her growling stomach rang through my ears.

I picked at my fingers as we reached the edge of the market, and our pace slowed. Dirt was perpetually encrusted under my nails, not just from gardening, but also from our laboring job in the fields. It was humble work, but it kept a roof over our heads and provided enough pay that we didn't completely starve, although last winter it'd been close.

Nerves buzzing slightly, I lifted my chin and tried not to dwell on our shopping failure or what I'd heard those old females gossiping about. Surely, the gods wouldn't allow us to starve, not when it was their doing that had allowed our race to colonize the most northern continent in our realm. Our land's magic had *always* kept us fed despite our frozen climate.

But my brother's warning from last summer brushed against my mind like fluttering wings. *Maybe I should go to the council. They're saying the king won't listen.*

I locked down the ache that spread through my chest every time I thought of Tormesh, then brushed off the older females' comments once and for all.

Nothing good had come from talk like that. Cailis and I knew that all too well.

When we reached the edge of the city, I looped my arm through Cailis's. We were of similar height, so it was comfortable walking side by side.

"Thanks for having my back at the market."

She patted my hand. "Always. You know how I feel about bullies."

I glanced down and picked at my fingers once more.

"Has Vorl been bothering you again?"

"No, nothing more than usual." But I said it too quickly and didn't believe it enough to fool her affinity.

Her expression darkened.

The sun was setting by the time we reached the road to our village. We still had a long walk to get back home.

"You can fly if you want," I offered to Cailis when we finally maneuvered out of the narrow streets.

"And leave you to walk alone? Never." She squeezed my arm.

Guilt burned under my skin again, but I didn't argue with her. It never mattered if I did anyway. She always chose to walk at my side.

❄

IT TOOK two hours at a clipped pace to reach our small home on the edge of our village. Snow covered the front yard, and the old wooden boards of our single-level house needed a fresh coat of paint, but the roof was sturdy and didn't leak, the windows mostly unbroken—save for one small pane in the kitchen—and the fireplace provided enough heat to keep the living area warm. And even though our house was only four rooms, it was our family's home. Cailis and I had grown up here, and I wouldn't trade it for the entire realm.

"I'll get a fire started," Cailis said when we reached our property's edge.

I blew into my palms, trying to warm them. Heavy snow had fallen during our entire journey, and the temperature had dropped at least twenty degrees. The thin gloves I wore weren't cutting it.

"Are you coming in?" Cailis asked when I didn't follow.

"I'm going to check on the garden first. I'll be inside soon."

"But a gale's coming."

"I know. I won't be long."

She put her hands on her hips. "Just because we came home empty-handed doesn't mean you have to go work in the garden tonight. You've got to be as tired as me."

I smiled, forcing cheer into my voice. "I'm not tired. I'm fine. I'll be in soon." Not waiting for her to argue, I picked up a jog.

Her loud sigh followed, but without me hindering her further, she took flight. Her black wings lifted her effortlessly from the ground as she sailed the remaining distance to our home's front door.

Within seconds, she was inside, and my stomach twisted, knowing she would have been home hours ago if not for me.

Pressing my lips together, I hurried through the six inches of fresh powder on the ground as numbness spread through my toes.

Banging sounds came from inside our home as light glowed through the back windows. Cailis was stacking wood in the fire, and thanks to one of our neighbors giving us a kernel of his fire elemental affinity, she had it roaring in seconds. Following that, she dug through the kitchen cupboards, probably trying to find something for us to eat.

I stopped at the shed in the back and pulled out a few gardening tools. I knew it could probably wait until morning—and that Cailis thought I was only here to appease my guilt—but I had a feeling that now was the right time to harvest the acorlis. If plucked at just the peak moment, the thick root vegetable had a sweetness to it that was unparalleled.

The shed's door protested when I tried to pull it open against the accumulating snow. It took several tugs, but soon enough, I had several heavy tools in my arms. They clanged together and vibrated in my palms as I hefted them over my shoulder.

Angry-looking indigo and navy clouds swirled above. A gale was definitely on its way as the northern sky grew darker with each second that passed. But the richness of my garden that waited ahead soothed my anxiety at the upcoming winter.

I stepped over the edge of my field, and a tingle of magic brushed over my skin like an old friend saying hello.

Around me, my crops shone in a rainbow of colors: emerald green, bright periwinkle, burnt orange, vibrant magenta, and sunny yellow. Each vegetable, fruit, grain, and plant thrived in the rich soil blessed with *orem* in our frozen land, and seeing my plants made me feel as though I'd come home.

"Hello, friends," I whispered. Running my hands over the soft petals of a berry plant, I plucked a leaf off and studied the fine veins that wove throughout it. The leaf bent easily in my palm, which meant it was only days away from being ready to harvest. "I'll get to you soon enough, little one."

"Do you need a hand with those tools, sweet Ilara?" a male called from behind me.

A scent hit me next—cloves and tobacco.

I stiffened and dropped the leaf. It fluttered to the ground as more snow fell from the sky, but the thriving magic in my garden meant that most of the snow evaporated before it hit the ground.

Breaths coming faster, I was loathed to confront him, but if I didn't, he would follow me to the edge of my garden where I would be alone, magicless, and at his mercy.

It wouldn't be the first time.

"I'm fine, Vorl." I spun slowly to face him.

My village archon's smooth complexion always reminded me of my wheat in the spring. His cool blue eyes hid a heart of ice, and his leathery and heavily muscled black wings were so large they nearly dragged on the ground. Like all other Solis fae, he had near-white hair. In the dying light of the impending gale, it shone faintly silver.

"Why aren't you at the council meeting?" I asked him.

He shrugged and leaned against my shed. A piece of bread was pinched in his hand, and he ate it languidly. The scent and look of it . . .

I bristled. "I see you let yourself into our home again. Are you enjoying the last of our bread?" I cast a quick glance over his shoulder.

Sure enough, Cailis was visible through her bedroom window. She was putting laundry away and probably had no idea Vorl had let himself in through the front door and helped himself to the last of our loaf. The large fae male, heavily blessed with magic, could move as silently as the wind.

Vorl popped the final bite of bread into his mouth, his strong jaw working through the doughy ball. "Very much so. It's almost as delicious as you are."

He pushed away from the shed, straightening to his full height as a pulse of magic drifted from him when he rubbed his fingers together. His magic cleansed the butter and crumbs from his palms, his skin once again clean.

A moment of envy filled me at how powerful he was, and I wanted to kick myself for it. Of all the fae in my village to be envious of, it would *not* be him.

"Doing some late-night gardening?" he asked, nodding behind me.

My grip tightened on my tools. "No, I was just heading back inside. The weather is going to—"

"Don't lie to me, Lara." His voice turned icy. Brutal. The beast within him flared in his eyes, because that was what he was. A heartless, cruel, vindictive beast of a fairy.

I flinched, and a flicker of perverse delight shone in his eyes.

Don't show weakness. Do not *show him weakness.* Squaring my shoulders, I kept my chin up. "I'm not lying."

In a move so fast it was a blur, his hand locked around my throat, and my tools clattered to the ground just as a boom of thunder shook the land.

He spun me so fast the realm turned. A split second passed, then my back slammed into the shed as his grip on my neck tightened. The welcoming magic of my garden disappeared in an instant since we'd crossed the barrier. Icy wind bit into my cheeks as the shed's cold planks heaved at my back. My heart thundered as I struggled to breathe. I thrashed against him, fighting as hard as I could, but it was no use.

Vorl always overpowered me.

He leaned in close until his entire hard body was flush against mine. My small breasts were squashed under his powerful chest, and the sadistic light in his eyes grew. A gag worked up my throat, but he squeezed harder, and it stayed trapped in my chest.

"Do not lie to me, sweet Ilara. You know how much it displeasures me when you do that. I know you were just about to tend to your garden. You and I both know that the weather doesn't affect your land. Or do you think I didn't notice?" He increased the pressure of his palm, and I clawed at his large hand more, but he didn't budge.

"Lara?" My sister's distant call came from the house.

In a flash, Vorl released me and widened the distance between us. I gulped in air, my throat burning as I scrambled from behind the shed just as my sister emerged from our tiny home.

"Tell no one. Or you know what happens." That sadistic gleam glowed in his eyes again, and the heavy weight of his magic shot around me.

Warmth seared my throat, and the scent of casting magic fell over me like a heavy cloud. I knew he'd just hid the bruises he'd inflicted since Vorl's affinity was illusions. He excelled at them above all others.

Cailis's pace increased as she ventured across the crisp, frosty snow of our small yard. The second she saw Vorl, she stopped in her tracks, and her eyes narrowed to slits. "What are you doing here?"

He shrugged. "I was flying by on my way to the village when I saw Lara struggling with her tools. I offered to help."

Cailis's gaze dropped to the tools that lay in the dirt, bending several stalks of berries. She slowly returned her attention to Vorl's guileless expression. "If Lara needs help, I can do it."

My sister's fingers drummed against her thighs, and her wings flexed. She didn't stand a chance in a fight against Vorl, but she'd go down trying.

"Vorl was just on his way, weren't you?" I tried to say loudly, but my voice came out hoarse. I hurried back to my garden and carefully pulled my tools from the berry plant. Magic clouded around me. Familiar, warm, comforting magic pulsed from my garden's land, and some of the tension eased from my shoulders.

Vorl cleared his throat, and I turned back to him and my sister.

Cailis was still watching him. Poised. Ready.

He scoffed. "Another time then."

Vorl flexed his wings and gave me one last warning look before he shot into the sky.

The energy thrumming from my sister evaporated. "He's a fucking prick, that one," she said through clenched teeth.

"That he is."

Against the impending storm, Vorl's outline looked like a phantom on the wind. He flew high and fast, already so far away that he was a small figure in the sky. No, not a figure. He was more like a dark demon who had come from the underworld to wreak havoc on my soul.

"Are you okay?" Cailis helped me collect my remaining tools.

"Fine. I'm fine," I said firmly.

She studied me, her eyes darting down my throat and along my body even though my worn clothing and thick cloak hid my limbs and torso. My neck was exposed, though, but Vorl's illusion affinity was strong and hid the bruises that were no doubt blooming across my skin as assuredly as my acorlis needed harvesting.

I gave my sister what I hoped was a reassuring smile. "Go back inside and stay warm. I'll just be a moment. It won't take long to dig them up."

"But—"

"It's fine, Cailis. Truly, it is." I forced a bright smile. "I don't always need saving. I'm not hurt. See?" I held out my arms and tilted my neck even though my throat ached. It was such a familiar feeling that I barely noticed it. Choking me was one of Vorl's favorite pastimes when he got me alone. It had been ever since we were children.

Cailis's frown remained, but after looking me over a second time, she finally acquiesced.

When she disappeared back inside, and the door had shut firmly behind her, guilt spread through my veins like wildfire. Cailis had tried so many times to save me from Vorl because none of the other villagers knew how the male brute tormented me. I'd tried to tell them. Once. But Vorl's retaliation had quickly put any further uprising from me to rest. He was our village archon after all, and he held more power than I ever would.

Still, it didn't stop me from fighting back every time he

❄ 13 ❄

pinned me, but I was never strong enough to break free, especially since I held no magic, and the bastard knew that. It was no doubt why he'd chosen me as his favorite victim.

Alone in our yard, I tightened my grip on my tools as snow skittered on the wind, flying and blowing as the gale let loose.

When I stepped over my garden's magical barrier, though, the gale vanished. Warmth flowed across my skin as my small patch of land welcomed me into its fold. I took a moment, reveling in my garden's energy as it seeped into my soul.

I used it to calm my breathing, because I hated being the weak one. The one who was different. The one who was *less*.

A true defective.

But I was good at gardening, and it would keep us from starving.

At the end of the day, that was what mattered most.

CHAPTER 2

The storm raged above my garden as my fingers ran through the black dirt that felt as soft as butter. I crooned and sang softly to the acorlis as I plucked one after another of the ripe large root vegetable from its underground vine.

Its bright orange skin shone like the sun as I stuffed each vegetable deep into the pockets of my cloak. As I slashed through the vine's bounty, I thanked it for its life that would sustain our bellies through the long winter.

Despite the angry storm, I worked until it was so dark that I could barely see the thick vine snaking through the soil. I'd pulled over twenty feet of it and still hadn't found the end.

"You grew quite deeply into our Mother, didn't you, my friend?" I murmured to it, then stood and brushed dirt from my pants and cloak. "I shall have to finish tomorrow, though. For now, I think we should both rest. Don't you?"

I gave the acorlis a gentle pat before hurrying to the shed to grab a large bucket. Snow and ice needled my skin when I stepped over my garden's barrier. It was so cold that for a moment, my breath caught.

Closing my eyes against the storm's biting sting, I carefully made my way back to my garden. Once the bucket was overflowing with the succulent vegetable, I struggled to stand under its heavy weight.

Wind raged outside of the field, but despite the gale, my garden shone like an oasis, the colors vibrant and beautiful amidst the winter landscape.

"Goodbye, my friends. I shall see you tomorrow," I called when I reached my garden's edge.

A small smile curved my lips even though my arms were aching and my back sore. I held the bucket tightly as I trudged through the snow, struggling to get to the house.

When I reached it, I kicked the back door open just as goosebumps of awareness prickled the nape of my neck.

I swung around as Cailis leaped out of her chair by the fire to grab the bucket from my hands.

"What are you waiting for?" Cailis asked as she tried to pull me inside.

My feet planted at the threshold. Nothing but darkness, cold, and swirling snow stared back at me from our yard. But I felt . . . *something.*

I shook my head and rubbed my neck again. "Nothing," I said sheepishly. "For a moment . . . I thought I was being watched, but there's no one out there. It's nothing."

Cailis rolled her eyes. "You're probably just tired. You were working for over two hours. Come on inside and clean up." She eyed the bucket of acorlis, her eyes widening. "So many!"

"There's more. That's only from one vine."

"One?" Cailis's eyebrows shot to her hairline. "Didn't you plant six acorlis seeds this summer?"

"I did."

"You mean, there could be *six times* this much? But this bucket alone is what a dozen vines normally produce."

"I know. Amazing, isn't it?" I grinned. "There's still more on the first vine too. It got so dark that I couldn't finish."

"How is that possible?"

I shrugged and finally shut the door behind me as warmth from the fire kissed my cheeks. "The Mother has blessed us."

A hopeful expression stole over Cailis's features. "If there truly are as many as you say, we definitely won't starve this winter."

I took off my snow-laden cloak and hung it near the fire to dry, then loosened my braided hair and ran my fingers through the soft locks, not looking at its embarrassing black color as I worked the strands free.

Cailis shook her head, transfixed by the bucket, her face still a mask of wonder. "So many."

I held my hands to the fire, warming them as my smile returned.

Cailis picked a few acorlis and placed them on the counter, excitement buzzing around her. "These will be delicious with a drizzle of syrup. I think we have a little bit left. I'll boil a few for dinner while you're washing up."

After drying my damp hands, I made my way to the bathing chamber and stripped my dirty clothes before peeking out the window's curtain. A pot of water heated over the chamber's fire, and goosebumps pimpled my skin in the chill air as I waited for it to warm.

With the curtain parted just enough for me to peer outside, that strange feeling swam through me again. Something was out there.

Watching. Waiting.

But all that stared back at me in the glass was my own reflection as the storm continued to rage.

Shivering, I dropped the curtain.

I HELD onto my bowl as Cailis and I waited in line at our village's field kitchen. The large one-room barn provided our only shelter and a place to rest during our breaks from laboring. The wooden benches and sturdy tables that filled its expanse were a welcome reprieve from the long days on our feet.

Wind still howled through the barn's vertical wall slats since they weren't perfectly sealed, but a fire was always roaring in the kitchen's hearth, and the flames beneath the cooks' pots took the chill from the air.

Around me, the other field laborers from my village waited patiently for their bowls to be filled. Those in the front of the line joked and laughed, while those in the back wore irritated expressions. By the time they would be served, there would only be minutes to eat before the bell struck to return to the crops.

It'd been a rough morning since the weekend storm had raged for two straight days, dumping three feet of snow by the time it finished. No one had been able to fly during the gale yesterday since the air currents had been so strong, but today the sun burned bright and was quickly melting most of the autumn snow.

Still, even our field's *orem* hadn't been enough to clear the snow completely as was common in the winter months but less so in autumn, so we'd spent most of the morning scraping snow from the land. Thankfully, beneath the heavy piles of white flakes, the plants shone bright and healthy. Their leaves seemed to expand before my eyes, welcoming the low-lying sun that kissed their stalks. Seeing that always brought a smile to my lips.

"Good thing we wore our thick boots today," Cailis said as her wings wrapped around her upper arms, giving her extra warmth from the autumn chill.

I tightened the scarf that covered my head and made sure it was still pulled low over my brow. Everyone in my village knew of my hair color, but I still didn't like advertising it.

"Yes, I was thinking the same. My toes are already curling from the thought of what winter will bring." I tapped my work boots, and snowflakes fell from them.

"Do you think there's any meat in the broth today?" Birnee asked hopefully. She linked her arm through mine, drawing me closer as she wrapped a wing around me. Like all of the Solis fae in my village, her hair was silvery white and her eyes blue. Her wings were small and slight, though, much like her, but they still radiated warmth to my chilled skin. "Last week they had meat on our first day back to the fields following the weekend."

Finnley laughed, the sound low and deep as he gave her an impish grin. "That was only because a snow fox got into old Dorn's coop and ate most of his hens. They salvaged what they could from the carcasses. Don't count on it happening a second time."

Birnee pouted. "Pooh. I was looking forward to that."

I squeezed her hand and met her stare at eye level since we were of similar height. "We could try our hand at hunting again to see if we can catch a hare. If we do, we can enjoy supper together."

"Does that offer extend to me too?" Finnley asked, elbowing me playfully.

Cailis rolled her eyes. "No, you'll probably eat the entire thing in one bite."

Finnley brought a hand to his broad chest. "Are you saying I'm fat?"

I eyed his large frame that was anything but overweight. The only one bigger than Finnley in our village was Vorl, and their imposing masculine builds weren't from being soft.

Cailis snorted a laugh. "If only we had the luxury of being fat."

Birnee giggled, the sound carrying through the rafters.

Vorl eyed me from the corner of the barn, standing stoic as he kept watch. As our village's archon, his main job was to ensure the work was done on time and our yields met the Winter Court's quarterly requirement, which really meant he used every opportunity allowed to bully and demean any field laborer who wasn't working fast enough.

I grumbled as he tracked my movements. Of course, I was his favorite victim, even though I worked hard. He never physically attacked me in the field as long as others were around, but alone, that was another story.

"Why can't he just leave me be for one day?" I murmured under my breath to my sister as Birnee and Finnley fell into conversation about the upcoming winter races and some royal trial they heard would be happening in the capital next month.

"Ignore him. He can't hurt you here," Cailis replied.

I fingered my throat. Despite two days passing since Vorl's

visit to my garden, his illusion magic held. The tender bruises that I knew bloomed along my skin weren't visible to the eye, but any pressure on the area made me wince.

Sighing, I dropped my hand and pulled my cloak tighter around me as our turn for our broth neared. In a way, I was thankful that Vorl's affinity was so strong. If not, everyone would see what he'd done to me, which would only remind them that I was defective and had no magic to fight back.

Scents of the hot broth wafted in the air, and my stomach grumbled in anticipation. The two older fae males in front of us held out their bowls, and I fingered mine. I was next.

Steam clouded around Krisil's face as she served each field hand. Her wings were tucked close to her back as heat from the broth rose around her.

"They say that he was in Firlim yesterday and that he's traveling to all of the villages in our territory, one after another," Krisil said to Evis, the serving cook handing out the bread. "He was last spotted in Coolisbar."

"Coolisbar?" Evis replied as she grabbed a hunk of bread to give to the male. "That's only a thirty-minute flight from here. But they only have one field there. Why would the crown prince be visiting them?"

I stilled. *The crown prince?*

Krisil shrugged as she filled my bowl with broth, barely giving me a passing glance. "'Tis just what I heard. Could be rumors. Would be strange to have anyone from the capital this far east at this time of the season. The court's nobles usually never venture this way as long as we send our territory's due each quarter, and Prince Norivun has never set foot in the croplands of Mervalee Territory as far as I'm aware."

KRISTA STREET

My hands clenched into fists as my chest tightened. I'd never met the crown prince. Had never even seen him. I'd only heard of him, even though Cailis and I personally knew the death and destruction that his terrible affinity brought.

"What do you reckon he's here for?" Evis asked as she grabbed a new loaf of bread.

"Couldn't tell you, but I heard he was asking about—" Krisil's ladle stopped right above Cailis's bowl, and her lips parted in surprise. "Oh, Cailis and Ilara, didn't see you there."

I managed a thin smile despite my heart beating erratically.

Evis placed a chunk of bread onto my plate. "Krisil, why would the prince be—"

Krisil cleared her throat and thumped her foot on Evis's.

Evis scowled. "Why in the bloody realm did you—"

Krisil cleared her throat again and angled her head toward me and Cailis. Both of us stood silently in front of them.

"Oh, it's the Seary girls." Evis gave us an awkward smile. "Um, bread? Here ya are. I'll even give you both extra today." The cook hastily deposited two of the largest pieces of bread onto our plates beside our bowls of broth.

Cailis and I shared a pained look before we left the line and went toward the table we usually sat at. Birnee and Finnley quickly followed, both wearing overly bright smiles as they launched into a conversation about Firlim's upcoming autumn ball that was only a few weeks away. None of us had ever gone, but that had never stopped us from talking about it, even though Finnley declared it one of the most boring subjects on the continent.

But even though I knew our friends were trying to distract us from what Krisil and Evis had revealed, both Cailis and I struggled to get into our usual banter of who would wear what and dance with whom. Instead, we only hummed and nodded when our silence grew painfully awkward.

"There's no way that he's actually here," Finnley finally blurted out. "It's probably rumors. You know what the villages are like."

"Fin!" Birnee hissed.

"What?" He held his hands up. "Why are we beating around the bush when we all know why they look like they've seen ghosts?"

Beneath the table, Cailis's hand found mine. I squeezed her tightly as the bread I'd been chewing felt as though it'd lodged in my throat.

"Fin, not another word. I mean it!" Birnee warned, her blue eyes shooting daggers at him.

He finally sighed and nodded toward the second piece of bread on my plate. "Are you going to eat that?"

Birnee rolled her eyes as I handed it over. But before she could admonish him, the sound of heavy boots came from outside the barn's door.

Vorl pushed away from the wall, a frown tugging at his features just as the door burst open.

Snow flew inside as a light gust hit us from the north, and a few villagers shrieked and yelled in complaint. But the second the newcomer stepped across the threshold and the blinding sun reflecting off the snow outside was shielded from our eyes, the entire room fell silent.

My heart thundered in my chest as the tall male scanned the room, his sapphire eyes narrowed and assessing as a commanding, powerful aura pulsed from his skin. Huge muscled, black leathery wings tipped with talons were tucked close to his back, and he seemed to dwarf the village males around the room.

The newcomer wore the Court of Winter's colors: black, silver, and blue. A thick tunic stretched across his broad chest, the court's seal proudly displayed on his arm.

Cailis's hand gripped mine even tighter as a light sheen of sweat burst across my entire body.

Everyone around the large male dipped into a bow, the rest of us dropping our heads.

Because the crown prince of the Winter Court had just entered the village barn, the Bringer of Darkness himself standing among us in the flesh.

Which meant the rumors had been true after all.

CHAPTER 3

"Who's in charge here?" Prince Norivun Deema Melustral Achul, first son of the king, Bringer of Darkness, Death Master of the continent, son of Prinavee Territory, and crown prince and heir to the Winter Court's throne, asked as he scanned the room. His deep voice resonated in my chest, and my heart beat even harder.

"My prince." Vorl immediately fell into a low bow as the rest of us waited mutely, nobody moving. Nobody breathing. "I'm in charge. It's truly an honor, my prince."

Snow laced the top of Prince Norivun's head, light dancing off the flakes in his silver hair. The top half of his hair was pulled away from his face and secured at the back of his head with an ebony leather band. His locks fell to just below his shoulders as his strong jaw worked while he scanned the room. Behind him, four powerful guards waited.

My fingers itched to move upward and secure my scarf more, but I didn't dare move other than to squeeze my sister's hand harder beneath the table as a deep burning anger began to bloom in my chest.

This royal, this *fairy* was the reason for all of our heartache. I hated him with a vengeance that was so potent I could barely breathe. Never mind that he was the crown prince of the Winter Court. He was my personal nemesis. Even if he didn't know it.

Prince Norivun signaled Vorl to rise. "What have your yields been this past month?"

The village archon straightened, and even though his wings stayed tucked in, he lifted them slightly, putting their impressive height on full display. "We yielded twenty percent more this month than last." Vorl's tone turned boastful, as if he'd been the one bent over all day, farming the land, tending to the crops, and was personally responsible for our village's prosperity. "It's been a successful transition from summer, more so than last season."

The prince's eyebrows drew together. "And your techniques, have you been doing anything differently?"

Vorl cocked his head. "No, my prince. We continue to labor as we always have."

The prince scanned the room again, except this time, his attention focused on each and every laborer, his steely gaze zeroing in on one individual at a time, as though if he stared hard enough, he could see through each villager to the heart of who they really were.

Shallow breaths lifted my chest as my gaze dropped to the floor. Despite the fury swirling in my gut, I didn't move, even though internally I was envisioning rising from my seat, dashing across the room, and smashing the prince's face in with Vorl's club before the Bringer of Darkness could blink. It was such a violent thought, so unlike me, but I *hated* this male.

Cailis's grip tightened, and I couldn't help but wonder if my sister was also envisioning rage-filled vengeance.

Minutes ticked by as the prince assessed everyone. There were so many of us that I wondered why he bothered. Like Vorl said, our yields were up. Our village was supplying what the court demanded, so it made no sense that the prince was here interrogating us and questioning our techniques.

Heat crawled up my neck when I felt the weight of Prince Norivun's gaze finally land on me. It was as though it had an actual presence, as if his magic spiraled toward me on a beam, falling upon my scarfed head in a blaze of might as I waited in a submissive bow.

But instead of shifting his interest to Cailis, Birnee, or Finnley, the prince's attention didn't falter. Instead, I felt every ounce of his powerful aura focus on me with numbing clarity.

Nobody moved as his heavy footsteps started up. First one step, then two, then three, and more and more as he crossed the planked floorboards in a quickened pace.

The tips of his black boots suddenly appeared in my line of sight. He ground to a halt right in front of me.

A bead of sweat trickled down my back even though I wasn't hot, but the energy radiating from the prince continued to cloud me, like a shroud that threatened to smother my breath. I squeezed my eyes shut as power radiated from him in waves, and not for the first time, I understood why the continent feared him. I'd never felt this much magic from anyone in my life, not even Vorl.

My earlier visions of besting the prince before he could react withered and died. It was such a foolish dream to have, something a child would romanticize. But I wasn't a child anymore. I was twenty-four winters, magicless, wingless, weak, and more of a burden to my village than an asset, yet I'd been born here and was one of them despite my defective state, so I tried my hardest to be useful.

Most had come to accept me for who I was, and the teasing and bullying from my youth had faded as the other fae grew and matured and realized that they actually pitied me, well, almost all of them. Some of the nastier ones still made comments, and then there was Vorl . . .

Still, every day I tried as hard as I could to prove my worth, even though the Mother hadn't blessed me with much.

But here, before the Bringer of Darkness, I felt every ounce of my lacking magic that my slight form didn't hold.

I was nothing before this male.

"Look at me, female," he commanded, his tone irritated and short.

Cailis's nails dug into me as I slowly lifted my head. My gaze crawled over the prince's thick boots, heavily muscled thighs, flat waist, and broad chest. Everything he wore was decadent and fine. Thousands of tiny stitches interlaced the thick cloth of his black tunic that looked so smooth and warm that I knew it was spun from the finest wool. Intricate embellishments adorned the leather straps crossing his chest and back and were so perfectly sewn that they could only have come from a tailor blessed with a creation affinity.

A glint of metal peeked out from behind his toned waist, and I realized he carried swords on each side of him, one beneath each of his talon-tipped black wings.

Yet the prince wore such finery as though it were nothing. As if it were trivial given his casual stance and ticking annoyance that I hadn't met his gaze yet.

My jaw clenched again, but I refused to show any emotion. I would not cower in front of him even though I knew he could end me with only a thought.

With a final lift of my head, I met his stare unflinchingly and filled with boldness.

Cobalt irises that sparkled like twin pools of stars stared down at me. His eyes narrowed, and a moment of clarity hit me at the insolence I was showing the crown prince.

Cailis dug her nails tighter into me, and I flinched, but it was enough of a warning—a reminder—of what this male was capable of.

Thankfully, it snapped me back to my senses because the last thing I wanted was to die today, which would leave my sister alone with no family left to speak of.

"My prince." I dipped my head and averted my gaze. A tiny notch was grooved into his chin, the only imperfection on his smooth skin.

The four male guards who'd accompanied the prince still stood by the door, their stances casual as they leaned against the doorframe and barn walls, yet their alert expressions told me they missed nothing.

The prince's firm yet full lips pressed together, and my attention shifted to his mouth. Of course, he would not only be the Death Master of the continent but an absolutely beautiful fae male at that. It made me hate him even more.

"Stand." His single command fell with such authority that I knew he was used to being obeyed without question.

Cailis gave me one last warning squeeze before releasing me, and I quickly slipped my legs over the bench to rise before him.

I kept my back straight and my eyes on his chin, but I still had to crane my neck back. Even standing tall and square, I barely came to his collarbones.

For the briefest moment, his gaze drifted to my throat, to the area clouded in Vorl's illusion affinity that hid my bruises.

"Remove your scarf."

My heart lodged in my throat. "My prince?"

His eyes hooded, and a wash of irritation radiated from him. "Remove. Your. Scarf."

A flurry of whispers erupted around the room, but a sharp yell from Vorl had them quietening.

I darted a look at my sister, then Birnee, and finally Finnley. They all stared at me wide-eyed, as the fear on my sister's face grew.

With trembling fingers, I lifted my hands to the back of my neck and slowly undid the knot that held my scarf in place.

When the scarf fell, my hair tumbled down my shoulders and around my breasts in a shameful ebony waterfall.

The prince didn't move. His gaze was unflinching as his attention traveled over my winged eyebrows, the tips of my ears, and then down the length of my hair.

Every villager sat frozen around us.

With a swift turn on his heel, the crown prince of the Winter Court gave me his back.

My eyes widened as I took in the thickest wings I'd ever seen. The height of those appendages was higher than any wings I'd ever encountered.

The prince glanced over his shoulder, his expression as cold as ice. "You're coming with me."

CHAPTER 4

"N o!" Cailis leaped from her seat and positioned herself in front of me.

Denial jolted through me as my breaths came faster. Surely, I hadn't heard him correctly.

"You're not taking her! She's done nothing wrong!" Cailis yelled.

But the prince merely walked toward the door. His steps didn't falter. He didn't even deign her with a reply.

"Cailis," I whispered as the rest of the villagers wore shocked expressions. *Mother Below, is this really happening?*

"He can't!" Cailis wailed.

I grabbed her shoulders. "Cailis! Don't. *Please.* I can't lose you too." Because if she fought the prince, he would end her without a second thought.

"But, how can he—" A sob shook her chest as her wings extended, then retracted. "Not you too."

"See to it that her last wages are given to her next of kin," the prince said to Vorl, as though he didn't know—or care—that Cailis was my only next of kin. "She won't be returning."

I won't be? My heart beat so rapidly that it felt as though it would beat out of my chest.

"My prince, what did I do?" I called.

The prince dipped his head to his four guards and began speaking quietly, my plea entirely ignored.

"No, no, no," my sister wailed. She wrapped her arms around me and pulled me close, burying her face in my neck.

I clung to her, holding her tightly, as the shock of what the prince had just said slammed into me like a tidal wave on the Tala Sea. *She won't be returning.*

But *why*? Did he mean to kill me? Apprehend me? End me because I was different?

It was as though he'd known when he'd asked me to remove my scarf that he'd find me without silver hair, but since when was being an outcast cause for the Court of Winter to intervene?

My thoughts tumbled around in my mind like a swirling cyclone.

"But I've done nothing," I whispered. "Absolutely *nothing* against the court. How can he be allowed to take me?"

Cailis sobbed harder.

"The prince has summoned you," Vorl called from the corner. A glint filled his eyes, and I knew he would relish bringing me to heel if I resisted.

I held my sister tighter. "I love you," I whispered and stroked her hair. "I love you. I love you. I love you. Please know that, sister. I will always love you."

Another sob shook her frame as tears pricked Birnee's eyes, and pity filled Finnley's. The rest of the room was silent as the fire flickered in the hearth. In the serving line, both Krisil and Evis watched everything slack-jawed.

"Look after her. Promise me that you will," I said to Birnee and Finnley as my sister dissolved into a bigger mess in my arms.

Birnee nodded quickly as Finnley stood in a swift move and wrapped both of us in a hug. His large muscular arms felt warm and comforting. He'd been like a brother to me, even more so since Tormesh had gone. But the joking expression Finnley usually wore, an expression my brother had also commonly bore as he teased Cailis and I mercilessly, was absent. Stoic resolved filled his face.

A soft wail came from Birnee, and then she was there too, standing with us as we all held one another while the rest of our village's laborers looked on. The four of us had been best of friends since childhood, and I knew Cailis would need Birn and Fin now more than ever.

We gripped one another harder.

The Death Master stood with thinned lips and a hard stare, but damn the Winter Court and its heir. He was robbing my sister of the only family she had left.

Glaring at him, I gave him my back and cradled my sister's cheeks in my palms.

One of the prince's guards, the one with hair shorn close to his head, said loudly, "The prince has demanded you come with us. If you do not come willingly now, we shall have to use force."

Vorl's shoulders tensed, his hand going to his club.

"Stay strong, Cailis." I kissed her on the forehead as she turned to Finnley and buried her face in his chest. Birnee gave me one last pleading look. "Take care of her," I begged. "Please."

Birnee and Finnley nodded solemnly as my sister's shoulders and wings moved up and down with each sob.

Standing tall, I locked down the pain that threatened to overwhelm me. I might have been the weakest fairy in our village, but I wouldn't let that define me now. Not here. Not in this moment.

Vorl's focus burned into me as I walked stiffly toward the prince and his guards. A moment of hysteria filled me, but I managed to contain the ironic laughter that almost spilled from my lips. Without me in the village, who would Vorl torment now?

My village archon's expression was filled with mixed emotions. Disbelief. Anger. Perhaps even resentment. But his hand remained on his club, just waiting for me to balk.

The prince cut Vorl a sharp look, then brought his attention back to me. For the barest second, the prince's gaze dropped to my throat again.

"This way," one of the prince's guards said. A braid whipped from around his back as he gestured toward the door.

The prince did a one-eighty, and I followed blindly, my feet moving of their own accord as I put one foot in front of the other.

"My prince?" I called to Prince Norivun again. He towered over me, his midnight attire shining like obsidian. His aura screamed of death and violence, but I still stepped closer to him. "If I've done something against the court, I can assure you it was entirely in ignorance. Please tell me what I've done so I can make it right."

"You've done nothing against the court." He slipped on a pair of supple leather gloves and disappeared out of the barn. He hadn't even glanced at me when uttering the words that proved my innocence.

My jaw dropped as confusion froze my tongue. The guard

with shorn white hair nudged me through the door after Prince Norivun, and I nearly slid on the ice when a burst of wind hit me in the chest, but I managed to right myself as the rest of his guards joined us and closed the door behind us.

Inside the field kitchen, an eruption of conversation broke out. I couldn't decipher what anyone was saying, but I could just imagine what their whispers and hisses hinted at, though nobody dared open the door to see what was happening. I did catch a few hovering near the window, as though I was a side show at Firlim's market and they were debating if they should drop a few rulibs in payment for the entertainment.

If the prince used his affinity on me now, it would indeed be a show. Albeit a quick one.

Shivering, I wrapped my arms around myself as the sun blazed all around. Since we stood outside of the field's land that was infused with *orem*, it was freezing.

I held up a hand to shield my view as the sun's reflection on the snow made the landscape blinding. Another gust of wind shot through the valley, and without my scarf, my hair flew around my face as coldness seeped into my bones. I couldn't remember the last time I'd been so exposed outside. I never left my home without my hooded cloak or headscarf.

"How shall we proceed to the capital, my prince?" one of his guards asked. He was of medium height with a thick white beard, yet his stance was strong, his hands large, and like the prince, two swords peeked out from beneath his wings.

All of the prince's guards appeared to be of similar age and wore the court's signature colors. They were young, strong, trained soldiers who undoubtedly knew how to wield those weapons.

The prince eyed me coolly, assessing my frame through an emotionless mask. "You have no wings."

I flinched. It was something anyone could see, yet it'd been so long since someone had so blatantly pointed it out.

"You're very observant." The sharp comment slipped off my tongue like a thrown arrow as that stirring rage began to simmer in me again.

The bearded guard scowled and stepped forward. "You dare to speak to—"

Prince Norivun held up a hand. "It's all right, Sandus. I'm sure she meant no disrespect." His voice turned glacial, and the magic around him stirred.

I froze, realizing what I'd done. Such insolence would likely garner punishment, even though I was innocent of any actual wrongdoings, but my innocence didn't matter. He was the crown prince, and the prince could do as he wished. He didn't need a reason to take me, and nobody cared that the prince had torn my family apart, that he was forcing me from my home and destroying my sister in the process, or that he was humiliating me on top of everything else. Even if he was doing it all on a whim, even if I'd done nothing against the court, it *didn't matter*.

That shocking realization made me take a deep calming breath. Because dying right here and now would in no way help my sister. Cailis needed to stay safe and continue her life peacefully and hopefully happily, but if I died for deliberate acts of contempt of the crown, her world would be shattered.

With stunning clarity, I knew that staying alive was the best thing for my sister, regardless of what it cost me. I needed to stay safe, keep breathing, and make my way back to her if at all possible. Which meant I shouldn't do anything prideful or stupid.

"I apologize, my prince." I dipped my head, the words like acid on my tongue. "It's been some time since anyone has pointed that out."

The tall, lean male, the one with his hair shorn close to his head, scoffed. "Is she even fae? No wings, and her hair's—" He shook his head. "How can she be Solis?"

The prince brought a hand to my face, not even hesitating. He stroked his pointer finger along my temple, his touch like a feather as he threaded a lock of hair around his finger and lifted it back.

Stunned, I didn't move.

Heavy magic pulsed along the prince's skin, his immense power coiled beneath that one fingertip.

The prince nodded toward my exposed ear, to the delicate point on the tip. "She's fae."

The lean male frowned. "Ock, but not Solis fae, nor Nolus or Lochen fae, and certainly not Silten."

The prince dropped his hand. "She's Solis fae, Nish," he answered in a firm yet exasperated tone.

Nish snapped his mouth shut and said less argumentatively, "Yes, my prince."

"What's your affinity?" the prince asked me.

Another flush stained my cheeks as the cold wind continued to blow around us. "I don't have one."

"No affinity or wings, yet she's still Solis?" Nish shook his head. "How shall we take her back to the capital then, if she can't fly and has no magic? Mistphasing is out of the question."

My eyes widened when he mentioned mistphasing—the ability to move from one location to another with magic alone. Most fae didn't harbor enough magic to do that.

"You're able to mistphase?"

Nish smirked. "We all are, but *you* still have to contain magic, or he can't cross with you."

Humiliation burned through me again as Prince Norivun stroked his jaw. The movement drew my attention to that tiny cleft in his chin. He studied me without pause as my heart pattered wildly. Not only was he scrutinizing me as one would a complicated puzzle, but he'd also touched me when he'd moved my hair, as though he had the right to do anything at all to me.

My lips thinned.

"You really have no affinity?" he finally said.

"No, I don't."

Something flickered in his gaze, but it was gone too quickly for me to decipher. Dropping his hand, the prince raised an eyebrow. "I suppose I shall have to carry you then if you're unable to fly and mistphasing is out of the equation."

My eyes bugged out. "*Carry* me?"

He cocked an eyebrow, a hint of amusement rolling through his features. "Unless you have a better idea?"

My mouth grew dry at the thought of being held in his arms for the entire flight to the capital. To be held by the very hands that had destroyed my family . . .

I took another deep, calming breath, then let it out when a solution came to me. "I could ride a domal, my prince."

"A domal?" Sandus shook his head. "Solis fae don't ride domals. Domals are for the Nolus fae, the *weaker* fae." He sneered, making it clear how he felt about the fae who lived south of our continent and regularly rode the animals that galloped about on four hooves and whinnied whenever they were displeased.

Domals weren't common on our continent, but some Solis fae had them. The large creatures were useful for transporting goods in wagons when magic couldn't be utilized.

I stiffened but forced myself to keep my tone steady. "Whatever you deem best then."

Prince Norivun took a step closer to me, and my breath caught in my chest. With him standing this close, the scent of cedar and snow drifted toward me, crisp and alluring.

I immediately began breathing through my mouth as I craned my neck back.

His sheer size dwarfed me, and before I could mentally prepare myself for the inevitable, his arms were around me, and he was lifting me to his chest. In another beat, we shot into the sky.

I clamped ahold of his neck as a survival instinct roared to life inside me. The ground disappeared beneath us much faster than had ever happened when my brother or Finnley had carried me, and I released a frantic prayer to Armarus, the goddess of the sky.

I glued my eyes shut, my breath locked in my chest as icy wind needled my skin, and my stomach bottomed out at how quickly we spiraled upward.

The prince's giant wings flapped hard and fast, but it was more than just his wings that propelled us. Magic clouded around us, making me wonder about his affinities, as though his magic moved him faster. The entire realm knew of his most powerful affinity, the one that made him feared by all, but I'd heard whisperings over the seasons that he possessed more than one—a trait rare in the Solis.

Neither of us said anything as the ground became distant,

and even though questions still burned through my mind about *why* this was happening, I stayed silent.

The rhythmic movement of the prince's flapping wings eventually slowed, and then we were gliding, riding the currents as we traveled west toward Prinavee Territory, where Solisarium, the capital, waited.

The entire time, the prince cradled me easily to his chest as the pastel-colored clouds drifted sporadically around us on this mostly clear day.

"At least you're not heavy," he finally remarked, breaking the silence.

"That's what happens when you're starved," I said beneath my breath.

He gazed down at me momentarily, but I refused to make eye contact.

A wind gust abruptly caught us, sending us higher into the atmosphere. A scream lodged in my throat, and even though I hated myself for it, I clung tighter to him.

"I won't let you fall," he said calmly, as if having a petrified female millees above the ground was a daily occurrence for him.

I forced my arms to loosen, but when I tried to let go completely and allow him to hold me entirely . . . I couldn't.

As ridiculous as it would be for him to take me from my village only to intentionally drop me thousands of feet to my death, I didn't trust him to keep me safe. I knew what he was, so despite my pride slugging me in the gut, I kept my grip on him.

"How long will it take to reach Solisarium, my prince?"

"Two days."

My head whipped up to see if he was serious, but all I saw

was the undercut of his jaw and his long lashes as he stared straight ahead.

"Two . . . *days*, my prince?" I was to endure being held by him for two full days?

"Yes." He glanced down at me. "Have you never been there?"

"No, of course not." I vaguely knew where the capital was on a map, but it was so far away that I'd never even considered traveling there. In fact, I'd never been beyond my village, Firlim, or the other villages surrounding that small city.

I tried to remember what I could from the seasons I'd been in school. We'd learned the geography of our continent and this realm, but that was so long ago. All I could remember was that Solisarium was at least a thousand millees from where I lived. Perhaps even farther.

Keeping my hands clasped around his neck, I dared a look over his shoulder to search for Sandus, Nish, and the two other males who traveled with the prince.

Their distant specks were visible through a smattering of pink clouds. "Aren't you afraid you'll lose your guards?"

"They know the way."

I tried to ignore how his hard chest felt against my side as he breathed evenly, so I glanced down, but the ground was so far beneath us I couldn't make out any details. I had no idea where we were.

Swallowing the uneasiness in my throat, I asked, "So we'll fly like *this* for two days straight?"

His brow furrowed, and a moment of fear stole over me when his power rumbled around me. "You seem to be forgetting how to address me properly."

My breath caught when I felt his affinity brush against me. A wave of coldness and bottomless darkness gathered around my soul.

I recoiled, and my heart beat as rapidly as a trisilee's wings. *My prince.* I was supposed to add "my prince" to the end of every question. I was not to speak to him casually, like I would to Finnley.

My hands turned clammy as I stuttered, "I'm sorry, my prince. I forgot . . . I mean, I'm not used to addressing royalty, my prince."

"As I'm coming to see."

That comment shut me up, and I vowed not to say another word during the next two days, but a minute later, the prince broke the quiet again. "We often stop at the same spot whenever we're patrolling the continent, so no, we won't fly like this for two full days. Even if I lose my guards in the clouds, they'll eventually end up in the same location as us."

I nodded tightly, not trusting myself to speak further without offending him again. I needed to remember what was best for Cailis. Stay alive. Get back to her. Don't anger the prince.

I could only pray that when my time with the prince came to an end, that my death wasn't waiting.

CHAPTER 5

The hours drifted past, and my arms grew so sore that I debated lowering them from the prince's neck.

I hadn't felt the brush of his affinity since his admonishment, so I was no longer concerned that he'd drop me or kill me. Not yet at least.

Tentatively, I let go of my death grip and bit back a hiss. My limbs would barely move. It was as though they had frozen around his wide frame. The prince's expression gave away nothing as I slowly and painfully curled my arms stiffly to my chest.

The landscape continued to be a blur. We were flying over mountains—I knew that much, and if we were traveling west, then I assumed they were the Gielis Mountains—the large mountain range that separated Mervalee from Prinavee Territory.

"Our lodging for the night is just up ahead."

I started at the sound of his voice. After hours of traveling in silence, with only the wind howling through my ears, I'd forgotten how deep and commanding his tone was.

KRISTA STREET

We abruptly dropped from the sky. Swallowing a scream, I grabbed a hold of him even though pain shot through my limbs from the unintended movement.

The air whizzed past us, blowing my hair around my face and covering my eyes, but I couldn't bring myself to release him again.

Down, down, down we went, spiraling and dipping from the atmosphere, and I wondered how high up we'd been.

He tightened his grip on me, as if in reassurance that he wouldn't let me fall, but when he shifted my weight as he maneuvered from a horizontal position to a vertical one, I realized it had only been to accommodate his landing.

Snow flattened beneath his large booted feet when we returned to the ground as lightly as falling mist. Around us, a thick forest covered a towering mountainside. The pale green sky above was still visible in the setting sun that was quickly disappearing behind the highest mountain peak.

I breathed heavily, and a moment of panic hit me when I realized how incredibly vulnerable I'd become. The clearing we'd landed in was devoid of life. No birds, creatures, or plants other than the towering pines whose needles were a sapphire blue surrounded us. If the prince left me here, I would be frozen and dead by morning.

"May I ask where we are, my prince?" Thankfully, my voice sounded calm despite my fear.

He released me from his grasp, and my stiff legs protested from the shift in movement. If it wasn't for my determination to act as though the day's long flight hadn't affected me, I would have crumpled to the ground.

"Near High Liss. The mountain village is just beyond those trees." He pointed toward the setting sun, which meant the town was west. "Our lodging for the night is down that path. Now, before we go . . ." A pulse of his magic fell around me, like a veil. It was so subtle that I almost didn't detect it.

I gasped when, before my eyes, my hair turned from pitch black to pure silver, just like all Solis fae.

"What . . . how?" I stuttered. "Is this a glamour?"

"No, it's an illusion, to draw less attention to you. Glamours aren't strong enough to conceal your hair for a long duration. Come." He tucked his wings in tight and headed toward the trail leading out of the clearing.

Curling smoke from a chimney rose above the trees, which meant our lodging had to be close. Marveling one last time at my hair, I finally stopped fingering the locks and followed him, placing my feet where his had been in the deep snow, which meant my strides had to nearly double in size.

Heaving, I finally caught up with him as a sprawling lodge appeared through the foliage. The rugged two-story abode with a wide porch and a towering chimney was a welcome sight. Lights blazed from the windows, and faint music stirred the air. A sign hung over the door, reading *Liss Lodge*.

"This way." The prince strode ahead, and since the snow here had been cleared down to inches, it made walking easy.

His heavy steps trudged up the stairs, and I tracked the movement as a terrible thought came to me . . .

Perhaps those stomps had been the last sound my parents and brother had heard when the prince had climbed the executioner block.

Perhaps that would be the last sound *I* would hear.

I halted mid-movement, my body freezing.

Soft music that sounded as though a hundred violins played

in harmony drifted to me when the prince opened the lodge's door. He arched an eyebrow at me.

"Are you coming?"

My feet wouldn't move. "My prince, will you please tell me why you've taken me?"

"Are we back to this again?"

Despite my frozen limbs and the lure of the warm lodge, I *couldn't* move. Blood thundered through my veins as fear paralyzed me.

"Will you at least give me a hint as to what's going to happen to me?"

He faced me, then let the door close before he inched closer on deceptively quiet steps. He moved silently until he towered over me, letting me know that when he wanted to, he could move like a phantom.

"Not yet."

My breath shuddered out of me. "Not *yet*?"

A swell of power rumbled around him, and I briefly realized that I was playing a very dangerous game again, but Blessed Mother, I was *terrified* of what was to come.

"Would you rather stay out here and freeze?" he asked.

"No." My voice shook. "But I don't know what's waiting for me in Solisarium, so maybe freezing would be best, my prince."

"And if I told you why I took you, would that make you more agreeable?"

My eyes widened. "You'll tell me?"

"No. As I said, not yet." He gave me his back and called over his tall wings. "Now come inside. If you don't come willingly, I'll have to assist you."

All of the blood drained from my face, as I ducked in after him.

Despite fear and trepidation pounding through me, my muscles loosened when the lodge's warmth caressed my skin.

A large fire roared in the center of the room, the chimney rising to the roof. Around the fire sat tables and chairs with a few sofas. To the right, a long bar ran the room's length. Several fae sat on the bar stools as other patrons were seated near the fire. None had bothered to glance at us.

"My prince!" a female called from behind the bar. Short wings were tucked in at her back, and a long skirt flowed to her ankles. She dusted her hands on an apron and sashayed around the bar's edge.

Everyone else straightened, their relaxed positions disappearing as all heads swiveled in our direction.

The female lodge employee smiled brightly as she approached us, a dimple appearing in her cheek. "I didn't realize you'd be joining us this fine eve, Your Highness. Come sit by the fire while I ready your room."

"Thank you, Milis. I'm sorry this is short notice." When she just waved a hand, the prince added, "The others will arrive shortly, and we have an extra guest with us tonight."

The female's eyes widened when she beheld me. She took in my worn clothing and wingless back, gawking more and more as I stood there.

I resisted the urge to fidget, because the female wore the same expression everyone did when they saw an adult Solis fairy without wings. But at least my hair was concealed. Silver linings. I almost snorted when that pun struck me.

"Like I said, she's my guest," the prince said tightly. "I expect her to be treated as such."

The female immediately dropped her stare. "Right, I'll—" She dipped in a curtsy. "Of course, my prince."

She hurried from the room to the back stairs leading to a second floor, which I assumed was where the lodging rooms waited, as an enchanted tray floated past us. Laden with drinks, it glided across the room to a table of three males. From there, the drinks floated off the serving tray, coming to rest in front of each patron.

Now that the surprise of the prince's arrival was wearing off, more and more looked in my direction. Whispers erupted, and comments drifted toward me.

"No wings? How peculiar."

"Were they shaved, do you suppose?"

The prince stepped in front of me, shielding me from their obnoxious curiosity. "Hungry?"

His question had my attention snapping away from the curious onlookers as Milis reappeared, hurrying from the stairs to our side.

"I suppose, my prince." I didn't add anything further. I was always hungry, even though at the moment I doubted I could eat.

"Your rooms are being readied. Would you like refreshments while you wait?" Milis asked, her smile overly bright.

When the prince inclined his head, she nodded toward the table nearest the fire and gave the couple sitting at it a sharp look.

Both hastily stood, their chairs squeaking against the floor when they pushed them back in a flourish. The prince didn't so much as utter a *thank you* when they moved to the empty corner booth far away from the fire and its heat.

My lips thinned as Prince Norivun settled onto the chair, the wooden seat protesting under his heavy weight as his wings settled into the divots created to accommodate them. I pulled out the chair across from him, looking anywhere but at his handsome face as an enchanted tray floated to us.

Two large bowls of stew glided off the tray to our place settings, along with mugs of ale and plates of heavily buttered bread. The portions were generous, easily four times the size of Krisil's ladle. It all smelled delicious as scents of herbed meat wafted up to greet me, but my stomach protested despite its hollow hole as another terrible thought struck me. Perhaps this would be the first meal of many I would have without my sister.

The prince was on his third bite before he nodded toward my bowl. "You need to eat."

I met his gaze, unblinking. His beauty struck me again. Sitting as he was, his sheer size dominated the room, yet he held himself with ease, his large bulk moving fluidly—gracefully even. I skimmed over his symmetrical features, deep-set eyes, and strong nose. His masculinity was the kind spoken of in sonnets and sung in melodies that seduced a female with only a few syllables. He was utter perfection, a living sculpture. It only riled me further. Such unparalleled beauty wasn't fair in a male such as him.

"Is that a command, my prince?"

His eyes narrowed before he leaned forward in his chair. "Your life as you knew it is over. I suggest you adjust to that and stop sulking."

"Sulking?"

"Yes, sulking."

"And have you ever been taken from your home, your family, by the fairy who . . ."

His eyebrow arched, a perfect wing of silver. "The fairy who what?"

His expression remained guileless, truly unburdened. He honestly didn't know what he'd done to me, to Cailis, to our lives.

Righteous anger burned inside me, which was much more preferable to the fear I'd previously felt, but I pinched my lips closed.

"The fairy who what?" he repeated.

"Nothing, my prince. I'm quite tired. I apologize." My heart beat painfully hard as I took a deep breath.

What he'd done to me, he'd probably done to countless other families, so it shouldn't be a surprise that he didn't know of my family's fate. He not only hadn't asked my name, but he'd also probably lost count of his atrocities. He was the Death Master of the continent after all.

I fiddled with the napkin by my plate as he took another bite of stew. "When will I learn why you took me, my prince?"

His lips sealed around his spoon as his jaw worked through the stew's tender meat and vegetables. "Soon enough."

A biting retort was on the tip of my tongue until I caught the seriousness in his eyes. He wasn't lying. Even though I didn't have Cailis's affinity for truth, I knew he was being honest. He would eventually tell me.

"Now, eat." He pointed his spoon at the bread. "You won't stay warm during the flight tomorrow if your belly's empty."

Looking down, I tore a piece off the bread and forced it into my mouth. The soft dough and smooth butter nearly melted on my tongue, yet despite that, I had to force it down because another horrible, awful thought came to me. Maybe he wasn't telling me why he'd taken me because my fate was much worse than mere death.

Soft violin music continued floating around us as the prince slowly finished his meal. I couldn't take another bite.

I had to know.

"My prince, are you going to torture me? Is that why you won't tell me of my fate?" I asked quietly.

His hand stilled from scooping his last spoonful. A moment ticked by. Then another. A muscle in his jaw began to pulse.

"What makes you think that?" he finally asked.

Because it's what you do. And if it's not torture, it will certainly be death because that's what you did to my brother and my parents. Yet you obviously don't know that. You probably don't even remember murdering my family.

But I kept those words sealed in my mind, locking them down as far as they would go. "Because what use could you possibly have for me—a weak, wingless, defective fairy if not to purge the Solis race of my existence and perhaps punish me for ever having been born?"

His eyes burned with an intensity that put a fire elemental's affinity to shame. "Is that how you see yourself?"

"Don't you?"

But instead of answering that, he simply said, "I'm not going to kill you, and I'm not going to torture you."

With that, he leaned back in his seat, his wings settling behind him just as the door opened, and Nish, Sandus, and his other two guards poured into the lodge.

Nish ran a hand over his short, shorn hair, then sauntered

toward us. He smelled of wind and snow, and the cold air still clung to him.

After pulling out a chair by the fire, Nish straddled it and signaled Milis over, then took in the prince's empty bowl and half-drunk mug of ale. "How long have you been here?"

"Oh, the usual," the prince replied. "Hours upon hours. If you bastards weren't so slow, we could have flown all the way to Solisarium tonight."

My jaw dropped because we'd not even been here an hour, and the prince's tone had been *joking*. I never would have thought the Death Master could have a sense of humor.

Sandus grinned and pulled out the chair by Nish before shaking the snow from his beard.

The other two—the one with round cheeks and the other with a long braid down his back that settled right between his wings—pulled over chairs until our table was overflowing with the large males.

Snowflakes fluttered from their clothing, wings, and hair, but the second the flakes made contact with the floor, they fizzled out of existence, letting me know the magical wards surrounding this establishment kept the elements at bay. If only my village's field barn had contained that kind of magic.

At the bar, Milis filled another tray with drinks and food, and the enchanted platter lifted, the heavy weight inconsequential to the magic that propelled it.

"Are your arms sore from the long flight?" Sandus asked the prince.

Prince Norivun cocked an eyebrow. "She doesn't weigh more than eight stone. You insult me."

But Sandus just grinned again, his smile peeking through his bushy beard.

"She give you any trouble?" Nish asked, nodding my way.

"*She* has a name, you know." The words shot out of me, and all five males' easy smiles vanished.

"And what name is that?" the round-cheeked male asked. His voice was joyful and smooth, yet he looked to be the oldest of them. He had a broad nose, light-blue eyes that were as bland as a small pond, and firm lips. Even though his features weren't typically handsome, he was still attractive, and of all of them, his demeanor seemed the kindest.

I brought a fist to my heart in traditional Solis greeting and replied more calmly, "Ilara Seary, daughter of Mervalee Territory. And you are?"

The prince's eyes widened slightly as a hint of a smile ghosted the guard's lips before he also brought a fist to his chest. "Haxil Hubberline, guard to the crown prince and son of Isalee Territory."

I sat up straighter, the mysterious words from the fae females at the harvest market over the weekend returning. "Is it true the crops are dying in Isalee?"

All movement at the table stopped. The male by Sandus, the one I hadn't met yet who had the long braid, lowered his drink as the prince's eyes narrowed.

"Where did you hear that?" the prince asked in a voice so cold that it sent a chill down my spine.

I resisted the urge to fidget and clasped my hands in my lap. "I overheard two fae talking about it at Firlim's market last weekend."

The prince's eyes turned to slits. "What did they say?"

"That the plants are black, the soil is gray, and the fae in Isalee are starving. She said our land's *orem* is failing. That the celestial events aren't replenishing it, and we're all going to die."

Prince Norivun and his guards all gave one another side-eyes, and if I hadn't already been curious about the rumors, I was definitely curious now.

"Is it true then?" For the first time, genuine alarm pulsed through me.

"How many others have spoken of this?" the prince asked.

"I don't know."

"Have any fae in your village or in Firlim spoken of being discontented?" Haxil asked, the earlier warmth radiating from his round cheeks gone.

My brows pinched together as all of them watched me intently. "No, not that I'm aware of."

Haxil's shoulders relaxed, and I wondered what in the realm was going on. "Is something amiss in Isalee? Is the *orem* there—"

A door burst open to the side of the lodge, and a female fairy came stumbling over the threshold. My breath sucked in when blood dripped from a long slash down her wing. She nearly fell to the floor but caught herself on a chair.

"My prince!" she called. "Please, I beg of you. Help me! He's going to kill him tonight. I'm sure of it. He won't stop!"

Milis rushed forward, her arms going around the female as she hushed her. "Not here, Mealow. This isn't the place. Alert the patrol."

The female grabbed onto Milis's arms. "I tried, but they're busy with a snowgum." The female gripped the bartender tighter. "I don't know who else to turn to. He's full of leminai and angry tonight, Mil. So angry, and I heard the prince had come."

The prince let out a long tired-sounding sigh.

"Want us to handle this, Nori?" the guard with the braid asked. He had angular cheekbones and looked as though he'd been crafted from a steel arrow.

"No, Ryder. It's my duty. Not yours." Prince Norivun rose from his seat and approached the female. Milis gave him an apologetic look, but all he said was, "What's amiss?"

The injured female fell to his feet, blubbering and crying. "Oh, my prince. It's my son. He's lipped off to my husband again, and he's got my son pinned to a wall, using his affinity to hold him. My son can't fight back. Not even to defend himself. He's going to kill him this time—I'm sure of it—and I'm not strong enough to stop him."

Haxil, Nish, Sandus, and the fairy with the braid—apparently named Ryder—circled around the prince.

Prince Norivun placed his hands on his hips. "Your husband's committed these acts?"

"Yes, her husband's a real brute of a fae," Milis said under her breath. "When he's drunk on leminai, he's dangerous and cruel."

The female with the torn wing cried louder. "I tried to stop him, but his claws—"

"What's his affinity?" Nish asked as a swirl of magic flowed around him.

"Ice bear."

My stomach dropped. Of course it would be one of the large animal affinities and not something easier to contend with like a superficial affinity.

The prince muttered something under his breath, then nodded toward the door. "This'll be messy. Let's go."

CHAPTER 6

"Haxil?" The prince inclined his head toward me as he followed Mealow. Haxil nodded and moved to my side.

"Keep that stew warm for us, Milis," Ryder called, throwing her a wink. His silvery white braid whipped between his wings as the prince and the two other guards headed after the female fairy.

"Thank you, my prince. Thank you!" Mealow called as she rushed toward the side door.

Their boot steps filled the room as the other patrons watched. When I just waited by the fire, Haxil gave me a sly smile. "What do you think you're doing?"

I frowned and raised my hands. "Waiting here with you?"

Haxil cocked an eyebrow. "Where the prince goes, I go, which means you're coming with me."

"You're not staying here to guard me? I thought that's what the prince wanted."

"No, I mean, you're correct that he wants me to guard you,

but not here. That was merely his way of telling me to stay at your side."

"Why? I'm a magicless, wingless, defective fairy, not a precious treasure that needs to be kept within eyesight at all times. You could just go with him and leave me here."

Haxil's eyebrow rose higher as an amused smile split his lips. "Just do as you're told, Ilara Seary, daughter of Mervalee Territory."

Knowing I wouldn't win this fight, I stood, but I couldn't help the annoyance that prickled my skin at once again being commanded against my will, so I gave a small yet dramatic bow. "As you wish, Haxil Hubberline, guard to the crown prince and son of Isalee Territory." I twirled my hand to add to the effect, then stood.

He chuckled, his eyes sparkling as he pulled me toward the door. "I would say I detected a hint of mockery in that bow."

"Really?" I asked innocently.

His grin grew. "You know, I think I'm going to like you, Ilara."

I snorted a laugh. Strangely, I was coming to the same realization, even though I'd just met him, and his archon was my sworn enemy.

Outside, the wind bit into my skin and was even more of a shock after an hour's rest in the warm lodge. Ahead, the prince and his guards were following Mealow down a path to High Liss.

"Are you worried about encountering a fairy with an ice bear affinity?" I asked Haxil. While animal affinities were common, the larger predator affinities were less so.

"Nah," he replied as he extended a wing, stopping the harsh wind from hitting me directly. "We all have warrior affinities and have yet to encounter a fight we can't handle, but the prince will likely deal with this fairy himself. We'll just stand watch and guard his back."

"You don't help him?"

"He doesn't need our help."

Of course. Considering the prince had no qualms about using his affinity and did so freely, he wouldn't need anyone's assistance, but only a true monster would use an affinity such as the prince's unchecked.

"So why are you guarding him at all if he's so capable?"

Haxil pulled back a tree branch as we entered the forest. "The crown prince doesn't need us to protect him if he's aware of a threat. It's just when a threat sneaks up on him or tries to catch him unaware, then we come in."

I nodded, realizing it only made sense that Nish, Sandus, Ryder, and Haxil would all have warrior affinities. What better guards to surround oneself with than fae who were naturally blessed fighters?

"Was your affinity a job requirement when you became one of the crown prince's guards?"

"No," Haxil replied as dim lights appeared ahead through the thick foliage. It appeared that High Liss was only a short walk down the mountain. "If you have the skills to guard the prince without a warrior affinity, you could be chosen, but very few fae are able to match our skill without it."

I could only imagine. I'd never encountered another fairy with a warrior affinity as far as I knew, but it wasn't as though fae wore their affinities on their sleeves. Unless one chose to reveal it, or you witnessed firsthand a fairy using their affinity magic, it was easy to keep it hidden. For all I knew, I'd been living beside a warrior fae in my village my entire life and had never known it.

Haxil kept his wing curled around me as we followed the others, but it didn't give me the creeps like when Vorl had done so. With Haxil, the movement felt natural, as though he used his wing to protect me and didn't give it much thought. Versus when Vorl had used his wings, it was to trap me and hold me hostage.

A yell reached my ears a moment later, then the mountain village of High Liss appeared. Rows upon rows of small homes, shops, and winding roads teetered on the mountainside. The village was perched on such a steep slope that I knew the founder of the village had either a constructo affinity or some ingenious engineering had been invested into its creation.

Ahead, Mealow was running toward a home on the valley side. Lights blazed from the windows as another yell came from within, this one filled with pain.

I stopped midstride. Those screams were probably coming from her son.

"We'll stay outside their home," Haxil said calmly and propelled me forward. "The prince won't want you in harm's way."

"Staying at the lodge would have been safest," I replied as uneasiness crept through me. "You could have left me there while you stayed with the prince."

"Not necessarily. What if someone tried to harm you?"

"Why would they do that? I've done nothing wrong."

"You're traveling with the Bringer of Darkness now. He has many enemies."

My stomach turned. "Meaning, harm may now come to me as a way to get to him?"

"Exactly." He quickened our pace as the prince and Mealow

ducked inside her home while Nish, Sandus, and Ryder guarded the perimeter.

The three guards positioned themselves around the small house, watching the village's citizens. Ryder even took flight, going to the opposite side of the house that overlooked the valley. His wings flapped as he hovered just outside of the home's back door that had a pad, almost like a balcony, attached to it for landings. In their current positions, they had all exit and entry points covered.

Haxil and I reached them just as ferocious roars came from within. I wrapped my arms around myself as the prince yelled, "Morph back to your fae form, and no harm will come to you!"

I dared a peek through the window. The prince faced something in the corner of the room as Mealow twisted her hands. She stood just to the prince's side, her attention fixated on whatever lay in front of them.

"Please, let him go," Mealow pleaded to who I assumed was her husband. "He didn't mean any harm by what he said."

I angled myself to get a better view, and my eyes widened when I beheld her husband drunk on leminai. He was fully transformed within his affinity—a huge monstrosity of fur, claws, and fangs. His ragged head touched the ceiling, brushing against the wooden planks. White fur covered his entire body, and hands that had become paws sported six-inch claws.

Naturally born ice bears were known for being deadly. Thankfully, they stuck to the mountain ranges, so we'd never had to deal with them in my village, but stories would circulate throughout the continent now and then, speaking of the treacherous creatures that lived on our frozen lands and roamed the forests and mountains.

The only mountainous creature more lethal than an ice bear was a snowgum—a huge feline with razor-sharp teeth and barbed claws. When it flared its magical essence, it grew invisible for brief periods of time, making an attack impossible to foresee and tracking them even more difficult. It was said if you were unlucky enough to encounter a snowgum, you didn't live to tell about it.

The drunk husband roared again as a young male lay on the floor beneath him. Blood trickled from multiple slashes across the youth's body.

My heart beat harder as I took in his pale complexion and closed eyes. He was unconscious, so his screams had stopped. Frantically, I searched for signs of life, and a relieved exhale escaped me when his chest rose in a shallow breath.

"He's still alive," I whispered just as a subtle throbbing sensation pulsed in my gut. I brought a hand automatically to my belly, but the throbbing stopped as soon as it'd begun.

Haxil's eyebrows knitted together as his full cheeks hollowed. "He won't be for much longer if he's not taken to a healer."

I studied the young male again, and for the briefest moment, that throb returned before it vanished.

"Last warning," the prince called. "This can end peacefully now, but you have to transform back."

The drunk husband only snarled and advanced.

"Poor choice, you foolish scum," Haxil said under his breath.

The prince's eyes narrowed. His shoulders tightened, but his hands stayed open and his arms loose. Rope veins bulged in his neck, and his jaw clenched as the air seemed to ripple around him.

Shallow breaths lifted my chest as I waited for his deadly

KRISTA STREET

affinity power to rise, but instead of letting it loose and killing the drunk male in a blink, the prince reached for his swords.

"Ah, he's going to give him a chance to come to his senses." Haxil chuckled, but nothing about this felt funny to me.

The male in his ice bear form advanced, swiping out a paw. The prince deflected it with the hilt of his sword, dipping with the movement.

Roaring, the fairy charged.

Everything next happened in a blur of power and speed. The fairy lunged, his gaping bear maw going right for the prince's throat, but the prince ducked and rolled at the last minute, his body moving with liquid grace despite his height and tall wings.

Coming to a crouch, the prince slashed out, his weapon arcing through the air right as the fairy reared.

A line of red appeared on the bear's belly, and his roar turned to one of pain. Behind him, the fae youth still lay listlessly. Time was running out.

"Last chance!" the prince called. "Transform back *now!*"

Despite the blood running freely along its fur, the husband gave a furious bellow and then ducked his head and charged.

The prince's lip curled. "So be it."

The fairy in his ice bear form swiped a massive paw toward the prince's face.

But his arm didn't connect.

A shockwave of magic unleashed from the prince.

My breath stopped.

Time stood still.

The prince's affinity rose so swiftly it speared the air.

Power radiated from the entire house.

I shuddered.

Jolted.

Nearly vomited.

An agonized roar came from the fairy. His massive head tilted back, revealing a mouth filled with fangs. Convulsions shook his furry frame, then he crumpled to the ground, his entire body spasming as a shimmer of energy vibrated the air around him. His figure morphed, the transformation happening too quickly for me to see.

I blinked, and a naked fae male lay still on the stone floor. I brought a hand to my mouth and took a step forward. Nausea churned in my gut. Blessed Mother, I had no idea if he was dead or only unconscious.

Before I knew what I was doing, I grabbed the door and pulled it open.

"Ilara, no!" Haxil called.

But I flew through the door before the guard could stop me. My focus zeroed in on the fairy. He couldn't be dead. The prince wouldn't kill him for being drunk and acting violently. Surely, he'd simply subdued him.

Prince Norivun's frosty gaze cut to mine, and then he was there, standing in front of me as a deadly coldness swirled around him.

I tried to sidestep him, but he met my attempts like a wall, his body once again *there.*

"Is he dead?" I whispered.

The prince's jaw tightened.

"Please don't kill him."

"I'm sorry, my prince," Haxil said as he encircled my arm from behind. "She ran inside before I could stop her."

"Don't kill him. *Please.*" Tears pricked my eyes as I gazed upward at the prince. "Surely, you won't. Surely, you're not that much of a monster."

The muscle in Prince Norivun's jaw ticked. "Remove her, Haxil."

"Yes, my prince. Apologies again."

And then I was being tugged backward, away from a sobbing Mealow as her husband lay still on the floor. Lifeless.

As soon as I saw that, I rounded on Haxil. "He killed him? He really *killed* him?"

The guard pulled me through the door, his grip firm. "Of course, he killed him," he growled quietly.

Shock rippled through me, and my feet planted to the ground, but the guard didn't hesitate. He picked me up and carried me the remainder of the distance away from the house.

Memories swirled through my mind of the moment I'd learned of my family being killed. The anguish, the disbelief, then the rising fury.

"He's a monster," I said in a choked whisper when Haxil placed me on my feet again. Once more, the prince had destroyed a family, even if the father had been abusive and feral. The prince had still torn that family apart.

"He did what was needed," Haxil replied gruffly.

I took a step away from him and then another, as the realization cut me to the quick that the sensations I'd just experienced were what it felt like to be in the presence of the prince's releasing affinity. My hand flew to my mouth as my breath seized. Was that what my parents and brother had felt when the prince enacted his affinity on them? Were those narrowed, crystalline blue eyes the last thing they saw before his affinity sucked their souls?

Tears flooded my eyes. One slid down my cheek as a sob racked my chest. The urge to vomit grew.

"That fairy didn't stand a chance. But why? Why kill him? The prince could have restrained him. That male didn't need to die."

Haxil's brow furrowed, his expression turning guarded. "Have you ever tried to take a fairy with an ice bear affinity into custody?"

All I could manage was to shake my head. I was breathing so fast. Too fast.

"Then you don't know it's near impossible to do so safely."

Near impossible, but not *impossible?* But I couldn't voice the question. I couldn't speak at all. Blessed Mother, my family had suffered what I'd just witnessed.

Inside the house, Mealow's wails rose. "He's dead," she said. "He's dead. He's dead." Her sobs rose higher, a piercing cry that seemed to echo down the valley.

"But your son's not. He's alive because your husband's dead." A disgusted snarl tore from the prince. "Ryder, seek a healer, now!"

A whoosh of air shot against my wet cheeks as the warrior fairy came careening from around the back of the house. Nish and Sandus immediately maneuvered to cover the gap that his departure left.

Dozens of villagers were now out of their homes, standing in the street, watching the spectacle unfold around them. A few glanced my way, raking over my frame.

"Who's she?" one hissed.

"Probably his whore," another replied under his breath.

A flare of shame crept over me even though I was anything

but the prince's whore, but the sneers in the crowd grew as did their looks of fear and revulsion. But those sneers weren't just for me. They were for Prince Norivun himself.

Ignoring them, Ryder called, "Who's a healer?"

Nobody moved.

Ryder's long braid whipped around his shoulder when he bared his teeth. "That young male is one of your own! Who will save him?"

A few shuffled their feet, then a slim boy pushed through the crowd. "I will, my lord."

The boy didn't have full wings—they were only half-formed. He was still in the midst of maturing, which meant his healing affinity had probably only recently manifested.

"I'm not a lord," Ryder replied, then gave him a once-over. "Do you know how to use your affinity yet?"

The boy's shoulders squared. "I'm learning, sir. I can help."

"There's no one else," an older female said, her arm curling around the boy's shoulders. "But my son's proven to be a quick learner. He'll save Mealow's boy."

Ryder picked the child up in one strong arm before sailing back to the house. Mealow still wept over her dead husband, tears pouring down her cheeks.

Watching, I dried my eyes and struggled to compose myself as I waited for Mealow to shift her attention away from her dead husband to her unconscious son who still lay listless on the floor.

"Isn't she worried about her boy?" I finally managed.

Haxil crossed his arms. "On some level, probably, but her reaction is typical in cases like this. Even though her husband's dead, her concern lays with the abuser. Some fae become dependent on the abuser, and the toxic cycle that forms between them is like an addictive potion in itself. She'll probably continue to mourn for him over the coming days instead of sitting at her son's bedside."

I wrapped my arms around myself, suddenly so chilled my entire body trembled. Haxil spoke as if he had experience with such matters. "Do you suppose she regrets going to the prince for help?"

"Probably." Haxil eyed the crowd. Dozens of scornful, wary fae stared back at us. "Everyone thinks it's a good idea to have the Death Master on their side until they see the absolute destruction that he's capable of."

CHAPTER 7

T he young healer's inexperience was apparent when he struggled to save Mealow's son, but after minutes of trying and refusing to give up, the teenage boy was finally able to slow the bleeding.

It took another aching moment for the injured male to open his eyes, but when he did, his foggy gaze slid around the room. When he beheld the crown prince hovering above him and his mother weeping over his father's dead frame, he sat up, wincing.

"Keep working on him," the prince said to the young healer. "His wing's broken from the looks of it, and that gash on his head probably means he sustained a concussion. And if your magic is deep enough, his mother also has a torn wing to tend to."

The boy dipped his head. "Yes, Your Highness."

I lurched back from the house when the prince burst through the front door. A thunderous expression scoured his features, and that look only strengthened when he saw me. I had no idea if he was angry that I'd tried to intervene, or if he was pissed off about having to deal with the attack, but fire burned in his eyes—a white-hot fire that turned them an icy blue.

I took a fearful step away from him as my breath quickened.

A low growl rumbled in the prince's chest, and then his gaze cut to my neck, his attention fixating on the area where Vorl had choked me. With a tight clench of his jaw, he pivoted and strode back toward the path, not saying a word to anyone.

My heart pattered even faster. I felt like a trisilee on the verge of a heart attack and was certain everyone could hear my pulse. That belief only increased when Haxil ushered me after the prince, and all of the villagers' stares shifted from Prince Norivun to me.

Their questioning assessment, confusion, and disgust hit me all at once. Unlike a pre-pubescent child, who one would expect to be wingless, I was a fully grown fairy, and their morbid interest made heat creep up my neck.

"She must be a strange sort of defective," a female hissed to her friend.

"But defectives still have wings. Where are hers?" the friend replied.

"Maybe *he* shaved them off." The first gestured toward the prince.

The other nodded. "He would do something like that. Evil, that one. Pure evil."

The male standing behind them snorted. "She probably didn't ride his cock hard enough, and he clipped her wings in punishment."

His friend elbowed him, then snickered. "You think that's why her clothes are so dirty too? Punishment? Or do you think he likes his whores filthy?"

The female in front sniffed. "Disgraceful, the lot of them."

I shot them all a glare, but their sniggering continued. I didn't know what was worse. The truth or their conclusion that I was the prince's whore, and he'd shaved my wings in punishment for a poorly executed fuck session.

But obviously, the truth wasn't even on their radar. The prince hadn't shaved my wings. I'd just never developed them. That truth had made shame follow me my entire life, even though I tried to accept myself for who I was. But the truth still hurt. I was the only adult Solis fairy, as far as I knew, that had never grown wings. And considering my age, I never would.

I clamped my lips firmly shut as the mountain's coldness sank into my bones. At least those villagers were completely wrong about me being a whore. I had that going for me. I would never touch the prince, not even if he offered me payment beyond my wildest imagination. I would rather die than let him touch me.

Despite knowing that, ice slithered through my veins. The villagers' comments stung. Deeply. But I knew I'd have to get used to it, because comments like that would likely continue. If the prince was taking me to Solisarium, a city of a million fae, I would have many more watchful eyes and scathing remarks coming.

"Imbeciles," I whispered under my breath.

Haxil grunted. "Couldn't agree with you more."

I gave him a small smile, at which he just patted my shoulder.

Ahead, the prince stormed toward the lodge, his movements as fierce as a gale roaring through a valley.

"Why is he so angry?" I asked Haxil.

The guard shrugged. "I suppose you'd have to ask the prince that."

But there was something in Haxil's expression that made me think he knew exactly why the crown prince was in such a foul mood.

As we trudged up the mountain, the prince's expression was hard and unforgiving, and the energy rippling from him was enough to make my shoulders want to fold inward while keeping my chin tucked to my chest.

Thankfully, whatever the reason for his rage, he kept it inward, not turning his affinity on me or his guards.

The village fell behind us when we entered the trees, and soon, smoke appeared from our accommodation's chimney. When we finally entered the lodge's main room, fragrant scents of freshly baked bread and succulent stew drifted through the air.

"Right over here!" Milis called, gesturing to the table nearest the fire that she'd preset with the guards' meals, hot and ready.

"See that Ilara gets to her chamber," the prince called tersely to Haxil before he disappeared up the back stairs.

Nish, Ryder, and Sandus headed toward their dinner. Numbly, I followed Haxil, once again realizing how my life was now completely out of my control. I was a prisoner of the crown prince. I now ate, slept, traveled, and probably relieved myself when he told me to.

Scowling, I pulled out a chair by the fire as my stomach let out a rumble.

"Hungry?" Haxil scooted over, making room for me at the table.

"I'm fine."

"Ock, from that growl I just heard, you're not fine," Nish replied, giving me a sniggering grin after he swallowed a large gulp of ale.

"Leave her be, Nish," Haxil said.

Nish cocked an eyebrow as Sandus also inched his chair over and waved toward the open spot. "Come and eat, Ilara Seary, daughter of Mervalee Territory."

"Is that an order?"

Sandus gave a crooked smile. "I can't order you, love. Only the prince can do that."

I glanced back toward the stairs, but wherever the prince had ventured off to, he was long gone. I frowned as the image of Mealow's husband collapsing beneath the prince's rumbling power filled my mind again. Seconds. It had only taken him *seconds* to kill that male. He'd brought down an enraged ice bear with only a thought.

My fury burned hotter, and I stoked my hatred for the crown prince until it roared as brightly as the fire in the lodge's hearth. Yet again, the prince had destroyed another family so easily. Even if the husband had been abusive, fae could change. But now, Mealow and her son would never know if that would ever be a possibility.

My chair scraped against the floor when I finally joined the guards. Despite my anger, they were right. I was hungry, and now that the prince wasn't around, perhaps I could stomach eating.

We ate in silence, with only the crackling of the fire and music floating through the air as company. Somehow, I managed to eat half a bowl of stew. My stomach protested at more, not used to the generous portions that Milis served. It didn't help that as each spoonful disappeared into my belly, I felt more and more eyes from the other patrons fall upon us.

Word must have gotten out at what the prince had done in High Liss, because the lodge's patrons stayed hushed—speaking in low tones to one another while casting wary glances toward the stairs, as though afraid of disturbing the dragon that slept in his cave above.

"Does the prince do that a lot?" I finally asked, breaking the silence. The guards had wolfed down their food, but now that everyone's bellies were full, they were leaning back in their chairs as their wings slackened, and the fire roared.

"Do what, love?" Sandus asked.

"Kill fae?"

The guards stilled.

"Is that how you see it?" Nish's eyes narrowed. "That the prince kills fae?"

"Isn't that what just happened?" I challenged.

"What happened," Nish replied, his teeth grinding together, "was that Prince Norivun acted in the realm's best interest. That fairy's wife came to him for help, so he did what was asked."

My hands clenched together underneath the table. Nails biting into my palms, I retorted, "I don't think she asked him to kill her husband. Besides, don't the supernatural courts usually deal with domestic matters like that? He didn't need to murder that fairy, especially since the prince is obviously a capable fighter. He could have restrained Mealow's husband even if her husband had been in his ice bear form. Or at least, he could have tried."

Nish's glare increased, and he leaned back in his chair, crossing his arms. "How many fairies in their ice bear form have you restrained?"

I frowned. "None. Obviously."

"Then you don't know the death rate significantly increases for bystanders when such an arrest is attempted."

I swallowed, remembering what Haxil had hinted at. "No, I didn't know that. But wasn't it worth at least trying? Until it became apparent it would be too unsafe?"

Haxil gave me a warning look, but I ignored him and leveled Nish with a heavy glare.

"And risk lives?" Nish snorted. "No. On the continent, when troubles rise swiftly and justice must be enacted quickly, the Death Master does what's needed and must make decisions without a second thought. So stop your righteous judging in matters of which you know *nothing*."

My pulse leaped, and I barely contained myself from lashing out at him. Because even if he was right that the prince had made the best decision in Mealow's house, I'd seen other kinds of *justice* the prince had delivered. When one went to him with concerns about the crops or concerns about a missing son, the prince didn't help those troubled fae. Oh no. He silenced them by murdering them. So I *did* know a thing or two about the prince's *matters*.

Sneering, I replied, "I suppose murder is one way to keep the peace."

Nish's wings extended, the leathery appendages nearly knocking into the chimney.

Ryder clamped a hold of Nish's shoulder as he gave me a withering glower. "Enough."

"Fine with me." Pushing back from the table, I stood. "I'd like to go to my room now."

"And what if I'm still finishing my ale, princess?" Nish replied, his eyes dark as he finally pulled his wings back in tight. "Wouldn't want you roaming around these halls and coming to any harm."

✳ 74 ✳

"Nish," Haxil growled. "Enough for you too."

Nish waved an angry hand toward me. "She disrespected our prince."

Haxil nodded. "As I'm aware."

Nish's lip curled. "If the prince didn't want her, I'd—"

"Enough!" Haxil roared.

Sandus crossed his arms, and though he remained quiet, he gave me a surly expression, as if *I* was to blame for the discontent growing within their group.

Ignoring both of them, I followed Haxil to the bar.

Haxil drummed his fingers on the bar top. "Milis? She's ready to turn in for the night. Can you show me which room is hers?"

Milis gave an overly bright smile. "Of course, follow me."

She led us toward the stairs, then up to the second floor. A long hallway waited, and my eyes immediately darted about, wondering what room the prince had disappeared into.

Milis's small wings fluttered slightly, and she lifted inches from the floor before flying slowly down the hallway. Only Solis with small wings could maneuver such tight quarters within buildings. The prince and his guards certainly wouldn't be able to.

Milis led us to a room several doors down, then inserted a key in a lock.

"Here? Really?" Haxil asked.

Milis shrugged. "That's what he said."

She opened the door to a large sleeping quarter. A huge bed, which could easily sleep two adult fae with their wings slightly extended, sat near the wall. Beside it was a glass table with a fairy light hovering above it, and across from it, a small living area complete with a couch and two chairs.

"Blessed, this is so—" I didn't even know what to say. It was by far the nicest room I'd ever seen. My entire home could fit into this one chamber. "It's wonderful. Thank you." I rubbed my arms, trying to ward off the chill. Frost iced the windowpanes.

Milis gestured toward the windows. "The hearth below will warm this room through the night, but it will still be cool. At this time of the season, as you know, winter starts creeping in."

"It's fine, truly. Thank you," I said again because it was. This lodge room was warmer than my home by at least twenty degrees. Last winter, Cailis and I had nearly frozen to death since we hadn't been able to afford the firewood needed to keep our hearth going around the clock.

Haxil prowled the room, checking the wardrobe and attached latrine. "Are the wards the same as always?"

Milis's wings stopped fluttering as she drifted to the floor. "Yes, Haxil. Without being granted the key or allowed entry by me or the room's recipient, visitors are not allowed to step over the threshold. The magic forbids it. Your guest shall be safe."

Haxil grunted, apparently satisfied with that answer.

Milis returned her attention to me. Her expression was painfully polite, and I couldn't help but wonder what her features would be morphing into if the prince hadn't warned her that I was his *guest*.

She surveyed my worn, dirty clothes. "There are bathing pools here on the second floor if you'd like to clean up before bed."

After the long day's flight, I was covered in a fine layer of dust, so I nodded. "That would be nice, if it's not too much of a burden," I added hastily.

"Not at all. The prince has asked that I supply you with fresh clothes. I'll show you to the bathing pools and will have clean clothing waiting on your bed when you return."

"Really?" I couldn't help my stunned question. I would have never suspected that the prince had thought of my comfort. I'd thought for certain that I would be wearing my field clothes to bed and for the foreseeable future.

"Indeed. Follow me. I'll show you the way." Milis lifted into the air and flew from my room down the hall and around the corner. She led Haxil and me to a set of exterior double doors. My breath caught when she opened them. Steamy mist wafted into my face from outside.

When it finally cleared enough for me to see, my surprise grew. The doors opened to the outdoors, to the mountainside resplendent with snow and moonlit pools.

A trickling waterfall cascaded from the mountaintop and fell into the pools' multiple bodies of water. Plants and vines wove throughout the natural rock formations, their lush foliage and colorful leaves in complete contradiction to the pines that I'd seen upon landing near here. Steam rose from the water, letting me know this area was either heated from magic or that they were naturally hot springs. Whatever the case, that warmth also explained the diverse plant life.

A smile parted my lips, and I stroked one of the leaves nearest us. "How hot is the water?"

"Quite hot," Milis replied. "But also very enjoyable. It soothes one's muscles after a long day's flight." She coughed abruptly, as if realizing I'd never known what wing muscles felt like after a day in the sky.

But I'd received such comments all my life, so I simply ignored her and waved a hand through the steam. I itched to take my clothes off and submerge into the crystal-clear liquid. It was beckoning me with its promised heat and tranquil atmosphere.

"Do you need to stay?" I asked Haxil.

While I didn't relish stripping my clothes with him watching, the thought of getting into the pool outweighed that. I'd never been in a body of water like this before, and there was no way I was turning it down.

The guard's eyes shifted to the waterfall, then back to me. He shook his head. "No, I shall leave you here to bathe at your leisure."

My eyebrows rose since that definitely didn't align with the prince's earlier command that he guard me, but I didn't argue.

"There are bathing soaps and cloths right over there." Milis pointed to the opposite side of the pool. "Enjoy."

She and Haxil sauntered back inside, leaving me alone at the pool's edge. I lifted my chin, a smile parting my lips at the plethora of stars and the three moons that shone above.

Glancing around, I searched to see if anyone else was lurking about, but I didn't see a soul. Not wasting any time, I took off one layer of clothing after another until I stood naked in the moonlight. The cold air chilled my skin, and my long hair brushed my waist. Goosebumps sprouted along my limbs, and my nipples peaked in the frosty temperature. My ribs were apparent as were my jutting hip bones, but even that didn't bother me as it usually did.

I couldn't remember the last time I'd been naked outside. Most likely when Cailis, Tormesh, and I were children and had run from our mother when she was trying to bathe us before bed, but even thinking of my siblings wasn't enough to dampen my mood at the thought of submerging in the pool.

I dipped a toe in, and my smile spread into a grin when the pool's heat kissed my skin.

Stairs had been cut into the natural rock, and with each step down, I shivered in glee. When I was finally fully submerged, I moaned in absolute delight.

Back home, we usually used a small wash basin to clean up each night. Rarely, we would lug out the tub to do a proper wash, but even that wasn't large. I would have to sit with my knees drawn to my chest while Cailis dumped water over my head.

But this . . . this was what luxury felt like.

I swam to the side of the pool, near the area where Milis had said bathing soaps lay. Sure enough, there was a large dish of scented mixtures. I picked one up and took a small whiff. *Sandalwood.* Too masculine for my taste. I tried another, then another, until I settled on a floral elixir that smelled of freshly cut jasmine and a hint of mint.

Using one of the cloths at the bowl's side, I poured a hefty dose onto it, then set about scrubbing myself until my skin shone pink and my still-silver hair hung in damp curls around my face. Even the dirt beneath my nails was coming loose.

With a frown, I cleaned them too, wondering when the next time would be that I would dip my hands into fresh soil and feel all of the life that the Mother gave us.

When I finally finished bathing, I lay back in the pool and let the water buoy me up until I floated on my back and stared at the twinkling stars above.

My breasts peaked in the cold, and goosebumps rippled over my exposed flesh, but I didn't care. The heat of the pool beneath my back and the serenity of the water cascading down the mountainside made my muscles un-bunch for the first time since the prince had taken me.

I drifted along the water's surface, letting the soft currents take me where they chose. Vines from the plants growing around the pool hung in suspended twists of braids and coiled strands near the water's edge, and when I bobbed toward them, I reached up and fingered the soft petals.

"How are you, my friend?" I murmured before going to the next flower, then the next vine, caressing all of them and bidding them hellos.

I floated like that for I didn't know how long, but when my eyes began to close in sleepiness, I finally straightened and swam a few laps across the water to wake back up before my interest drifted toward the waterfall.

I kicked closer to it, and my brow puckered when I realized it didn't run against the mountain's rocky side as I'd initially thought but instead covered the opening to a cave.

Interest piqued, I toed closer until the rushing water was only inches from my face and then took a deep breath before pushing through it. Only seconds passed before the pounding of the swiftly moving falls disappeared behind me.

Opening my eyes, I gasped when I beheld a dark hidden cave beneath the falls. The ceiling above glimmered with a thousand diamond-like stones that shone like distant stars. I stared upward, taking in the radiance of it. The cave itself wasn't more than ten feet in diameter, but the smallness of it didn't distract me.

Finding my footing on the pool's floor, I stood to my full height. While I wasn't what anyone would call tall, the cave's waters were actually quite shallow, allowing me to rise until the water licked my waist.

Reaching above, I tried to touch those beautiful stones, but a stirring in the pool's water stopped me. It felt as though someone had shifted, and a small wave lapped against my skin.

Swinging around, I gasped when two piercing blue eyes glowed from the darkness.

Goosebumps sprouted across my entire body as the crown prince gazed at me from a hidden seat within the cave. His gaze was hooded, his expression impossible to read, and he didn't say a word when his focus slid from my face to my breasts and then to my bare stomach.

I quickly submerged, resisting the urge to cover myself as fury glowed in my gut.

"I didn't realize you were there, my prince." I stepped quickly backward, putting as much distance between us as I could, until the prickly cave rock met my bare back.

Prince Norivun's wings shifted, and I figured he'd had to curl them behind him, bending his appendages to accommodate the shallow pool. They were probably dragging on the pool's floor, and it was sheer luck I hadn't stepped on one.

"I figured as much. You certainly looked like you were enjoying yourself."

My breath sucked in when I realized there were openings from the cave on each side of the waterfall. One glance outward told me that from the edge, a fairy would have a perfect view of the entire bathing pools. And the prince was sitting on the edge.

My cheeks reddened, and I wondered if this entire time the prince had been watching me.

"Did you enjoy the show?" I bit out, not caring when anger laced my words, but I hadn't hidden my naked form at all, and considering the prince was only feet away from where I'd been trying to touch the glowing stones, my breasts had practically been in his face.

The corner of his mouth kicked up. "Quite."

My breath sucked in at his smug arrogance. I shot a hand out, throwing a wave of water into his face before thinking better of it. "You're a cad."

An amused smirk lifted his lips as he wiped water from his eyes. Droplets clung to his long eyelashes. He ran a hand over his silver hair, slicking it back, and if the crown prince of the Solis continent was at all offended that I'd just shoved a wall of water in his face while calling him a name, he hid it well.

"I suppose it was bad manners not to let you know of my presence, so I shall forgive you for your actions."

I snorted. "It was more than bad manners. It's what a creep would do."

His smile wiped clean, and he inched closer to me, coasting along the water's surface like a feared predator in the Tala Sea. "Are you calling me a creep?"

My heart beat harder when he stopped only a foot away. Water ran off his broad shoulders and down his muscled form as his defined pecs appeared just beneath the surface. He was so big that I knew he had to be kneeling in the shallow pool.

I swallowed the ball in my throat. "I'm saying that only creeps watch naked females when they're unaware."

His gaze drifted to my neck again, right where Vorl's illusion spell hid my bruises.

"And did a creep do that to you? Or was that something you welcomed?" he asked quietly.

My hand flew to my throat. "You can see it?"

His eyes darkened, turning into cobalt chips of ice, as he gave a single nod.

"But how? Vorl's illusion affinity is so strong."

"Not stronger than mine."

My jaw dropped. "So you truly have an illusion affinity too? You weren't just glamouring my hair?"

"I have several affinities," he said, still looking at the bruises on my neck. His jaw began to tick.

So it *was* true. The crown prince of the Winter Court had been blessed with multiple affinities. "What else can you do?"

His eyes shuttered, and his expression turned impatient. "I believe I asked you a question."

I fingered my throat. The skin was still sore but not as tender as it had been a few days ago. "I wouldn't call him a creep, my prince."

One of the prince's eyebrows rose, yet the tension in his shoulders remained. "So you were a willing participant when it happened?"

"I didn't say that. I just said I wouldn't call him a creep."

The prince frowned as the aura off him rose. "Then what did you mean?"

"I meant that Vorl isn't a creep. He's a bully."

The prince stilled. "So he forced himself on you?"

I glanced away, unable to meet his penetrating stare. "He forced himself on me numerous times."

In a movement too quick for me to see, the prince's fingers enclosed my chin, and he jerked my head in his direction. "He raped you?"

I jolted back, breaking the contact as a thousand nerve

endings came alive within me from that single touch. "I never said that."

"Then what did you mean?" he growled, his voice low and deep and rippling with barely leashed power.

I shivered at the absolute menace rolling off him. "I meant that he forced himself on me in other ways but not in *that* way."

The prince's jaw ground together. "Explain."

"I . . . he . . . Vorl's bullied me since I was a child," I said in a rush. "Pushing me around, tripping me, hitting me on occasion when others weren't looking, but his favorite pastime was choking me. He loved that one the most. That's why I have bruises."

The prince's jaw locked even tighter, and that brewing power within him rippled out across the water, causing small waves to lap against the cave's walls. "And he did this regularly?"

My brows drew together as I recalled how many times over the seasons Vorl had bullied me, belittled me, tortured me, hurt me. I finally gave a swift nod.

The prince's nostrils flared, and he ran a hand through his hair. The movement made his bicep bulge and his wings flex. I tried not to notice, tried to stop my attention from shifting to that gesture, and tried to stop from noticing how incredibly thick all of his limbs were. The male was pure muscle. Everywhere. And it wasn't the bulky type that some males had who tried to increase their build. It was the type that came from a naturally powerful frame with muscles that had been honed from actual combat and use.

"I wasn't sure what the reasoning was behind your bruises when I first saw you," he finally said, his words like ice. "So I didn't ask. But if I'd known that archon had done that maliciously to hurt you, I would have—"

"You knew it was Vorl?" I blurted out, then remembered how the prince had glanced at my throat and then to Vorl back in the barn. "But how?"

The prince took a deep breath as his aura still pounded out of him. "Illusions leave residual magic. When a fairy with an illusion affinity casts their magic, it leaves a mark, like a flavor or calling card. If you're in tune enough with your affinity, you can pick up on that mark and track what fairy did it. The magic woven around your neck has a very distinct mark that was tied directly to that archon."

"Oh." I shook my head, stunned. "I had no idea."

"It's not something fae like to advertise. When one's illusion mark is able to be identified, it can be embarrassing. Only fae with stronger illusion affinities are able to see through the illusion of a weaker fairy."

"Meaning you can see through Vorl's illusions, but he can't see through yours because your affinity is more powerful than his?"

"Correct."

The prince didn't elaborate. Anger still swirled in his eyes, and his strumming aura kicked up another notch, causing a second round of ripples to shoot across the pool.

Seeing as how the prince didn't seem inclined to say anything further, I asked, "So . . . why did you think this wasn't done maliciously?" I gestured toward my bruises.

"Sometimes females welcome choking," he replied distractedly.

My head cocked. "They do? When would a female ever want to be—"

I snapped my mouth closed just as the prince smirked.

Blessed Mother. How embarrassing. I might be an untraveled fairy, but I wasn't entirely naïve. I'd heard that some females liked to be choked while their partner pleasured them, that it could heighten the experience. Granted, it wasn't something I was into, and I'd never asked the males I'd been with to do such a thing. Still . . .

Cheeks aflame, I said, "I didn't realize you were into those types of kinky activities, my prince. Not that I'm judging," I added.

"I never said I was." He arched an eyebrow, some of the rippling anger around him morphing into amusement. "But you sound quite surprised that royalty could have a fondness for such bedroom activities."

I wanted to submerge in the pool and drown right there.

The amusement on his face grew.

I fiddled with my hands and cursed the large male for making me feel so ridiculous. "Whatever fae choose to do in the bedroom is their business, not mine. So if you do like choking, choke away, my prince."

That infuriating tilt to his lips remained as he drifted closer to me and said in a low tone, "And what about you, Ilara Seary, daughter of Mervalee Territory? Are there any kinks that you like?"

My eyes widened, and I shoved another wall of water in his face. The wave splashed him, and since he once again didn't try to prevent it, I guessed that meant he didn't have a water affinity too.

Aghast, I managed to say, "Are you really asking me about my sex life?"

He wiped the water from his face for a second time, his sly

grin lifting even more. "That's twice now you've assaulted me in this pool."

I snorted. "Well, arrest me then." I tapped my chin. "Oh no, wait, sorry. I forgot that you already have."

His smile spread. "Have you always been this insolent to authority?"

I ground my teeth. "Well, until you and Vorl, I never had the need to be."

His smile disappeared. "You're comparing me to him?"

I shrugged. "In all honesty, my prince, I'm not sure how much you two differ. You both take what you want when you want it, except you . . ."

"Except I what?" His jaw clenched, the muscle bulging in the corner.

I'd almost told him that Vorl hadn't murdered anyone, at least as far as I knew, and that he certainly had never killed anyone in my family, but with one glance at the prince's lethally cold expression, I stopped. "Nothing."

The prince studied me a moment longer, the tension flowing from him sending another ripple through the water.

My heart beat harder, and I didn't move.

He abruptly stood, and water cascaded down his chest. I shoved back against the rock as he prowled past me, and despite willing myself not to look at him, my traitorous eyes drifted from his square jaw to the rounded balls of his shoulders, past the heavy slab of his chest, and then to the defined abs beneath it. The water hid what was below his waist, but a clearly defined "V" headed south.

The second my eyes drifted toward his cock, I firmly forced them back up.

When I did, I found the prince watching me at the waterfall's edge. "And you're calling *me* the creep?"

With that, he ducked through the waterfall, and his giant wings disappeared with him. Embarrassment flamed through me until the prince's next words snapped me upright.

"Follow me, Ilara Seary. You're not to be left alone out here."

CHAPTER 8

It struck me on the walk back to my room that the only reason Haxil had left me at the bathing pools was because he'd known the prince was there, so I wouldn't be unprotected. If only I'd been astute enough to realize that.

It also explained why none of the lodge's other patrons had been enjoying the hot springs. When the Bringer of Darkness lounged within its depths, one could hardly blame a fairy for being skittish and unable to relax.

Back inside the lodge, I followed the Death Master down the hall as a perpetual scowl painted his features. Apparently, he didn't like being called a creep and was so bothered by it that he also didn't care that he was strutting around half-naked.

He hadn't used one of the lodge's robes. Instead, a simple towel was looped around his waist, which only amplified his toned abdomen. Wings tucked in tight to his back were like a narrow slit down his spine. Muscles bunched and moved in his shoulders, and ridges that I had no business seeing seemed to beckon my attention as he dipped around corners.

The prince was masculinity incarnate, a beautiful sculpture of death that would delight any female in the throes of her demise. It took everything in me not to throw a dagger at him—if I had a dagger, that was.

Cool air brushed over my skin as we made the final turn to my room. Since I didn't have wings, the slits in the back of the robe allowed a breeze to flow freely across my backside. I just hoped that my bottom wasn't on display. Normally, I had to buy my clothing from the youth vendor booths in Firlim's market. Since pre-pubescent fae didn't have wing buds, their clothing was still complete in the back, which meant that it kept my bare back covered, unlike adult fae clothes.

"Do you have your key?" the prince asked when he reached my door. He faced me, which put his firm chest in my line of sight.

I craned my head up. "Yes, my prince." I held it up, then tucked my dirty clothes under my arm and went to insert it into the lock.

"Allow me." He took the key in a large, calloused palm.

"Such a gentlefae, my prince."

He gave me a side-eye, and in turn I provided a saccharine smile.

With my door open, I expected him to step aside and return to wherever he was residing, but instead he crossed the threshold, and the hum of the protection wards surrounding the room vibrated against my skin.

Bristling, I followed him, then crossed my arms as he surveyed the room. "My prince, aren't you returning to your chambers?"

He fixed his piercing blue eyes on me, and I was once again

confronted with the planes and angles of his sculpted features. "This is my chambers."

My eyebrows knit together as a thrum of confusion pulsed through me. I ran a fluttering hand through my hair. "There must have been a mix-up. I thought they told me this was my room. Which bedroom chambers do I reside in?" An image of a frozen barn came to mind. *Blessed Mother, hopefully it won't be that bad.*

"There hasn't been a mistake. You're staying with me."

My hand fell. "What?"

"I said that you're staying with—"

"I know what you said, but why am I staying with *you*?"

He cocked an eyebrow. "Do you always ask such asinine questions?"

My nostrils flared as I pumped my hands into fists. "Only when encountered with ridiculous fae."

"Are you calling me, your prince, ridiculous?"

"Oh, no, of course not. I'm sure that would be considered treason, my prince."

His eyes lost their luster as they turned into chips of ice. "You're right, so I'm glad you're not that foolish."

Fuming, all I could do was watch as he prowled around the room, testing the doors and windows and sending out pulses of his magic to gauge the protection wards. When he finished his perimeter inspection, he nodded toward a pile of clothes lying at the end of the bed. "I see Milis did as I asked."

I planted my hands on my hips. "You're seriously staying here with me?"

"I believe it's actually *you* who's staying here with *me*. This is my chambers after all."

Tapping a foot, I replied, "Which again, begs the question,

why am I staying with you? Surely you can at least explain that even though you claim it's an *asinine* thing to wonder?"

He straightened more, and his shoulders seemed to stretch across the room as a dark cloud fell over his features. I took a step back, not even realizing I was doing it until I ran into the doorframe.

"Did you not hear the villagers' comments?" he asked in a deceptively quiet voice.

"Of course, I did."

"Then you know that some wish me, and by extension *you*, harm."

My throat turned dry when I forced a swallow. "Do you really think they would try to break in here and hurt me?"

He shrugged. "It's hard to say, but it could happen. Many attempts have been made on my life."

Too bad none of them were successful . . . "Then why doesn't one of your guards stay with me in another room that has two beds?"

The corner of his mouth kicked up. "Are you scared of staying with the Bringer of Darkness?"

Scorching hot anger abruptly raged through me, like an uncontrolled wildfire engulfing the mountainside. It came from out of nowhere, but that cocky smile ignited what had been simmering within me all day—fury over what this male had done to me.

"Is everything a joke to you?" I snapped.

"Hardly."

"Then why do I have to stay with you?"

He stepped closer, with lightning-fast speed, until we stood toe to toe. My breath sucked in, and I stumbled back until my spine was plastered against the door. Instinctively, I gripped the firm edges for support.

"Be careful, Ilara Seary, daughter of Mervalee Territory. I might be offended by how much you despise me."

Forcing myself to raise my chin, I met his cold gaze. "One would think you would be used to it by now. Doesn't everyone hate you, my prince?"

His eyes shuttered. For a moment, he didn't say anything at all, but then that frostiness returned to his expression, and he said in a menacing whisper, "And pray tell, why would someone, such as yourself, have reason to hate me? A simple farm girl from some unknown village on our vast continent, who's never once encountered me before today. Tell me, why do *you* hate me so?"

Because you murdered my parents and brother when Tormesh had done nothing other than report his concerns of the dying crops to the court, and my parents' only crime was asking the court what had become of him.

That bold statement was on the tip of my tongue when a knock came on the door.

I jumped just as the prince's head lifted, his nostrils flaring. "It's just Nish." He reached past me, his thick forearm brushing my side when he gripped the door handle and pulled.

"How do you know—" But I didn't bother finishing my question. Nish stood in the hallway.

The guard ignored me as he addressed the prince. "I'm first watch tonight. Just thought I'd let you know I was here."

Prince Norivun gave a curt nod.

"After me, it'll be Sandus, then Ryder, and Haxil's taking the last shift."

The prince inclined his head again. "Thank you."

"My pleasure, Nori." Nish gave us his back, and the two swords tucked in sheathes beneath his wings glinted in the hallway light.

The prince shut the door and began walking toward the latrine. "I suggest you try to sleep tonight. It'll be another long day's flight tomorrow."

"But—" I hurried after him, at which he promptly closed the latrine door in my face. An enraged howl worked up my throat, and I was two seconds away from pounding my fist on the door when he opened it again, except this time he was dressed in sleeping shorts that clung to his toned waist.

The scent of fresh magic surrounded him, and I knew he'd probably cleansed his teeth with it since a slight puff of peppermint lingered on his breath.

"Did you need something?" he asked, not even a flicker of guilt in his gaze.

I stared at his firm chest, akin to a solid wall. Smooth, slightly golden skin spanned his entire upper half. Not one flaw or birthmark covered him, but he did have a long scar running along his side.

He was so huge that I didn't even reach his collarbones. Despite that, I gritted my teeth, determined not to let his intimidating presence deter me. "Why must I stay in the same room with you?"

He crossed his arms. "How many guards do I have?" I scoffed, at which he quirked an eyebrow. "This isn't a trick question."

I blew forcefully through my nose. "Fine. You have four guards, my prince."

"And what do you suppose their job is?"

"To guard you when you're unable to guard yourself."

"Correct. Now don't you suppose that they would also like to get some rest tonight?"

"Well, of course they would."

"And do you really think that they'd be able to rest well if they were guarding me while I slept in one room and you while you slept in another? That would require two guards on each room during the night versus four guards on one room. I'll leave the mathematics to you. I'm sure even your simple mind can deduce that they'll get more sleep if there's only one room to protect."

I rolled my eyes. "So you're actually claiming that you're sharing a room with me to be less of a burden to your guards?"

He continued to stare down at me from his imposing height and didn't respond.

Even though my hatred for the male still burned hotly inside me, a small part of me paused at his strange courteousness. As the crown prince, all he had to do was snap his fingers, and he would be granted any wish of his choosing. One would assume with that kind of entitlement, he would be selfish and uncaring, but apparently, he actually thought about his guards' comfort.

Or it was all just a ruse to trick me.

Of course. It had to be a ruse.

The prince leaned down, and I could have sworn darkness gathered around him. "What's the matter, Ilara Seary, daughter of Mervalee Territory? Does that surprise you so much? Does it not coincide with your preconceived notions of the Death Master?"

Even though his words dripped with sarcasm, I still detected something in his tone. Something that hinted at my reaction being what he was so used to hearing.

"I shall leave the latrine to you. Fresh clothes are on the bed." He sidestepped me before I could stop a sliver of guilt from burning through me.

But any shame I'd felt at assuming he was horrible in every way was doused when a pile of clothes abruptly landed on my head.

I swung around to find him smirking.

"Did you really just throw my clothes at me?"

"No, I simply gave them to you."

"You're not a gentlefae at all." I snatched the shirt off the floor that had fallen off my head.

"I figured I'd save you the trip back to the bed."

Seething, I tucked the clothes under my arm and faced him as he doused one of the fairy lights. Since it was becoming apparent that I was sharing a room with him whether I liked it or not, I said, "Okay, fine. We'll share a room, but tell me something, my prince. How do you know that *I* won't harm *you* during the night?"

His gaze dipped, and he did a slow perusal of my body, his stare like the strength of a hundred suns, burning a path into me.

"Let's see . . . you're small, underweight, wingless, magicless, and most importantly, weaponless." He stroked his chin as he lifted the covers with his free hand. "If you were actually able to kill me in my sleep, I would deserve it for being so weak."

"So I'm too minuscule to be a threat? I see." Thankfully, my reply came out haughty because inside, I was dying with embarrassment. The prince was right. Even if I managed to secure a weapon, I wouldn't know how to use it.

"Now, are you satisfied?" He sank onto the mattress while his wings bent to accommodate him. "Or do you have more questions I need to address before I finally go to bed?"

I clenched my teeth. "One last question, my prince. Why must we share a bed?"

"Because there's only one."

"Can't you sleep on the floor?"

He settled the covers over his bare chest, and his rounded shoulders stayed visible over the top while his giant wings seemed to take up half the mattress.

"Why would I do that?"

Blessed Mother . . . I made myself count to ten before responding. "Because we're not sharing a bed, my prince. And since I'm the one who's been taken captive and held prisoner for no discernible reason, I think the least you can do is give me the bed while you take the floor."

"Why would we do that when this bed is more than large enough for us both?"

"Just get on the damn floor!"

His eyes widened, and the bastard actually looked like he was going to laugh. "I believe you're my subject, and I'm the one who gives the orders."

"And I believe you know I'm in the right, and you should act like a gentlefae."

He leaned back, his lips splitting into a wide smile. "I thought we'd already established that I'm *not* a gentlefae."

A shiver ran through me when a cloud of his magic drifted toward me. Power. Might. Horrible destruction. It was all rolled into one misty essence that he'd unleashed. The sheer presence of the male—even from across the room—threatened to consume me.

Yet . . . a part of me wondered if that was who he truly was. It could all be a show. Perhaps he played this heartless role because everyone assumed it was who he was, me included.

Frowning, I realized accommodating his guards *didn't* play into my preconceived notion of his brutality.

But before I could form a coherent reply, his magic dissipated, and the prince turned on his side and doused the last light. "We leave at sunrise to finish the trip to Solisarium. I suggest you stop yammering and go to sleep."

I sputtered, once again unable to form a reply when the creak of the bed broke the silence. He shifted into a comfortable position while his wings relaxed behind him.

I spun toward the latrine and slammed the door behind me. I couldn't be sure, but I could have sworn that a faint deep chuckle came from the room, which only confirmed he *was* a heartless monster, and my brief hesitation to believe anything but had been foolish.

Sighing, I knew that meant one thing. I would be taking the floor.

CHAPTER 9

"Please, my prince. Please! I beg of you. Don't kill us. Spare us! We have children. Two daughters remaining. They need us. They'll starve without us!"

My parents' pleas filled the throne room of the Court of Winter. But instead of King Novakin staring down at them from his icy throne, it was his son, the crown prince, whose judgment reigned.

"Silence," Prince Norivun commanded. His giant wings draped behind him, the huge black leathery appendages in complete contradiction to the whites and blues of the court's inner room.

My father dipped his head. "Please, my prince. My daughters will starve. My youngest, Ilara, has only just started working full-time in the fields, and my other, Cailis, has only been working them one winter. They're lowest on our village's pay. Without my income to help support them—"

"I said, silence!" the prince roared.

My father's lips clamped shut as my mother wept beside him.

Both were on their knees, their features twisted in pain as they faced their judgment.

"We only came to ask of our son," my mother said softly, her sweet voice carrying through the room like a bird's call. "To ask what became of him when he traveled to this court to voice his concern over the dying crops. Please let us go."

Prince Norivun's jaw ticked. "Guards."

Ryder, Sandus, Nish, and Haxil appeared, hovering over the prince's side before they descended the throne's steps to my terrified parents.

"Hold them." The prince's eyes turned icy. Brutal. It was the same look he'd worn right as he took the life of Mealow's husband.

"No!" I screamed. I tried to run from the back of the room, but wisps of fog drifted around my limbs, holding me in place. I pumped my legs faster, but I didn't move.

"Please don't kill them!" I shouted.

Tears ran down my cheeks as I pushed myself harder. I needed to move. Needed to get to them. I had to save them.

But no amount of effort propelled me forward. I stayed locked in the back of the room as sweat beaded on my skin and my muscles burned. It was as if my legs had been anchored to the floor, stuck to some sort of magical treadmill that kept me from saving my parents no matter how hard I tried to reach them.

"Please, Prince Norivun. Don't kill them. I beg of you!" I called again. I cried harder, sobs racking my chest. "Please! Please!" I said over and over.

But the prince ignored me, and his guards' grips tightened around my thrashing parents.

My eyes scrunched closed when the Bringer of Darkness unleashed the terrible strength of his affinity. I felt it wash over me *after it passed through my parents. Felt it when their lives ended as swiftly as the raging northern winds.*

My breath came out in a rush as I forced my eyes open. A twitch convulsed my father's body, then my mother's, before they both lay still as the prince's horrific magic sucked back inside him.

"No, no, no. Please no. They can't be dead. They can't be." I fell to my knees, suddenly able to move as sobbing overtook me.

But my pleas didn't stop even when my parents' vacant eyes gazed skyward from the cold stone floor.

"Please, don't let it be true. Please, no."

"Shh," a deep voice whispered in my ear. Strong arms lifted me from the cold floor, then I was moving out of the throne room as the scent of cedar and snow drifted around me.

"But they're dead. They can't be dead." Another sob shook my chest, and the strong arms slowly lowered me.

Then I was lying on a cloud of warmth as softness settled over my skin, and a hard and heated slab nestled against my back.

I cried harder as the throne room around me faded, and then all I felt was warmth, a slight stroking of fingers untangling the hair from my face, and a deep voice that shushed me to sleep.

My eyes fluttered open when a knocking sound roused me, but I wanted to keep sleeping and stay buried in the mountain of warmth that encased me.

I snuggled deeper into the bed, loving the feel of the soft mattress and the thick covers keeping me warm. This was heaven. A true luxury. Like no bed I'd ever slept in before.

Wait. A bed?

My eyes flew open.

I bolted upright in an actual *bed* just as a knock came again. A young female was calling through the door, telling me that it was time to get dressed.

All I could do was stare at the sea of pillows, sheets, and thick soft blankets surrounding me.

I was in the prince's bed, when I specifically remembered going to sleep on the floor. My attention snapped to where Prince Norivun had slept.

He was gone. The bed was entirely empty save me. I reached a hand across the mattress. Cold sheets slid beneath my fingers.

"Thank the Mother," I whispered. I must have crept into the bed after he'd left, probably when I'd grown too frigid on the hard floor.

"Lady Seary!" the female outside of the room called again when I continued to sit there.

"I'm up!" I finally called. "And I don't need assistance. I'll get dressed!"

Another knock came. "Apologies, but the prince insists."

I grumbled as I rubbed my eyes, and then a flash of a dream came to me. My parents. The Winter Court. Strong arms around me.

I frowned as the knocking resumed. "Please, he said I must assist you."

The foggy dream vanished as I processed her words. Reluctantly, I pushed the covers back, then padded to the door and opened it. A young timid-looking female stood in the hallway beside Haxil. The guard gave me a nod, a slight smile curving his lips.

I returned the greeting, then shifted my attention back to the young servant. She was probably less than twenty winters, and she bobbed her head multiple times as she held out an armload of folded clothing. "These are for you. I'm to help you change into them."

My confusion grew as I stared at her, then I looked to Haxil for answers, but he just shrugged.

"But I have my own clothes." I opened the door wider to let the girl inside, then shut it behind us.

She didn't waste any time smoothing the rumpled bedsheets before holding out her hands to assist me out of the sleepwear Milis had provided. "I'm afraid you can't wear your own clothing."

"Why not?"

She wouldn't meet my gaze as she lifted my shirt. "I'm sorry, my lady. The prince said we were to burn them, not wash them."

My hair—still silver from the prince's illusion—brushed my shoulders when I spun to face her. "He did? And is that what was done? They're gone?"

The young servant's eyes widened. "Yes, 'tis correct. I'm very sorry. I was simply following orders. The prince gave me your clothing this morning and said to destroy it."

My chest heaved, but I forced my breathing to calm. It wasn't her fault, and even though my pants had been worn threadbare in some areas and engrained with dirt and stains in others, it still infuriated me.

Once again, the crown prince was doing as he pleased, not caring nor considering that those were *my* things.

Arrogant cad.

"My lady?" the young fairy said as she twisted her hands. "May I help you dress?"

I forced my tight-lipped smile to smooth. "Of course. I'm sorry. It's not you I'm angry with."

She bobbed her head again, a relieved exhale escaping her, then she held the fresh undergarments out for me to step into.

Somehow, amazingly, everything the young servant had brought fit. On top of that, the shirt didn't have wing slits in the back, and the pants felt as though they'd been crafted specifically for me. I marveled at that when the clean material spun from the softest cottonum and warmest woolen blend settled over my skin.

Eyeing my new pants, I was relieved that the prince hadn't commissioned a dress for me, as was the common choice among noble fae females. Instead, I'd been given supple black leggings that were thick and warm.

The rest of the clothes were all done in the Winter Court's palate. The sweater was a thick cable-knit that rose to the top of my neck and slid down my arms to the base of my fingers. The beautiful royal blue brought out the natural sapphire in my eyes. Coupled with the silver stitching woven throughout the pants and top, along with the fur-lined black cape rimmed in silver and blue flowers carefully stitched along the outer edge . . . well, I felt like a true princess, which would probably make Nish snicker.

"Where did these clothes come from?"

"They were sewn yesterday in High Liss, my lady. The prince requested it of Milis, so she commissioned our local seamstress."

I frowned, trying to think of when the prince would have had the time to ask that of Milis, then realized he must have done it after he'd left me with the guards in the great room downstairs.

I held out my arm, marveling again at how well everything

was tailored. "The seamstress must have a creation affinity if she could sew everything so fast and so precisely."

The girl bobbed her head again. "That she does. She sews most of the clothing sold in High Liss and is quite adept. With her magic, she can create an entire wardrobe in one night."

"Please thank her for me, although, I'm not sure how I'm going to pay for—"

"'Tis already been paid for, my lady. The prince covered the expense."

I sighed. He'd probably spent more rulibs than I made in a full season. "I'm sure he'll expect me to repay him, and I'm not a lady. You really don't need to keep calling me that."

The girl's blue eyes grew curious. "I apologize. I'd just assumed you were a lady since you were traveling with Prince Norivun. I've never seen him carry anyone, but I suppose since you don't have—" She cleared her throat and glanced toward my back, to where my wings should have been. "I'm sorry. I shouldn't have presumed."

"It's fine, really." I shrugged, then added, "If you really want to know, I'm his prisoner, not a lady."

Her eyes bugged out. "You're a criminal?"

I laughed. "No. I'm entirely innocent of any crimes, but one would never guess it." I quickly recapped how the prince and I had come to meet. "So, as you can see, I honestly don't know why I'm traveling with the prince or why he took me. He has yet to explain anything." Remembering that made annoyance flare within my gut, causing my irritation over my destroyed field clothes to strengthen.

The girl tapped her chin, her finger slight and slim, just like the rest of her. "'Tis definitely strange, but still rather exciting, don't you think?"

"In what way?"

"You're not being convicted of any crimes. You're traveling to a new territory, and you're going to see the great capital. *And* the prince hasn't harmed you. Not to mention, you've been fed, had a nice bed to lay your head, and now have warm clothes specifically tailored for you to wear into the heart of our continent." She sighed. "Sounds like a grand adventure to me."

I gave her a sad smile. Her optimism reminded me of my brother. Tormesh always looked at the bright side. He'd been so hopeful that the court would listen if he only presented his concerns about the crops. Instead, that optimism had gotten him killed.

Shaking my head, I realized that the young servant's perspective and mine were the epitome of the differences between childish dreams and mature stark reality. While the prince hadn't mistreated me, I was still a prisoner. Perhaps a prisoner currently kept in a gilded cage, but a captive nonetheless. Seeing it as a whimsical adventure would lead to nothing but heartache and disconnection from reality.

I turned toward the full-length mirror across the room and took in my appearance. Bathed last evening and refreshed following a good night's sleep made my skin glow radiantly. And the garments I'd been dressed in truly did make me look like a lady.

Clearing my throat, I hastily smoothed my top as the girl arranged a thick cloak around my throat, then handed me butter-soft leather gloves.

"I suppose I better get moving." It was well after sunrise. "Thank you for your help."

"Of course." The female bobbed a curtsy, then led me out the door to Haxil.

The guard did a once-over. "Well, look at you, Ilara Seary, daughter of Mervalee Territory. You look like a noble female."

"I had help." I nodded toward the serving girl.

She blushed, then curtsied one last time before scurrying down the hall, leaving me to follow Haxil downstairs to the great room.

A fire roared in the giant hearth, just like it had yesterday when we entered the area. I figured that a fairy with a fire elemental affinity had infused it with magic that allowed it to burn hot and bright around the clock, even when the wood fueling it ran low.

The three other guards along with the prince sat at a table, the remnants of their breakfast in front of them. A serving platter with a few portions of meat, eggs, and thick toast slathered in butter, along with dishes of fresh berries in cream, remained.

My mouth watered at the sight, and my stomach gave a ferocious growl. I'd never been around such an abundance of food in my entire life, and it seemed that my stomach was taking notice. Of course, the prince and his guards probably took it for granted. Unlike the rest of the fae on the continent, they'd probably never known a day of hunger in their lives.

The prince was drumming his fingers on the table and eyeing the windows when we reached them.

"Would you like to sit, Ilara?" Haxil pulled out a chair for me. "I'm sure the prince wants you to eat before we leave."

The other guards watched me, but my cheeks didn't warm until the prince glanced my way.

Prince Norivun's features remained smooth, giving no hint to anything unusual having happened between us.

I gave an inward sigh of relief. I must not have climbed into bed while he still occupied it. *Thank the Mother.*

But any gratefulness I felt vanished when his jaw ticked with annoyance. "You're late. I told you we leave at sunrise."

I settled onto my chair and waited for Haxil to also seat himself before I said in a biting tone, "Good morning to you too, and if someone hadn't destroyed my clothes, perhaps I would have arrived on time."

The prince's drumming fingers stopped. "Your clothes were filthy and better off burned. I did you a favor."

I snapped my napkin over my lap. "Is that how you see it, my prince? How kind of you to take one more thing from me and destroy it without my consent."

His eyes blazed sapphire. "I didn't—" But he closed his mouth as a frown knit his features. His jaw ground tighter, and a rumble of his power vibrated around him before he growled, "Just eat. We need to get going. A gale is moving in."

Those words left his mouth with such commanding force that my hands responded before my brain did. I found myself reaching for the plate of toast, then piling a spoonful of eggs on the bread.

"Would you like any of this?" Haxil held up the array of meats.

I grabbed several slices of crisp bacon as the guard also poured me a cup of tea.

"Thank you."

Haxil grinned, his cheeks round and his eyes sparkling. "Pleasure is mine."

I gave Haxil a small smile, and the prince's chair squeaked when he pushed it back and cast his guard an irritated glare before he stood and went to the windows.

Ignoring the crown prince, I munched on the toast, bacon, and eggs. The other guards remained quiet as they shared occasional glances between Prince Norivun and me.

Once again, a scowl twisted the prince's features. It didn't seem he was in a much better mood than me, which led to Nish glowering at me more than once. I figured the guard was blaming me again for causing problems, but if he thought I was going to simply sit back and become an obedient fairy, he had another thing coming. Granted, I couldn't do anything so stupid that it would get me killed, but I could goad the prince and do everything in my power to make him regret ever having taken me.

I was halfway through my last piece of crispy meat, the fat on it so succulent that it melted in my mouth, when the prince returned to the table.

"Time to go. You'll have to finish eating when we get there."

Dusting my hands off, I stood without complaint. Considering I'd eaten twice as much as I usually did, I gave him a sweet smile.

"As you wish, my prince."

His scowl deepened, which made a petulant thrill run down my spine.

"Safe travels," Milis called as we ventured toward the front door. "Ock, be mindful out there. A right gale's coming in. Best to take care."

The prince inclined his head, then ducked outside as his giant wings dipped to avoid hitting the doorframe.

Frigid wind pelted my face when I joined him, and the raging clouds made me pause and wonder if I should have hurried after all. Wincing against the icy onslaught, I brought the cloak's hood up as a large gust of wind shot through the trees. The soft fur rubbed on my cheeks, and despite my anger at the prince for burning my things, I had to admit that it was warmer than my previous cloak.

"Fly high," the prince said to his guards. "It's the only way we'll get through this."

The four of them gave swift nods before shooting into the sky, their huge wings flapping as they fought against the air currents of the incoming storm.

"Is it safe to fly in this kind of weather?" My throat bobbed when the prince stepped closer. I instinctively took a step back, causing him to smirk.

"Scared? You should be. Most fae can't fly in these conditions. And those that try often don't make it to their destinations."

"But you can?"

"If I have to, and since you didn't heed my call to leave at sunrise, you'll have to as well."

My stomach churned as the ominous-looking navy clouds grew in the sky. Fat snowflakes swirled through the air, coating the trees and layering the ground in several new inches.

"Is it truly possible to fly above it?"

Instead of replying, he swept me up in his arms, and with a huge thrust from his legs and a flap of his wings, we were airborne.

Like yesterday, the ground disappeared quickly beneath us as he held me tightly and climbed into the sky. Given how quickly he did it . . .

Mother, he's powerful.

Turbulence from the atmosphere jostled him, though, making us dip and roll. A crack of thunder shook the air, and then a flash of lightning shot through the sky.

"Fuck," the prince muttered under his breath.

I clung tightly to him as his wings flapped harder, but the air currents didn't abate. We'd climb and climb only for a huge gust of wind to shoot us down.

Above us, the prince's guards also struggled to gain altitude.

It was on the tip of my tongue to tell Prince Norivun I was sorry that I'd stalled our departure when a huge burst of magic abruptly shot out of him.

Suddenly, we were careening upward, moving faster and faster as his guards were propelled up with us too. It was as though a force pushed us from below, fighting with the Mother to free us from her stormy embrace.

The air grew thinner the higher up we went, and my ears popped at the sheer speed in which we ascended through the storm.

Lightheadedness from the thin air fogged my thoughts, but then the angry clouds parted, and we were above them.

The prince immediately halted his vertical ascent and turned us perpendicular to the clouds, flying over the cascading cottony sea of navy and indigo clouds beneath us as the pale green sky stretched in a dome above. Up here, the sun shone brightly.

"Blessed Mother!" I panted, still clinging to the prince. Below us, Nish, Sandus, Ryder, and Haxil were all free of the storm too.

Haxil gave me a thumb's up as the four leveled out into normal flight.

Still panting, I tried to gulp in air, but it felt as though I'd pass out.

The prince's arms tightened around me more. "Hold on."

I'd only just gripped him tighter around the neck when another swell of magic pulsed around us, and then we were catapulting forward, going so fast that his four guards turned into a blur before they disappeared behind us.

"Show off!" one of them yelled, their faint call already distant and barely discernable to the blasting wind in my ears.

The magic cloaking us grew, and a shimmer appeared around us. Then the wind abruptly died, and the thin air grew richer.

I breathed deeply as dense air filled my lungs. My dizziness abated.

"How—" I glanced down in confusion, but the clouds were still beneath us, and we still flew high in the atmosphere. "How am I breathing easier?"

"Magic."

"From where?"

He smirked.

My jaw dropped. "Another affinity you've been hiding?"

He glanced down at me, that arrogant curve to his lips that I was becoming all too familiar with on full display. "I don't hide anything. It's not my fault if you're unaware of my talents."

"So you have an air elemental affinity too? Is that how you got us above the storm?"

"Perhaps."

"And that's how we're breathing easier up here too? I'm assuming most fae can't fly at this altitude?"

"Also correct."

I glowered at him. "You know, for a simple farm girl from Mervalee, I seem to be making a lot of the correct deductions."

"You are. Perhaps you're not simple-minded after all."

I scoffed. "But how am I breathing normally this high up?"

"I've created a bubble around us filled with dense air, and I have a concentrated stream of air at our backs, propelling us faster than my wings can carry us."

For a moment, I just stared at him. His wings flapped occasionally, but for the most part he seemed to be gliding, letting his wings ride the currents in his magical bubble—currents that he'd probably constructed. No wonder he was so much faster than his guards.

"So let me get this straight, my prince. You have your *death*" —I could barely get the word out—"affinity, an illusion affinity, and you have an air affinity?"

"Among other things."

I gaped. "You have *more*?"

He gave a barely perceptible shrug. "I was bred to be powerful."

I frowned, but even though I was curious to learn more, I didn't want him to think that I actually cared. Because I didn't. It was just normal, is all, to be curious how a fairy could have so much magic.

I loosened my arms slightly from around his neck as the clouds drifted beneath us. Glancing over his shoulder, I searched for his guards, but they were long gone.

"You seem to be in the habit of leaving your guards behind."

He shrugged. "I don't need them at the moment, and they can be dreadfully slow."

Despite trying to contain it, a snort escaped me when he smiled wickedly. "In all seriousness, why don't you just create bubbles around them and use your magic to propel them at the same speed as us?"

"They don't need the extra help, other than the denser air. Their affinities give them incredible strength, speed, and endurance. That's why they were only an hour behind us yesterday."

"Yet, you're still faster than them despite their affinities."

"I am. Now surely you don't hold that against me too?"

"Well, I didn't say that. I intend to hold everything against you."

"As I'm coming to see."

I frowned. "But don't you want to keep them close, just in case you need their protection?"

He nodded toward the unbound atmosphere. "Their job is simply to protect me when I can't protect myself, but up here, nothing can hurt me."

He sounded so confident, so sure of that fact, and given the immense capability of his power that I'd seen so far, I had a feeling he was right.

CHAPTER 10

Despite the prince's magic shooting us across the land toward the capital, it still took hours of flying. Beneath us, the angry clouds of the gale pummeling the Gielis Mountains fell behind us after we finally crossed the mountain range and descended into Prinavee Territory.

The clouds thinned and shifted from indigo and navy to light pink, soft yellow, snowy white, and translucent summer green. And as we flew farther, the clouds thinned even more until there was nothing but clear seafoam sky above us and bare land below.

When the weather truly calmed—something I knew would rarely happen come winter—the prince dispersed the magical bubble we were encapsulated in and drifted lower, allowing me to decipher more details of the land beneath us.

"Are those villages, my prince?" I asked, pointing.

The prince's silvery hair was pulled back with another leather band, but today it was in a low ponytail. A few strands had pulled loose and twisted around his face, highlighting the planes and angles and his deep-seated eyes. "They are. As we get nearer to the capital, the city sizes grow, but we're still a hundred millees away, so out here, they're farming villages."

"Like where I come from."

"Correct. The land in my territory isn't blessed as richly with *orem* as in your territory, but we still grow crops."

The small village I'd spotted grew nearer. Within minutes, we were directly above it, and even sharper details were present.

Tiny houses and narrow streets ran in a gridwork pattern. The roads had been cleared of snow, but when I beheld the land around it and searched for the fields, I struggled to find any.

In my territory, the *orem* made the fields warm, and even if they were filled with snow, the crops still grew and flourished, often growing through the snow if the *orem* wasn't able to completely melt it. But the signature bright colors of blue, burnt orange, green, marigold, dazzling red, and fuchsia—the rainbow of colors I would expect from fields of wheat, vegetables, and fruits—were absent. All I saw was a sea of white.

I frowned. "I don't understand. Where are the crops?"

The prince's arms tightened around me. When I glanced up, searching his face for answers, he simply nodded ahead. "Do you see Solisarium?"

I shifted my attention forward, searching for the capital but not really knowing what to expect. All I knew of the great city was that it resided within Prinavee Territory, which was our continent's only landlocked territory, and that over a million fae called it home.

"I don't see anything."

"Look closer."

I squinted, then caught the flash of something bright shining above the snow, then another twinkle, and another. Glistening droplets of frosted glass, bricks of snow, and twisted white metal grew larger the more the prince's wings carried us.

The castle.

It stood highest in Solisarium, and I was able to see more fragments of its architecture with every millee that passed.

My heart beat harder as more and more details of the sprawling city emerged. The outer edges were mostly homes and small shops, barely discernible from the ground, but inward, the buildings grew taller and the architecture more extravagant. I'd never dreamed that I'd actually see any of this, had never even thought to imagine it since where I came from, the most a fairy could hope for was to work in Firlim if one managed to avoid laboring in the fields. But nobody in my village ever went to university, not even the closest one in Elsberda, which was only a two hours' flight away, let alone the prestigious Academy of Solisarium in the capital. It just wasn't done. Nobody could afford that.

And knowing that my dreams for the life I would one day lead were vastly limited, I'd never considered the possibilities outside of Mervalee. It'd been too painful, too final to know that any dreams larger than my village would be squashed before they'd begun.

Yet now I was seeing Solisarium, even though it wasn't under any circumstances I'd ever hoped for.

"Why do you look sad?"

The prince's question startled me so much that my grip slipped from around his neck. Of course, it didn't matter. He simply tightened his hold on me.

"I'm not sad. I'm fine."

He rolled his eyes, the movement so unlike him that some of the lingering pain from a life I'd never be able to lead faded away.

"Anyone with eyes can see that you're sad."

Not liking that he'd caught me in a moment of weakness, I scowled. "Don't you mean anybody with the ability to empathize is able to see that I'm sad?" His forehead scrunched together, so I added, "Fae without empathy don't sense emotions in others. They're not able to pick up on subtle body language."

"So you're saying I have empathy?"

I started. "No, um . . . no, that's not what I meant. I just meant that not everyone with eyes would be able to see that. I'm saying that you're wrong."

"So that definitely sounds like you're saying I have empathy, which would imply that I'm *right*."

Flustered, I wondered how I'd trapped myself in a corner, then realized it was because I'd felt vulnerable so therefore got defensive and started blubbering.

"Hardly," I finished lamely.

"Then what did you mean?"

"I meant that—" I paused. *Dammit.* What did I mean? Because if the prince had just picked up on the wave of sadness that had rolled through me, and he'd cared enough to ask about it, did that mean he *did* have empathy? The Bringer of Darkness, the fairy who wreaked destruction on our land, actually had some kind of heart?

He chuckled. "And now you look angry again. That's an emotion I've grown quite used to seeing on you."

"What makes you think I'm angry now?"

"You get a little line between your eyes, and your lips thin in the slightest way when you're upset."

My eyes widened. He wasn't wrong. Cailis had told me the same thing.

I shifted in his arms, not liking where this conversation was going, mainly because it was forcing me to concede that the prince, in whatever capacity, did have empathy within him, even if it was in minuscule proportions.

Blessed Mother. I'd actually just accepted that.

"So are you going to tell me why you were sad a moment ago?"

I unclasped my arms completely from around his neck and crossed my arms over my chest. "Fine. I'll tell you. I was thinking about how I'd never in my life thought I'd see the capital."

He frowned. "And that made you sad?"

"Yes, it did."

"Why?"

I rolled my eyes and then said sweetly, "Do you always ask this many *asinine* questions, my prince?"

He arched an eyebrow. "Is that sarcasm I detect in your tone?"

"Me?" I batted my eyelashes innocently. "I would *never.*"

He shook his head, but a hint of amusement rolled across his features. "So seeing the capital, after not thinking that would be possible, has made you sad. I have to say, of all of the emotions I'd expect a fairy to feel at seeing the richness of our great continent, sadness would have been the last one."

"Then perhaps you're not as empathetic as you thought."

"Or perhaps there's more to your story that you're not telling me."

"And why should I tell you my story?"

He shrugged, the movement causing us to lift slightly in the wind. "We still have thirty minutes until we reach the castle. Conversing seems like a good way to pass the time."

"Are you getting bored of the silence?"

"Not at all, but I have to say, now that I've asked you a question, which you seem Mother-bent on avoiding, I'm even more intrigued."

A smug smile lifted my lips. "Good. Then I won't tell you."

His mouth parted, a look of shock covering his face, before his eyes narrowed. The look was mischievous enough that my stomach flipped.

"And what if I said I'd drop you if you didn't tell me?"

I immediately curled my arms around his neck. "You wouldn't."

He shrugged again, except this time the movement was even bigger, causing us to career upward at an even faster rate. I swallowed a shriek just as he said, "Wouldn't I? We've already established I'm not a gentlefae."

Another scowl descended over my face as a dark light entered his eyes. "That's not fair. You're threatening me bodily harm simply to get what you want."

"I never said I'd harm you."

"You don't think dropping me would hurt me?"

"Of course not, because I'd catch you before you hit the ground."

I glanced downward, the land seeming even farther beneath us. "You're a bully."

His lips parted, then he laughed. "I'm many things, but a gentlefae and a bully aren't two of them."

"Oh really? I completely disagree, my prince. You're trying to force something out of me that I don't want to share. That makes you a bully."

"That doesn't make me a bully. It makes me a male who knows how to play his cards right."

"Oh, please. That just makes you a bully in sheep's clothing."

"Have I done anything to hurt you?"

"Besides ripping me away from my sister and everything I know and love?"

"Besides that."

"I think that's a pretty big one."

"But an unimportant one."

"How in the realm is *that* unimportant?"

"We're getting off track. I believe I asked you why seeing the capital, which you never thought you'd visit, would cause you sadness and not joy."

"And I believe I told you that I'm not answering."

His lips twisted up even more. "Now I'm *really* intrigued." His arms loosened abruptly, and I clung instinctively to him, plastering myself to his chest as my face pressed flush against his neck.

His steady heartbeat filled my ears, and the wind died down even more with his body shielding mine. But worst of all, his scent flooded me, and he smelled so rich and decadent. Mother, he smelled good.

I abruptly pulled back, my heart beating rapidly. From fear or from the unfurling sense of attraction that had just sparked within me, I didn't know. *Blessed Mother, how twisted is this? To feel a sense of attraction for the* murderer *of my family?*

I'd completely lost all sense. Cailis would give me a tongue-lashing if she knew.

Trying to calm my breathing, I bit out, "You're insufferable."

He grinned. "And you're a frightened little mouse."

"You would be too if you didn't have wings."

He shrugged, and we once again shot upward. I cursed him several times over, berating him for doing it, which only made him laugh again.

When we finally—thankfully—settled into a relaxed glide once more, he cocked an eyebrow at me. "Surely you know by now that I won't let any harm come to you?"

I gave him a bewildered look. "I don't know that. How could I possibly know that?"

"Because if I wanted you dead or hurt or maimed or whatever else your imagination has come up with, it would have happened already."

"Or perhaps it's still coming, and it won't happen until the capital."

"Why would I fly you all the way across the continent simply to postpone harming you until we reached the capital?"

"I don't know. Why would you?"

He frowned again as a look of discontent washed over his features. "You truly think I'm going to hurt you."

"I truly think you're going to do something to me that will either hurt me or make me wish I'd never met you."

His frown deepened. "Very well, then forget I asked about why seeing the capital made you sad."

"I've already forgotten, my prince."

❄

WE DIDN'T SPEAK the rest of the flight, and I was glad for it. Now that the prince had relinquished whatever sudden curiosity had overcome him, he'd returned to gliding normally with no further threats of dropping me.

And since I was determined to look anywhere but at him, I soaked up as much as I could from our bird's-eye view of the capital.

The closer we got, the more I was able to see that Solisarium was nestled in a broad valley surrounded by hills that rose in gentle snowy mounds and that buildings and homes covered every inch of them.

The entire city was a hodgepodge of streets. Some were parallel and perpendicular. Others were curved and looping around. It was as though the city had been built haphazardly, and I realized that since it had grown so much over the centuries, that it likely had been.

The outer rim seemed more structured, but the inner portion was a winding maze of streets and alleys that would be very easy to get turned around in for someone who wasn't able to fly above everything.

Snowy rooftops covered every building and home, but snow was less common on the steeper, ice-coated roofs. I marveled that none of the central city's buildings rose higher than five stories, making the castle at the heart of the capital's inner district that much more commanding and breathtaking.

My throat bobbed in awe as I beheld it. Even from a distance, its towers, huge turrets, and steeply peaked roofs screamed of wealth and decadence. A solid, thick wall surrounded the entire castle, and its exterior held glistening spears of decorative ice. A shimmering dome of sparkling magic as fine as dusted snow covered the entire expanse. I could only presume that dome was a protection ward that didn't allow anyone in who wasn't invited.

I tried to soak everything in, tried not to let one detail escape me, but it was hard as the congestion grew. Fairies flew everywhere, making it difficult to see, and the closer we traveled toward Solisarium's center, the more fae appeared in the skies.

Hundreds of fae flew at different heights and speeds. Some flew leisurely, obviously not in a hurry to get anywhere as they traveled just over the rooflines. Others flew as fast as their flapping wings could carry them as they climbed high into the sky, probably hoping to avoid the busier altitudes below. Some carried bags. Many carried children. But regardless of where I looked, fairies were everywhere.

"So many fae," I whispered, not even realizing I'd said it aloud until the prince responded.

"Over a million call Solisarium home."

He'd continued to look irritated in the few times I'd caught glimpses of him, but his tone didn't sound angry when he replied. I kept any further comments to myself, though, and returned to gazing at the capital and the castle ahead.

It wasn't until we were almost at the castle's boundary that I realized in the entire time the prince had been flying, he'd done so in a straight line. He'd never had to climb or dive or sweep out of the way to avoid the congested areas of flying citizens.

Everyone moved to the side for him.

My lips parted when I realized that. The prince's giant, talon-tipped wings continued to flap while his gaze stayed trained straight ahead. Even though some fae stopped to hover and watch us, he didn't greet anyone or show any signs of acknowledgment, and it wasn't lost on me that more than a few made the sign of the

Blessed Mother, as though hoping our land would protect them from any evil left in his wake.

And for the very first time, it struck me how incredibly hated the prince must feel. Everyone feared the Death Master, and fear often morphed into anger, revulsion, and then hate. Hatred was easier to feel than fear—I would know.

"Is something wrong?" the prince asked, not even slowing as we approached the outer ward of the castle's protective barrier. Magic pulsed over my skin, even from a distance, as though warning any flying fae not to come near unless they wanted to experience the castle's wrath.

"No, everything's fine," I said, doing my best to ignore his probing stare.

But as much as I tried to ignore the pang of curiosity that had filled me about the life the prince must have led, I couldn't suppress it completely.

It seemed Prince Norivun wasn't the only one who felt intrigued by the other.

CHAPTER 11

The minute we pushed through the castle's protective ward, the sound of steel meeting steel clanged around us.

"Fuck," the prince hissed under his breath.

He dropped from the sky, and my eyes widened at the horrific fight occurring by the castle's outermost wall.

Two guards were lunging at each other viciously. Deadly blows nearly landed on each male as they sliced and danced around one another.

The prince touched down and released me in the same beat. I stumbled back as he strode toward them, his affinity rising as a ripple of his aura shot out. The guards surrounding the two fighting males all stumbled back, then fell to their knees in deep bows when the prince passed them.

"My prince, I'm sorry," one of the guards called as he rushed after him. "I tried to stop them, but they're fighting over—"

"Let me guess," the prince seethed. "Lorinda, that barmaid?"

"Yes, my prince."

The prince reached the two dueling guards, and one of them seemed to finally realize the storm cloud that was about to unleash, because he glanced away from his opponent.

It was enough of a distraction for the second guard to land a blow. The sound of flesh tearing, then a gurgle of blood erupting filled the courtyard. The prince stopped in his tracks, and my hands flew to my mouth as the guard fell.

His opponent's sword had struck right at the base of his neck, severing part of his head. Blood pulsed in shooting sprays from the wound—a lethal injury unless a talented healer could be located immediately.

"Get Murl now!" the prince bellowed.

Several guards rushed away as two ran toward the fallen male.

"What in the realm is happening out here?" a portly, older male called, coming from across the yard as the prince rounded on the one who'd landed the blow.

"Not now, Lord Crimsonale," Prince Norivun bit out as he faced the guard.

The young male backed up, dropping his sword as his righteous anger morphed into palpable fear, but I didn't pay him or the approaching lord any further attention as my focus shifted to the fallen fairy, the one who was seconds away from dying.

A deep throbbing sensation started in my gut as a strange yearning began to fill me. And then the land was rushing past me as my feet carried me like the wind toward the fallen guard.

Everything happened as though time stood still. Breath rushed from my lungs. The throb in my belly grew. My attention focused with pinprick precision on the dying male.

I slammed into the crowd around him, pushing through the

guards hovering at his side, fighting to reach the fallen male. I had to get to him. Had to help him. Had to—

"Out of the way, the lot of ya!" a male roared.

The commanding demand fell on my deaf ears. A shadow shimmered along the dying male's form. My gaze was fixated on that shadow. *I needed to—*

Rough hands yanked me back just as the healer hunkered at the male's side. The healer's affinity rose swift and strong, clouding the nearly dead fairy as an awareness crept over me.

Something was rising from the dying male, like a translucent cloud. The throbbing in my belly increased just as the prince's head snapped toward the dying male's form, then to me.

My vision tunneled again, shrinking inward to that hovering essence. *Hold it. Protect it.*

I fought against the hands holding me, but then the prince was suddenly there, towering over me.

Disbelief swam in his eyes. "You're—" His mouth snapped shut, but his eyes widened more and more. Blood drained from his face as though he'd seen a ghost.

A guard tried to yank me away as Lord Crimsonale watched us with narrowing eyes, but a deep growl vibrated the prince's chest as he shot the guard a furious glare. "Release her. *Now.*"

The guard stumbled back as the chaos around the fallen guard increased. Magic surrounded the dying fairy, but Prince Norivun's attention fixated entirely on my face. His gaze roamed over my features as his eyes swam with confusion, awe, and something . . . primal.

"And who is this, Prince Norivun?" Lord Crimsonale asked.

The prince snarled, and then his arms encircled me before we shot into the sky. He moved so fast that I couldn't breathe.

The ground rushed by as the castle's yard disappeared behind us.

My breath stuttered. "What are you doing?" I gasped.

I tried to see over his shoulder. I had to know what became of that dying male, but the prince flew too quickly, and the sight was gone before I could blink.

I beat on the prince's shoulder. "Why did we leave?"

I had to . . .

The prince's hold tightened, his breaths coming rapidly.

"Why!" I yelled again.

But the prince ignored me as he descended over the castle's inner buildings. Steam rose from boilers. Smoke curled from chimneys. Fae dressed in working gear scurried about. Dozens of servants tended to who knew what within the kingdom's court as that guard was possibly dying.

My breaths came faster and faster and faster. Too fast.

"Will he live?" I finally asked, my chest heaving.

"Most likely. Murl got there in time."

My heart beat erratically as that strange throbbing sensation in my gut dimmed. I brought a hand to my belly, wondering if something at breakfast hadn't agreed with me, but then we were spiraling downward, and any thoughts over food sickness fled.

The prince landed in a small open courtyard, shifting me in his arms as his booted feet touched the ground. I still thought of the dying fairy. Still wanted to know what had become of him.

"Can we go back?"

"No," the prince bit out.

Snow covered the courtyard and kicked up when Prince Norivun placed me on my feet. My toes touched the powder, then met cobblestones slick with ice beneath it.

Shouts and yells carried to us from a distance, probably commotion around the healer and injured male. But it was muffled, like background noise. I would have barely noticed it if not for my heightened state.

I stepped away from the prince. He still held onto me, his large hand anchored to the small of my back. And his expression . . . He was looking at me so intently . . . almost *possessively*.

"Are you okay?" I asked uneasily.

His head snapped back, and his expression wiped clean.

Once accustomed to the slippery surface, I put more distance between us, needing to get away from the barely leashed energy surrounding the prince.

I wrapped my arms around my middle. "Who was that other male? Lord Crimsonale?"

The prince looked away. "An archon. Nobody you need to worry about."

I lowered the hood on my cape and forced my breathing to slow. That strange throbbing that had started in my gut finally vanished completely.

For a moment, the prince and I stared at one another. Two yards of distance now separated us, yet it didn't feel like enough. An intensity I'd never seen before carved his features into something that made me want to run. He looked so fierce yet also as if he were in shock. It was a conundrum I couldn't comprehend.

"Are you sure you're okay?" I asked again because he looked anything but.

He shook himself, and another moment passed, then he tore a hand through his hair and waved dismissively at the courtyard we stood in. "I'm fine, and welcome to the Court of Winter. Although that wasn't the introduction I'd hoped for."

Frowning, I studied him. Something still felt *off* about the prince, but for the life of me, I couldn't place it. "Why did we leave that guard so abruptly?"

The prince took his gloves off, first the left, then the right. He did it slowly. And with each pull of his glove, he took slow deep breaths. The aura around him still felt so high it was suffocating.

I didn't flinch, not even when his attention focused completely on me again, but that wild look I'd seen previously was now behind a carefully blank expression.

"Answer me, my prince. Please. Why did you make us leave like that?"

"There was nothing further we could do."

My eyebrows pinched together. *Nothing we could do.* He was right. Obviously. Yet the need I'd felt to go to that male . . .

I shook my head. Madness. My life had descended into absolute madness. I brought a hand to my forehead and finally looked at the small courtyard. "Where are we?"

"Within my private wing."

The courtyard was a perfect square. The castle's tall walls rose three stories on each side. Spires and turrets that soared to impossible heights hovered in the distance, but the courtyard was too narrow for me to see much of the castle past that.

A *bang* came from my left, getting a jump out of me, and then several fae bustled into the courtyard from a door near a silent fountain. Trickling snowflakes cascaded over its sides.

"My prince," they all said, each bowing low, one even getting on his knees despite the wet snow. All of their heads dipped simultaneously.

"Patrice, Balbus, Haisley," the prince replied. "I assume you've been well?"

"Of course, my prince, we've all faired fine." The balding fairy with the round belly straightened. Wisps of white hair clung to the sides of his head, the top as shiny as ice. He hurried to take the prince's cloak and gloves. "The court's been eager for your return, my prince. Lord Crimsonale was just announcing to everyone that you've arrived."

The prince's jaw tightened. "I'm sure he was. I know I took longer than anticipated. Has my father been notified of my arrival?"

"He's being told as we speak, my prince," Balbus replied.

"Undoubtedly, the king will want to see you within the hour," the skinniest male added, the one who'd dropped to his knees in greeting. "He's been asking daily if anyone's heard from you."

The prince's expression grew impossible to read.

"I told him how you dislike mistphasing back to the castle each night, my prince," the portly fairy added. "That you prefer staying among our fae to better understand our vast continent during your overland tours. The king wasn't happy, but he accepted that."

"Thank you, Balbus," the prince replied.

I clasped my hands in front of me, as my thoughts returned to that dying fairy. I couldn't help but wonder how he faired.

Thankfully, the prince's servants seemed caught up in the crown prince's arrival, and since my illusion-hidden hair didn't draw attention, and none of the servants had noticed my wingless back yet, nobody paid me any attention.

I mulled over what had happened, but then the prince gestured toward me.

"Patrice, Balbus, Haisley, may I introduce Ilara Seary,

daughter of Mervalee Territory. She is my guest and is to be treated as such. I would like her time with us kept discreet. None of you are to speak of her to anyone else in the castle, especially Lord Crimsonale. Is that understood?"

"Of course, my prince," they all replied in unison.

The balding fairy stepped forward and brought a fist to his heart in the Solis traditional form of greeting. "Ilara Seary, daughter of Mervalee Territory, my name is Balbus Greenthorn, son of Harrivee Territory. It is a pleasure to serve you." He dipped his head again as the other two also came forward.

"Patrice Hollarhan, son of Osaravee Territory, at your service." Patrice brought his fist to his heart, then inclined his head but didn't get on his knees—not surprisingly—as he had for the prince. He was the youngest of the three with a thin, wiry build and medium-sized soft-black wings.

"And I'm Haisley Bottomale, son of Prinavee Territory. How do you do?" Haisley said in a nasal tone as he rested his fist over his heart. He gave me a pleasant smile and then bowed as well.

"Nice to meet you all," I replied and brought a fist to my chest. It wasn't lost on me that not one of them commented on my wingless back.

The prince stepped closer to me, his hand slipping to my waist. "I would like Ilara placed in the Exorbiant Chamber. Please have it readied immediately."

I stiffened just as the three servants bowed before departing.

The prince hastily removed his hand and stepped back. He opened his mouth, then closed it. A low growl vibrated his chest as he looked away.

My entire body heated at his nearness and . . . how he'd just touched me so intimately.

KRISTA STREET

"How—" I cleared my throat. "How do you expect to keep my imprisonment here a secret when the entire capital just saw you fly me here?"

"The capital saw nothing, but unfortunately, all of my guards and Lord Crimsonale did."

I frowned. "What do you mean the capital saw nothing?"

"I cast an illusion over us before we reached the capital's edge. Nobody outside of these walls knows you're here. They all saw me flying solo."

"Your magic is that strong?" An ominous feeling coated my stomach as the prince looked me over again. His expression wavered between anger, then confusion, and then annoyance before he said, "I want to show you something."

He gave me his back as he headed toward a door opposite where the servants had exited.

"Show me what, my prince?" I called as I shuffled over the icy cobblestones. My heart felt as if it were hammering a million beats a minute. I was slowly becoming used to the prince's intimidating aura, but it had ratcheted up another notch in the past few minutes and was now nearly swallowing me in its strength.

"It's something I think you will enjoy."

"Does it involve a looking glass to my home in Mervalee?"

We reached the door, and the prince stiffened. "No."

"Then perhaps a fairy with even faster traveling abilities than you who's going to take me home?"

His eyebrows knitted together, and the scowl he often wore made an appearance. "No."

"Then I doubt it's something I'll enjoy."

His lips thinned, but he pushed through the door and beckoned me to follow.

Inside the castle, a tingle of magic rushed over my skin, and the temperature immediately warmed. I sighed in relief as I followed the prince down a stone hallway. Tapestries hung intermittently, mostly portraits of the royal family, as fairy lights suspended high above us, lighting the area thoroughly.

I was soon lost to the twists and turns as the prince led me from one hall to another, but what I found most surprising was how quiet it was. I'd expected to hear a hundred servants hurrying down the passageways or clinking and clanging from the inner workings of the castle, but it was unexpectedly *still*.

"Where is everyone, my prince?" I asked when curiosity got the better of me.

"Somewhere else most likely. My private wing is off-limits to others within the court."

Well, that explains the quietness. But that also meant we were entirely alone. My heart rate ticked up again.

The prince finally stopped at a solid-wood arched door just as it swung open from within, and Patrice, Balbus, and Haisley poured out.

"My prince," they said simultaneously before bowing. "Lady Seary's chamber is ready."

"I'm not a—"

But before I could correct them for also mistaking me for a lady of the court, the prince replied, "See that a platter of food and drink is brought here."

"Of course, my prince. It would be my pleasure." Balbus beamed, making me think he enjoyed being a servant a bit too keenly, but I supposed living in a castle beat laboring in a field or working in the outer boiler rooms.

The three servants left in a flurry down the hall, all three taking flight since their wings were small enough to maneuver the walkways.

"You'll be staying here." The prince led me through the arched doorway into what I could only assume was the Exorbiant Chamber.

I did my best to hide my surprise at my newest prison cell, and any concerns I'd had over being mistreated shrank.

The chamber before me was fit for a princess. It was easily three times the size of the prince's suite back at Liss Lodge. Crackling from a fire snapped in the room, and a sweeping view through a huge set of glass double doors revealed an attached snowy and private courtyard.

A four-poster bed draped in gauzy curtains sat against one wall. It was so roomy it could probably accommodate three fae with wings. Across from the bed lay a grand fireplace that one of the servants had already set alight, taking the chill out of the air. Decadent couches and chairs surrounded it, along with throws and cushions that would ensure snuggling up by the fire to be a cozy pastime. Each seating arrangement was made for adult fae with slits to accommodate their wings, but even for someone such as myself, it would no doubt be comfortable.

Through a door in the corner, I spotted a bathing chamber and latrine. A *private* chamber. I'd never in my life been privy to anything like that. Beside that door waited a large wardrobe that made me wonder if it was filled with clothes or lay empty.

I turned slowly until my gaze fell upon the last area of decadence. A bar made of ice sat in the corner of the room with a flare of magic running through it. Icy crystals and snowflakes danced within its translucent walls with glimmers of stardust intermixed. It was truly beautiful, obviously designed by a master craftsman and entirely extravagant given its living magic.

"Do you like it?" the prince asked, breaking the quiet. He was watching me again, his expression tense, his eyes back to that icy blue that were impossible to decipher.

"This is what you wanted to show me, my prince?"

"Not this specifically, but I'm still curious if it's to your liking."

"It's beautiful," I replied uneasily.

He raised his eyebrows. "Does that mean you like it?"

"Would it matter if I did?"

A shadow passed over his face, but in a blink, it was gone. "Come. What I wanted to show you is through the doors."

He strode across the room to the glass doors that opened to the courtyard.

When I passed through them, another hum of magic washed over me as a warded barrier tingled along my skin.

"Is everything here warded, my prince?"

"Yes. It's a necessity."

"Warded to keep fae out or fae in?"

A dusting of snow fell from the sky as he turned to face me. Several snowflakes landed on the top of his head, melting quickly and disappearing into his silvery hair. "Would it matter?"

"To me it would. Is this to be my new prison cell despite the fact that I've committed no crime against the court?"

"I had hoped you would like it."

I frowned. "But why? Why would you want me to like it? Why have you brought me here?"

His brow furrowed. "I told you. You shall know in time."

"But not now?" I balled my fists. That simmering anger was

beginning to rise again, chased by a clawing anxiety over what my future held. I could be kept confined within these walls for days, weeks, even *full seasons*. And for what purpose?

"Do you enjoy the garden?" he asked, bypassing my question completely and sweeping his arm to the private courtyard.

Begrudgingly, I surveyed the open area. Similar to the courtyard we'd landed in, this one was also surrounded by the castle's walls that were too narrow for me to see the higher portions of the castle, but unlike the first one, withering plants filled this neglected patch of land.

Snow covered every inch of every surface, and my fingers tingled, inching toward the ground inadvertently. My frown grew as I beheld trees without leaves, vines without fruits, and plants frozen in ice.

Before I could drop down and let my hand glide over the frigid soil, I straightened my spine. "How is this a garden, my prince? It looks terribly neglected and without any *orem*."

He shrugged. "True, but I figured since you're used to tending to fields that perhaps you would like it."

I stiffened and wondered if he realized how ridiculous that sounded. Most in my village hated laboring in the fields and only did so as a means to support their family. I was one of the few fae who enjoyed it, but that was only because of my love for the plants. However, the prince couldn't possibly know that, which simply implied that he assumed all field laborers wanted to work the land.

He inhaled sharply. "What have I said that's angered you now?"

"Who said I'm angry, my prince?"

"That line between your—"

"Right, I must be wearing my angry face. How could I forget?" I did my best to smooth my expression, then crossed my arms.

He cocked an eyebrow. "Are you going to tell me?"

I pinned him with a haughty glare. "You want me to tell you why only an arrogant, entitled fairy would assume that all lesser fae who labor the fields would enjoy their jobs and want to tend to crops in their spare time? Oh no, I don't think there's any need for me to tell you that. Only a prince entirely out of touch with reality would need to be made aware of that fact."

His eyes narrowed, and a rumble of his great power vibrated beneath my toes. "Careful, Ilara Seary, lest I remind you who I am."

My heart jumped into my throat as a kiss of his magic washed over me. Breathing rapidly, I lowered my gaze and wondered when I'd become so stupid as to goad the Death Master of the continent. But there was something about this male that positively set me aflame with scorching anger. Anger. Not fear. Fury was easier to feel after all.

Still, I needed to stay alive, even if I was to be kept in a gilded cage. I had my sister to think of.

"I apologize, my prince."

His nostrils were flaring when I dared a look up at him, and that earlier hopeful expression he'd worn had vanished. Instead, he was the portrait of annoyance.

A moment of guilt bit me, which was ridiculous, but it seemed as though he'd genuinely wanted to please me with this chamber.

But what had he expected? Beautiful or not, it was still a cage.

The prince lifted his attention over my head toward the Exorbiant Chamber at my back. "Food shall be brought shortly. Balbus is just outside the door."

"He is? How do you—"

"I have matters to tend to, so I suggest you find something to do in your chambers while I'm gone. I had thought that perhaps the garden would keep you occupied, but maybe I was wrong. Regardless, you can do as you see fit."

With that, he strode out of the garden, back into my chamber, before opening the door and passing Balbus in the hall, who carried a full tray of food and drink.

Blood thundered through my ears. I barely heard the servant when he called a greeting to me. Because one thing had become incredibly apparent. The prince intended to keep me here, locked within this room for a reason he refused to share, and I had no idea if I would ever escape.

CHAPTER 12

Balbus was quite possibly the happiest servant in existence. If he wasn't beaming and gushing over all of the luxurious items within the Exorbiant Chamber or joyfully tending to any food or drink I needed, then he was simply grinning for no apparent reason.

Despite myself, I found myself liking the male.

The servant's round abdomen pushed into the table when he bent over to pick up my empty tray. Straightening, he flashed me a wide smile. "Now that you've had your fill, what shall I get for you, Ilara Seary, daughter of Mervalee Territory?"

"A dose of magic big enough to mistphase me back home?" I asked hopefully.

His eyes widened, then he laughed as his large belly moved up and down. "Oh my, you are a funny one, aren't you, my dear?" He winked at me affectionately. "But I was thinking more along the lines of books or knitting materials or perhaps needlepoint. To help pass the time, of course."

My breathing picked up, but I forced myself to say, "Um,

books, I guess?" I'd never had much time to read nor had easy access to books following primary school, although even that luxury didn't make this situation any better.

Balbus bowed. "Lovely. There's a library within the prince's wing that he's instructed me to give you full access to. The castle also has a library, which you've been granted permission to use. I shall fetch reading material shortly. Now, as for your clothes, the castle's tailor shall be by later this afternoon to obtain your measurements. All right, my dear?"

I could only manage a nod.

"Splendid. Should you need anything until then, simply pull that golden cord near the bed, and Patrice, Haisley, or I shall return. Otherwise, you can expect to see Daiseeum later tonight when she pops in to help you with undressing and bathing."

"Daiseeum?"

"Your assigned lady's servant."

"My lady's servant. Right." I followed Balbus to the door, wringing my hands the entire way. "Might I go with you, Balbus? Please? Perhaps to help in the kitchen with the dishes I dirtied?" Mother, I just needed to get out of this room.

His jaw dropped. "Help in the kitchen? You can't be serious?"

"As serious as a whiteout on the Cliffs of Sarum."

His eyes widened further. "Ock, no, Lady Seary! The prince would shave my wings for that. You're to stay here in your chambers. I do apologize, my dear. Prince's orders." With that, he exited the room and closed the door with a flourish.

When I tried to turn the doorknob to follow him, the handle wouldn't budge.

"Blessed Mother!" I beat on the door, but it did no use.

Balbus didn't come back to rescue me, and nobody else came either. For all I knew, they couldn't even hear me. I had no idea how strong the wards were protecting this chamber, but they'd been thick when I'd passed through them, making me wonder if they trapped sound too.

My solitude didn't last long, though. Balbus returned with books as promised, but instead of allowing me to follow him despite nearly begging, he once again locked me in my chambers.

Fuming, I turned back toward my prison and for a moment just stood there. That lasted all of two seconds.

I quickly turned into a flurry of exploration, looking under every layer of bedding, upturning every piece of furniture, and prying under all of the artwork on the walls. I figured there had to be *something* that could help me escape or perhaps would yield a hidden exit. I just needed to find it.

HOURS LATER, my fingertips and knuckles were raw from endless tapping and scratching as I searched for hollow areas in the walls or hidden exits. All of my searches proved unsuccessful, though, and were only interrupted when the tailor arrived. He was quick, efficient, and the opposite of loquacious. Despite trying to pry information from him too—that could hopefully help with my escape—the only words he uttered were *turn* or *arms out* or *extend your legs*. He didn't even comment on my wingless back.

Grumbling, I resumed my searching after he left, but by nighttime the only interesting things I'd discovered were an old necklace stuffed deep within one of the couch cushions, an aged bottle of the greenest leminai I'd ever seen, and a magical safe hidden behind the small portrait of flowers near the wardrobe.

The safe was, of course, guarded with a spell, so I couldn't open it, but since the opening was too small for me to fit through, I knew it couldn't contain a hidden passageway to escape. Most likely, it held jewels or ledgers that needed protecting, which wouldn't help me in the least.

My stomach was howling in hunger by the time I conceded defeat. It didn't help that my throat also itched with a vengeance as Vorl's magic began to fade. Within a few days his magic would dissipate completely, although the bruises would be long gone by then—as they always were whenever Vorl purposefully hurt me and hid it.

My physical discomfort only amplified my situation, so I kicked the wall in frustration. That, however, only led to a stubbed toe, but dammit, there was no way out of here, not unless I could fly out of the courtyard, which the bastard prince knew I couldn't, and that would only be if a domed ward didn't encapsulate the courtyard's air.

Depressingly, this chamber was too warded for someone such as myself to breach, which meant that unless the prince set me free or I could convince one of the servants to help me, I was stuck here for the foreseeable future.

Only the forlorn nature of the plants in the garden had pricked any interest in me. The prince had been right in that aspect. Even though I'd stated it was asinine of him to think I would want to tend to them, I did.

It was cold and dark by the time I slipped out through the glass doors. At least it'd stopped snowing, but a new inch of fresh powder covered the ground. Dropping to my knees, I let my fingertips touch the soil as I searched for a pulse or hum that *orem* existed within the garden. Dry, frozen dirt greeted me. I pushed harder, forcing my fingers into our Mother's depths.

Nothing.

My brow puckered as I tried to comprehend the absence of magic. Even though some territories on our continent were more naturally blessed in *orem* than others, they all held our land's magic to some degree. But here, within these walls, I didn't detect an inkling of it.

"How odd," I whispered to the frozen shrubs, vines, and plants. "No wonder you're all dead. You poor things."

I went to each one, carefully removing the snow and ice from the leaves until my hands were so cold I could barely bend my fingertips.

Blowing on them to warm them, I surveyed what I'd accomplished. It wasn't much considering how vast the garden was, but I'd managed to clear off at least a third of the neglected plant stalks.

"My lady?" a voice called from inside the chamber, barely carrying through the crack I'd left in the glass doors.

I peered inside.

A female fairy, still young at around fifty winters, waited in the chamber as she surveyed the area, obviously searching for me.

"I'm here." I slipped through the door, and she gave a surprised "Oh" when she turned to survey me, then immediately dipped into a curtsy.

"How do you do, Ilara Seary, daughter of Mervalee Territory? My name is Daiseeum Wheatvale, daughter of Prinavee Territory. I'm to be your lady's servant during your time at the

Court of Winter, and I've been sent to help you bathe and dress before you retire for the night."

I took in her angular features and hair tied in a severe bun at the nape of her neck. Like Milis, her wings were tiny, but unlike the Liss Lodge owner, Daiseeum's wings were rounded at the edges and were a soft-black color. Given how delicate Daiseeum's wings appeared, they were pretty much the exact opposite of the prince's huge leathery, talon-tipped wings.

My stomach gave another growl, and Daiseeum's hand flew to her mouth. "Mother Below, have you not eaten yet?"

"Oh no, I did when I got here," I replied sheepishly as I slapped a hand to my stomach.

Her lips puckered. "But that was hours ago."

I stared dumbly at her as I tried to understand why she looked so aghast. After all, I was being held prisoner inside a chamber in the king's castle, nobody was to know I was here, and I wasn't allowed anywhere near the kitchen. How in all the realms was I supposed to get myself food?

I crossed my arms. "I was told I couldn't leave these chambers, and I'm afraid no food or drink was left behind when Balbus departed."

Well, besides the alcohol at the bar. I'd been tempted more than once during the afternoon to partake in it, but I figured stumbling around drunk wouldn't help me if I managed to find an exit from this warded chamber.

Daiseeum's frown grew. "Did Balbus not show you the cord near your bed? All you need to do is ring it, and we would be most happy to assist you. Oh my, oh my." She shook her head. "The prince will be most displeased when he learns that we failed to keep you contented."

"No, Balbus did show me." I hurried to correct her, not wanting anyone in trouble on my account. "He mentioned the cord, but I didn't realize I was to use it for food too. I thought it was for—I don't know—emergencies or something." Such as if I stumbled and fell in a drunken state and gashed my head open. At the rate my captivity was going, I imagined that scenario was inevitable, especially if I partook in the overly bright-green leminai.

"Mother, no," Daiseeum replied. "It's to be pulled for anything you need, anything at all. I shall ring it right now. Tell me, what does your heart desire?"

I raised my shoulders. "I suppose whatever the kitchen has on hand."

Daiseeum's lips pursed again. Apparently, that was the wrong answer. "I shall also have them provide a menu so you don't have to wonder what's available. Of course, anything you would like can be made, anything at all. All you need to do is ask, my dear."

"All right, thank you," I managed to reply as my forehead furrowed.

My time here was getting stranger and stranger. So not only was I staying in a chamber fit for a princess, but apparently, I was going to be treated like one too—only I was to be kept under lock and key.

Daiseeum proceeded to pull the cord. Following that, she insisted that she help me undress and bathe before my meal arrived. It was a bit like the serving girl's help at Liss Lodge—entirely unnecessary—but I didn't want to turn her away if it meant she got in trouble with the prince.

"Daiseeum?" I said cautiously to her as she pulled out fresh nightclothes for me after I'd washed in the large tub. "Do you by chance know what happened to a guard that was injured earlier today? He was fighting with another guard when I arrived, and he was on the verge of dying when the prince whisked us away."

"Oh, yes, t'was a most unfortunate incident. The entire castle is talking about it." Daiseeum smoothed my top, then held out the soft cottonum pants. "He's still alive, gravely injured, but Murl—the castle's head healer—believes he shall live. Although, he shall have to remain in the infirmary for at least three days' time."

My shoulders sank in relief. "And the other guard? Is he to be punished, or what's to become of him?"

Her lips pursed again. "Well, if it were up to Lord Crimsonale, he'd be sent to the Death Master for execution."

My eyes bulged.

"But never you mind about all of that," she said in a hurry. "He shall answer to his commander as all the guards do when aggressive events occur."

I cinched the pants and eyed her curiously. "Who's Lord Crimsonale?"

"The archon of Osaravee Territory. He sits on the king's council, but again, never mind about all of that." She *tsked* and made me sit so she could brush my wet hair.

Even though I was perfectly capable of brushing my own hair, it was pleasant to have her assistance. Daiseeum's hands were gentle, and she took care not to pull too hard when she encountered a tangle, and when she finished brushing, she used her magic to dry my hair completely so I wouldn't dampen my pillow.

Haisley arrived with a platter of food, just as Daiseeum's magical cloud lifted.

"Here we are!" he said with gusto.

The kitchen had sent several dishes at Daiseeum's insistence in order to find something that I enjoyed. But I'd learned long ago to eat any food that was put in front of me.

But what arrived surpassed my meager expectations by millees. The minted lamb, herbed potatoes, grilled acorlis, gravy-soaked hen, fluffy gelatin, buttery pastries, and sweet fruit pies were more delicious than anything I'd ever tasted. I took bites of everything, unable to help myself.

The lady's servant kept me company while I ate, and even though she was hesitant at first to share personal details, I eventually pried out of her that she was the youngest of four siblings, all girls, and that she'd been serving at the castle since maturing age.

"That young?" I replied as I popped a petite pie into my mouth. "I suppose that's like me too. I've been helping in the fields since I was a child, but I didn't begin officially working in them until last season."

"Do you enjoy field work? I do so enjoy my position here. I couldn't have asked for anything better."

"I do, or maybe, I did," I said with a frown. "Working with plants has always brought me joy."

She gave a pleasant smile and began to collect my dishes.

I reached for my glass and silverware. My belly was so full I feared Daiseeum would have to roll me to bed, but that didn't mean I couldn't help. "I can clean up my mess. You've done enough."

"Blessed Mother, no!" She frowned heavily and whisked everything away. "It is my pleasure to serve you."

"That's what Balbus said." I picked at my fingers. "I'm sorry,

Daiseeum, but this feels so weird. I've never had anyone wait on me before."

She smiled sweetly. "Well, I suggest you get used to it, Lady Seary. The prince has commanded it, so therefore, everyone is here to serve you. Now, is there anything else I can do for you tonight?"

"Please, call me Ilara or Lara."

"Very well, Ilara." She raised her eyebrows, and I knew she was waiting for me to dismiss her.

I sat on the edge of the couch near the fire, shifting a bit uncomfortably, but I figured I wouldn't know until I asked. "Actually, would it be possible to perhaps accompany you? I would love to stretch my legs and get out of this room. Even just a short walk through the prince's wing would be much appreciated."

The servant's pale-blue eyes dimmed. "I'm sorry, my lady. That's impossible. I'm under strict instructions not to let you leave. Besides"—her voice dropped to a hushed whisper—"the castle isn't safe right now. Fae have gone missing, there's been unrest, and Lord—" She abruptly cut herself off.

I frowned. "Lord who? Lord Crimsonale?"

Her cheeks pinked. "Mother, listen to me carry on. But anywho, no, I'm sorry, my lady. You must stay here."

My frown stayed as I tried to comprehend what could possibly be going on that would make it unsafe for me to leave this chamber, but just when Daiseeum was about to depart, I asked in a rush, "Then is there any way I could be given a looking glass? I would love to know how my sister's doing at home. Surely, that's safe."

The lady's servant shook her head. "No, my lady. I'm afraid not. The prince forbids those."

Of course, he does . . .

I forced a bright smile. "How about a quill and parchment? Could I write my sister a letter and have it sent via courier? I'm sure she's worried about me. I just want to let her know that I'm okay."

Daiseeum's lips pursed—an expression the lady's servant seemed to wear regularly. "That might be something we could accommodate. I shall speak with the prince."

"Speak with the prince about what?" a deep voice called from the doorway.

I stiffened as a pulse of Prince Norivun's aura filled the room. He'd opened the door silently, so much so that not even Daiseeum had sensed him.

"Oh, my prince." The servant immediately fell into a deep curtsy as my spine turned rigid. "Lady Seary was just requesting some writing supplies to contact her sister and let her know how she fairs."

"I see. I'll take care of that. Thank you, Daiseeum."

"Of course, my prince." Daiseeum gave another curtsy before she exited the room, leaving me alone with the Bringer of Darkness.

I didn't turn to greet him, nor did I stand from the couch.

"You know it's customary for subjects of the court to acknowledge their crown prince when he enters a room." His deep voice flowed to me from across the chambers.

A shiver rolled down my spine as I jutted my chin up. He prowled toward me, all lithe grace and huge wings. Fury began to roll through me at just the sight of him. This male was the murderer of my family members and had officially taken me prisoner. Never mind that my prison came with luxurious bedding, fine dining, personal servants, and a tailored wardrobe. I still wanted to scream my frustration at him.

"Good evening, my prince," I replied icily. "I trust you are well and had a pleasant afternoon?"

The corner of his mouth kicked up before he fell into the chair across from me, his wings stretching behind him. They were so long they nearly touched the bar. "Why is it that every time you address me, there's always an underlying tone of derision in your voice?"

"Is there?" I replied innocently. "I'm afraid I don't know, my prince."

A rumble of his power vibrated the floor.

I whipped my gaze away, anywhere but to look at his sculpted chest and broad shoulders that were clearly visible in his fresh tunic.

"I was told you only requested food in the past hour. Was the earlier meal not to your liking?" he asked.

"It was fine, my prince."

"Then why didn't you eat sooner? You're too thin as it is."

My lips pressed into a tight line, and I debated telling him that I hadn't realized my weight was also being monitored, but then a knock came at the door.

"Dear brother? Are you in here?" a male called. "I was told you'd escaped to your wing for the night, and I haven't been able to find you."

The prince was on his feet and crossing the room before I could blink. He reached the door just as it was opening.

"Nori?" the male called. "Are you in here?"

"What is it, Nuwin?" the prince growled.

"Ah, you *are* here. I just came to see how your travels were, and if—" The newcomer's voice abruptly cut off as the aura from the prince strengthened a thousand-fold. "What do we have here? Are you keeping a female in here?"

The prince tried to block the door and the newcomer's view of me. "Not now."

The male laughed, not seeming the least concerned by the crown prince's surly tone. "Is this what you were doing while you were traipsing around the continent? When you were supposed to be—"

"I said *not now*." The prince's tone left no room for argument, which only made me more curious.

I was standing from the couch and striding toward the door before the prince could stop me. If Prince Norivun thought he could hide me away in the castle and keep my imprisonment a secret, then he had another thing coming. I would relay my unlawful captivity to anyone with the authority to return me home, and perhaps this newcomer was just that.

"Hello." I brought my fist to my heart in traditional greeting as I peered around the prince's broad back to his apparent brother. "My name's Ilara Seary, daughter of Mervalee Territory, and I'm being kept here against my will."

Prince Norivun cast me a scathing look, but I ignored him and turned plea-filled eyes on Nuwin.

"Brother?" The male laughed, and my breath sucked in at the likeness of the two.

Nuwin was just as tall and imposing as the prince, but his black wings weren't as large, and a lighter aura surrounded him, making him less intimidating. One look at his fine clothes, sultry

KRISTA STREET

smile, and twinkling blue eyes told me that such likeness extended to his personality.

Blessed Mother, maybe he'll help me.

Nuwin shifted his attention to the prince. "So you *were* flying with a female when you returned today. I heard a few mutterings among the guards, and Lord Crimsonale is most curious, but I didn't know if it was true or some strange new political maneuver."

I tried to push past the prince, but he blocked me. "Please, help me!" I begged of Nuwin. "I just want to go home."

The prince cut me an irritated glare. "You're staying *here*."

Nuwin glanced between the two of us, but instead of concern, a delighted smile crossed over his face. "So you've finally found a female that intrigues you."

A low growl of discontent vibrated the prince's chest. "Ilara is none of your concern."

"I am a concern if you can get me out of here!" I interjected.

But the prince's brother ignored me completely and laughed again, a rich, booming sound that seemed to fill up the entire hallway. His jovialness was a complete contradiction to the gravity of this situation, and I wondered if he was perhaps simple-minded, but then his next comment knocked that thought clear out of my head.

"Why, dear brother," Nuwin said, clapping the crown prince's shoulder, "after all of these winters, you've finally taken a courtesan."

CHAPTER 13

"A courtesan?" I retorted. My cheeks flushed as a snarl cut loose from the prince. "No, I'm a *prisoner*."

"She's not a courtesan or a prisoner, and you're to address her with respect, brother," the prince growled.

"Excuse me?" I placed my hands on my hips, facing Prince Norivun. "I'm most *definitely* a prisoner."

Nuwin ignored both of us and pushed the door open before strolling toward the ice bar. He gave the Death Master an amused smirk, then pulled out a bottle of alcohol.

"Drink, Ilara?" Prince Nuwin asked, his eyes still twinkling, which got another growl from the crown prince.

"Seriously? That's your response?" I rolled my eyes at Nuwin when he continued to wait for an affirmation. "Fine, actually, yes. I think I need one."

Prince Norivun cast me an angry side-eye, but I ignored him and stalked back to the sofa. Nuwin handed me a drink in a crystal cup, then clinked his glass against mine.

"Solls." He flashed me a wicked grin as the prince fisted his large hands.

"Solls," I replied, because at this point, what did it matter if we celebrated our drink? It didn't seem anyone was going to help me.

The prince's eyes shot daggers at his brother, but Nuwin simply eased himself down onto the chair adjacent to the couch and peered at me over his glass's rim.

"So the whisperings among the guards that a beautiful, wing-less female had been brought to the castle by my dear brother were correct." He laughed. "And I thought they'd simply had too much to drink."

"Is there something you need, Nuwin?" the prince snapped.

Nuwin glanced at him before taking another drink. "Not particularly, but I would love to hear more about your travels over the continent and how you came to meet this pretty thing."

Veins swelled in the prince's neck. "Now's not a good time."

"Oh? Then when is?"

In two strides, the prince was towering over his brother and hauling him to his feet. Nuwin's wing caught on the chair as he tried to set his glass down.

"Really, Nori . . . such manners."

"Don't even think about it," the Death Master said under his breath as he dragged his brother to the door.

I watched them both wide-eyed from the couch.

Nuwin smiled devilishly. "Think about what?"

"You know exactly what I'm talking about." They reached the door, and the prince lowered his voice even more, but I still caught his hushed words. "She's off-limits. *Don't* touch her."

"Have you claimed her?" his brother asked, his eyes widening to saucers.

"No, but—" The prince dragged a hand through his hair, loosening half of the long strands. He cast a glance my way, then shoved his brother out the door, passing through the wards, which muffled any further conversation.

I strained to hear them, trying to pick up something, *anything*, but the prince was back in my chambers and firmly locking the door behind him before I could.

"I apologize about that." Prince Norivun's aura continued to pulse around him.

My eyes narrowed. "Why did you tell him I'm off-limits?"

The prince's agitated movements stopped. "You heard that?"

"And," I added, ignoring his probing stare, "what did he mean about claiming me?"

It was such a preposterous thing for Nuwin to say. Only mates claimed one another, and the prince was *not* my mate. Blessed Mother, I could barely stand being in the same room with the male.

The prince's jaw locked. "It's nothing. Forget you heard anything." He strode toward me and plucked my half-drunk drink from my hand.

"Excuse me. I was enjoying that."

But the prince dumped the remains in the bar's sink. The leminai trickled through the plumbing in the icy wall, and I watched as the bright-green liquid disappeared through the bottom, into the floor, and to the nether regions of the castle.

The prince set the empty cup on the bar's counter. "That drink is particularly strong, and my brother knew that."

"So?"

He rounded on me, his wings extending slightly. "It would have been an easy way to get you drunk."

"Again, so? At this point, being perpetually intoxicated may be the best way to exist."

His eyes flashed. "You're to stay away from my brother."

Heat rose in my neck. "Why?"

"Because I said so," he growled.

I stomped toward him until I stood only an inch away. My chest nearly brushed his, and I had to tilt my head back since the bastard was so tall. "Do you think I have any control over who comes in and out of this room?"

"Of course, you—" But the prince cut himself off and scowled heavily.

"Ah, so you've finally come to realize that it seems everyone else is free to come and go through that door, but if I grab the handle, it doesn't turn."

The prince raked a hand through his hair again, refusing to meet my gaze, but then his eyes caught on the double doors leading to the courtyard. "You cleared some of the garden."

I placed my hands on my hips, knowing he was steering the conversation away from my imprisonment, but also realizing I lacked the righteous anger to pursue it further. My shoulders slumped. I was tired. So tired. After two days of unknowns, long flights, captivity, knowing I was powerless to resist whatever happened to me, and now dealing with an angry royal heir . . . I was quite simply exhausted and ready for him to leave.

"Yes, I did," I replied with a sigh.

"And you enjoyed it?"

"I suppose so."

The prince strode toward the door, then stepped outside. I

followed him, wrapping my arms around myself as the cold air swirled around us. The three moons were bright, two of them full while the other was a waning gibbous. Combined, they lit up the courtyard in silvery light.

Frowning, I watched as the prince went to each plant that I'd cleared of snow. He fingered their dark stalks and brittle leaves, his face a blank mask. When he finished his perusal, his attention shifted to me.

A wave of his aura pushed toward me, hitting me unexpectedly.

Warmth bloomed over my skin as the heat of his energy consumed me. It felt even more potent than normal. Different, raw, and like barely leashed . . . something.

The prince prowled closer, and I instinctively took a step back.

The minute I did, he stopped in his tracks and drew himself up short.

I plastered myself to the doorframe, gripping its edges for support.

The prince's aura abruptly diminished, and his face wiped clean. "I shall bid you goodnight." He bowed stiffly.

He didn't look at me when he passed, and my skin prickled in awareness when his arm brushed against my forearm.

"What am I to do from here?" I called.

He faced me when he reached the door, his gaze skimming over my sleeping attire.

I thanked the gods that Daiseeum had chosen a modest pair of pants and a long-sleeved top. I supposed it didn't matter, though. The prince had already seen me naked in Liss Lodge's bathing pools, although that had been from a distance and when it'd been dark in the cave. Not like in here, where the fairy lights burned brightly and only twenty feet separated us.

I raised my eyebrows at him when he remained silent.

"You're to keep yourself in this chamber." With that, he strode out the door and locked it behind him.

THE PRINCE HADN'T BEEN KIDDING when he'd said I was to stay in my chamber. The next day he returned in thick clothing, similar to what he'd worn when I'd first met him.

He pulled on leather gloves, refusing to meet my gaze as he said, "I have to leave again for a few weeks to tend to business on the continent."

From his back pocket, hidden beneath his huge wings, he extracted several rolls of parchment and a quill. After setting the writing supplies on the desk, he added, "I've arranged for a courier to deliver letters to your sister after they've been read by my staff to ensure they don't contain damaging information."

Since I'd dressed myself right after waking in the garments I'd been given in High Liss, I felt less vulnerable when I placed my hands on my hips and scowled at him. "Information such as the crown prince keeping me locked in the castle for no discernable reason?"

His power rumbled. "Mind yourself, Ilara Seary, daughter of Mervalee Territory. You're to stay here until I say otherwise." With that, he stormed out of my chambers before I could ask anything further.

"Arrogant cad," I muttered when the door slammed closed,

then I gave him my pinky finger even though he couldn't appreciate the rude gesture.

Grumbling, I paced the room a few times, then tried to take a page from my brother's book and look at the bright side. At least, the prince would be gone. Knowing I wouldn't have to see him caused some of my stress to lighten. And perhaps with any luck, I would be able to find someone to help me escape without the prince's ever-watchful eye, but when Daiseeum arrived an hour later, stunned to find me already dressed, that hope quickly faded.

Days passed after the prince's departure, and the only servants I saw were Balbus, Daiseeum, Patrice, and Haisley. Each time one of them entered my room, I would scramble to their sides and ask if I could leave, but each and every one of them made it abundantly clear they were loyal to the prince, and his wishes were for me to stay in my chambers.

As days turned into weeks, my hope turned into fear, especially when time ticked by, and there was no sign of the prince returning to explain what my future held.

Even writing to Cailis didn't lighten my mood since I was pretty sure from her worried replies that the censor practically erased all of my ramblings. But at least she knew I was alive. That counted for something.

But even though Cailis knew I lived, I began to sink into despair despite the servants doing their best to buoy my spirits. Balbus and Daiseeum were the most constant fixtures in my otherwise gilded cage. Balbus checked on me every morning, sometimes supplying me with books from the prince's library, other times regaling me with stories of his time spent on the Cliffs of Sarum—the deadly cliffs on the tip of Isalee Territory that only the locals with skilled knowledge knew how to navigate. His perpetual cheer and constant smiles helped alleviate the unfailing anxiety that coated my insides day in and day out, but they didn't quell it completely.

Daiseeum did her best to distract me too. The clothes the tailor had created for me came hours after the prince's departure. Dresses in the finest silks, tops of the thickest cottonum, and pants of varying richness and warmth were only a few of the items in the vast wardrobe. I'd been speechless when Daiseeum had carefully stowed everything away. It was so much. *Too* much. But she insisted on dressing me up some days to provide me with something to do, and while I'd never been into fashion, her love of it did make me smile. But seeing how much clothing had been crafted for me and my wingless back inevitably made my anxiety return.

Just how long did the prince intend to keep me here?

My imprisonment would have undoubtedly driven me to insanity if not for the courtyard and neglected garden. I spent nearly every moment of the day in its frigid temperatures. At first, I'd simply cleared the snow from the wilted plants, spoken with them, and empathized with their plight. I'd thought for certain that the courtyard was devoid of *orem*, but on day three of my imprisonment, I felt a stirring of it, just a touch when I knelt beneath the large maple tree to clear its base entirely of snow.

The giddiness that discovery had instilled in me lasted the entire day. And then the next day, I felt a touch more of it near the boxwood shrub as I fingered a brittle leaf tenderly. By that afternoon, that brittle leaf had transformed into a shiny one covered in wax. Its succulent pink tone was the first shade of color to pop up in the neglected garden.

I poured my heart and soul into nurturing the garden back to health once I realized that *orem* did exist in it. And slowly, the courtyard's garden came alive, growing more and more each day. By the end of week two, the snow had entirely melted, and the temperature was no longer freezing. The soil grew looser, the rich dirt moister and suppler between my fingers. And by the end of week three, all of the plants were alive, some even thriving. The rich colors and decadent fragrances that each plant harbored bathed the small courtyard in a perfumed cloud of life and peace.

"This is so beautiful," Daiseeum proclaimed as an entire month of my captivity was upon me. "If only Lord Crimsonale and Lady Wormiful could see this, then maybe they'd stop their ridiculous talks."

"Who?" I asked, cocking my head as I tilled the soil. "And talks about what?"

A flush worked up the servant's neck. "Nothing, Ilara. Carry on."

But despite my world shrinking to the Exorbiant Chamber and courtyard, I still heard rumblings among the servants, when they didn't know I was listening, about life beyond my confining walls. More commoners had flooded the capital since the prince had left, bringing with them increasing worry over the state of our continent's crops.

Ice had flooded my veins when Haisley and Balbus had restocked the bar, and Haisley had hissed under his breath, "He was removed, some laborer from Isalee, just like the last two."

"By who?" Balbus had asked, keeping his voice low. "The prince isn't here to deal with them, so who's taking them?"

"No one knows," Haisley replied. "But it's best to watch your back. A serving girl in the kitchens has gone missing too. They say she was sympathetic to the commoner's plight."

Hearing that made the anxiety within me grow. *What exactly is happening in this castle?*

Throwing myself back into my garden, I concentrated on the plants, the soil, and the life growing before me. My father would have been proud. I tried to concentrate on that. Despite being a field laborer, he'd taken pride in his work, always boasting any time his crops grew tall and strong. If he were here now, he would have patted my shoulder and told me well done.

Smiling, I closed my eyes and remembered my father's horrible yet endearing singing every time he'd shoveled snow off the path to the front door. His ballads would be so loud he would scare the nearby nesting owls away despite their daytime slumbers.

And as the soil sank through my fingers, I would think of the softness of my mother's hugs and the scent of her lemony lotion every time she'd braided my hair. I would picture how she would bump me playfully with her elbow every time she'd beat me at a game of cards, or how we would knead dough side by side in the kitchen while she'd hummed under her breath.

I remembered my brother too, his jokes, his laughs, and how Cailis and I had always teased him mercilessly since he'd had a crush on Birnee but had never worked up the courage to ask her to be his mate.

So despite my captivity and the disturbing whispers filtering through the castle, I worked and remembered as I filled my days with thoughts of Tormesh's infectious laugh, my mother's gentle hands, my father's comforting hugs, and Cailis's sharp tongue.

Dirt encrusted itself under my nails again, and it was such a welcome return of the life I once led that I kept my hands close to my chest, refusing to clean them properly. Daiseeum was, of course, aghast, but when she tried to scrub it away or insist that I soak for hours to loosen it, I refused.

It was the only remnant of my former life that felt like mine, and I fiercely protected it.

CHAPTER 14

"This is unbelievable! I had no idea such beauty could be grown in this desolate patch of forgotten waste."

Nuwin's voice had my head whipping up so fast that a crick formed in my neck. Wincing, I set down the spade that I'd been using to dig into the garden.

"Prince Nuwin?" I blinked, then blinked again just to make sure I wasn't hallucinating.

I hadn't seen the youngest prince in over a month, and considering that solitude bred insanity, well, I figured it was a good sign that I was still questioning if I was seeing a possible apparition.

"Yes, it's me, and I know, I know. I've been quite neglectful in my attention of you." He sighed and crouched at my side, his black leggings flexing with the movement.

He looked so much like the crown prince that for a moment, I marveled at their similar features. But Prince Nuwin dressed more fashionably than his older brother. A rich-blue tunic covered his upper half, and all of the stitching had been done in silver—the court's colors on full display.

Nuwin gave a rueful smile. "Believe me, I would have come sooner, but my dastardly brother reworked his wards to keep me out." He waggled his eyebrows, a mischievous grin streaking across his face. "Too bad for him that he forgot about one of the trap doors, and I finally remembered it and gave it a try."

I laughed, unable to help it. "Is that why I haven't seen you? I have to say this is a surprise. I thought you'd disappeared with your brother, and that was why you'd gone missing."

During the past month, I'd thought of both Nuwin and Haxil, hoping the males would stop by to ease the monotony of my days, but I figured there was little chance of me seeing the guard. If the prince had left, then his four guards had probably accompanied him, but as for Nuwin . . .

I smiled pleasantly up at him.

"This is a good surprise, I hope?" the youngest prince replied with a wink.

"Yes, it's nice to see someone new."

Nuwin grinned.

"Does the prince know you're here?" I asked curiously, then wondered again why Prince Norivun would want to keep his brother away from me. I set my spade down and wiped a piece of silvery hair from my cheek.

Amazingly, the prince's illusion magic still held, not showing even a hint of weakness. All of my black hair was still concealed.

Nuwin's grin just broadened as he evaded my question by lifting a hand and wiping his finger across my cheek. "You had a smudge of dirt," he explained when I stiffened. "Although it did make you look quite adorable."

My cheeks warmed. "Does the prince know you're here?" I asked again. Not that I cared about following the prince's rules, but he did seem extremely concerned about me seeing his brother.

Nuwin rocked back on his haunches, then gave me a cheeky smile. "If he did, he'd be storming in here and bringing the wrath of the realm with him."

My heart beat harder. I'd strangely felt safe with the prince when we'd traveled here, but it'd been over a month since I'd seen him, and I'd started to wonder if my judgment had been impaired during the two days we'd spent together. The male was a murderer after all.

"That's ridiculous. Why would he do that? Surely, no harm would come from you?" I smoothed my shirt and wiped at the light sheen of sweat on my brow. Now that the *orem* in the garden was thriving, the temperature was comfortably warm each day.

The young prince's lips tilted up again, and this time, when he lifted his hand and wiped his thumb across my forehead, I ducked my head sheepishly. I always got dirty when I worked in the fields, and this garden was no exception.

"Oh, of course not, my dearest Ilara. I wouldn't harm you in any physical way. However, I have been known to harm a lady's reputation a time or two." He gave a sultry smirk and waggled his eyebrows again.

I couldn't help but laugh. "To their parents' horror undoubtedly?"

"Absolute horror," he replied with mock sternness. "A few even complained to my father about it." He held out his hand to help me up.

I accepted it, and his warm palm closed around mine.

"And were you punished?" I tilted my head up to see him better. Like his brother, Nuwin also had a cleft in his chin, adding to his handsome appeal.

"Of course not." He said it with such indignation that I laughed again.

"And what happened to those innocent ladies that you deflowered?" I batted my eyelashes playfully.

He chuckled, the sound entirely genuine, as he began guiding me back to my chambers. "Well, let's see. There's quite a few, so it might take some time to recall all of them, but the latest one—"

The door to my bedroom chamber suddenly banged open with such tremendous force that I yelped.

My feet stopped short when I beheld the crown prince seething at the threshold. His chest rose and fell quickly, his hair tousled and his expression thunderous. But the second he caught sight of my horrified expression, his face smoothed, and the pulsing aura rippling around him tempered.

"Ah, dear brother!" Nuwin called good-naturedly, as if not having a care in the world that the Death Master had appeared out of thin air and looked on the verge of enacting his terrible affinity. Not to mention, he'd been missing for weeks, and well . . . *that* had been quite the entrance.

"I wondered how long it would take for you to mistphase back as I'm guessing I triggered your perimeter enchantments." Nuwin's grin broadened. "Naughty indeed of me to thwart your attempts, I know, but it was quite rude to keep me from our guest."

"How did you get in?" the prince asked through clenched teeth.

Nuwin's cheeky expression grew. "That's for me to know and you to wonder."

The crown prince's gaze flickered from his brother's face to our joined hands. I hadn't even realized that I still held onto Nuwin after he'd helped me to a stand in the garden, but when I tried to let him go, his grip tightened.

"I was just about to recount all of my court conquests to Ilara." Nuwin tugged me closer to him. "Lady Seary has shown interest in hearing all of the tales."

The prince's lips thinned. "I'm sure the last thing she wants to hear about is the females you've bedded."

Prince Norivun's gaze flicked again to where his brother held my hand. His giant wings tightened into razors at his back as the talon tips glinted like obsidian claws.

"Oh, I don't know about that." Prince Nuwin stroked his chin with his free hand. "Some females quite enjoy hearing the details. It can get them quite arou—"

"That's enough, Nuwin." The prince strode toward us, his eyes narrowed. When he reached us, he looked his brother in the eye as his aura pulsed again. "Remove your hand from her."

Prince Nuwin's mouth formed a surprised "O" when he looked down. "Oh, I hadn't even realized. I suppose she and I are naturally quite comfortable with each other. It must have slipped my mind."

He finally let go, and I brought my hand back to my side while I wondered what in the realm was going on between the two brothers. It was obvious that an underlying game was being played, but why I'd been brought into the middle of it, I didn't know.

"Have you returned to take me home, my prince?" I gazed up at the Bringer of Darkness.

My heart hammered when he looked down at me. I told myself it was because of his sudden return and because he had the power to decide my fate. It certainly wasn't his scent that rolled toward me or the way his shoulder muscles flexed when he turned in his fitted tunic.

"No," he replied stonily.

I scowled, drawing on all of the anxiety and anger that had been swirling inside me since the morning he'd left. "Still no explanation for why I'm being kept here either, I presume?"

He glanced over my shoulder, toward the garden. His eyes widened, and his mouth dropped open. "You did it."

He strode toward the glass doors and was outside before I could reply.

Nuwin and I shared a confused look before following him.

Outside, a look of excitement lightened the crown prince's face as he moved from plant to plant, stroking each leaf, and testing their strength and flexibility. I watched in absolute bewilderment as the strength of his aura rose until it was a crescendo of epic proportions.

Taking a step away from the seismic energy that surrounded the prince, I crossed my arms and was about to demand that he finally return me to Mervalee Territory, but he turned to confront me.

A look of complete satisfaction covered his face. So much so that my words caught in my throat. In the same breath, a wave of his magic washed over me, and his illusion cracked and broke all around me.

My hair cascaded around my shoulders in soft waves, curling

lightly and returning to its true pitch-black color. I gasped at the sudden change just as Nuwin's breath sucked in.

"She's like Mother?" the youngest prince asked in shock.

The prince nodded, his smile still in place.

Nuwin glanced back at me, his eyes widening as he reached up to stroke a piece of my hair.

The prince growled, low and deep, and his brother's hand instantly dropped before Nuwin grinned. "But she's wingless."

"She still holds magic."

"What magic?" I finally said, volleying between the two of them as I reeled from the feel of the prince's magic touching me so intimately when his illusion affinity had peeled away.

"The magic to save our continent, Ilara Seary," the prince replied. "You have the ability to create *orem*, which means that you can save us all."

CHAPTER 15

"What?" There was no way I'd heard him right. The words he'd just uttered were pure lunacy.

"Your affinity is the ability to create *orem*," the crown prince repeated.

I blinked. Then blinked again before I finally found my voice. "I don't have magic or an affinity," I said patiently, in a way I often spoke to children who struggled to understand a topic. "And I most certainly cannot conjure *orem*. I'm a defective."

The prince's gaze cascaded over my black hair, his icy-blue eyes sharpening at my condescending tone. "You're not a defective. Your affinity bloomed late, but it's manifesting."

I frowned, my eyebrows knitting together so tightly they felt joined. "That's not possible. I'm twenty-four winters, a true defective. My affinity should have bloomed ten winters ago like all Solis fae at maturing age."

"No, Nori's right." Nuwin's eyes gentled. "It can happen like how it has for you. It's rare, but it can. Our mother, the queen, was similar. She bloomed late and has black hair, although she has wings." He shrugged. "But no matter, you and she are the same. She also has extraordinary magic, although her magic is different from yours."

My jaw dropped. "What are you talking about? The queen doesn't have black hair."

"She does actually," Nuwin insisted. "Her hair is hidden under an illusion to make it appear silver. She's lived that way her entire life. Most in the continent have no idea of her true hair color."

My jaw dropped so completely I was surprised it wasn't on the floor. *The queen has black hair? Truly?*

But despite that unbelievable revelation, I inched away from him, from *both* of them, since I didn't like the intent way the crown prince was staring at me or the wonder in Nuwin's eyes. Despite the queen's hair color, they were wrong about me. Totally and completely delusional. I was magicless, wingless, and defective. I didn't have power, and I certainly couldn't create *orem* and save the continent. Whatever that even meant.

I rubbed my hands up and down my upper arms. "Why do you think I have magic?"

The prince spread his arms wide. "*This* is why. I suspected you might when I saw you working in your garden at your home, and—"

"You saw me in my garden?"

He nodded.

"When?"

"A few days before I took you."

My eyebrows shot up when I recalled a moment in my garden, after Vorl had attacked me, when it felt as if I was being watched. That had been *real*? The prince had been the cause of that feeling?

My eyes narrowed to slits as I put my hands on my hips. "You were spying on me?"

The Death Master shrugged, and I was itching to tell him that made him a total creep.

"I had to know. Your garden was the most abundant, vivid, bright, and flourishing patch of land that I'd encountered during my entire span of the continent. I didn't think it was possible anymore to grow plants like that. With the *orem* diminishing and the crops dying, I no longer thought such life could be sustained in our climate."

My entire body grew rigid, especially after hearing those fae females gossiping in Firlim's market all those weeks ago, seeing the prince's reaction to that gossip when we'd been in High Liss, and then hearing the rumblings of concern that had been whispering through the castle during the past month. "So it's true? It's actually been confirmed that our *orem's* dying?"

Nuwin and the crown prince shared a veiled look.

"You might as well tell her," Nuwin said. "Word's getting out more and more. We've had several incidences since you left. If she's to help us fix this problem, she should know."

"You're right." The prince took a deep breath before addressing me. "It's true. Entire territories' crop lands have died out completely."

My heart beat harder, thundering louder and louder with each breath I took. The *orem* was dying. Crops were withering. Solis fae were going to starve to death.

All this time . . . Tormesh had been right.

My eyes squeezed shut when I remembered my brother

returning last summer after his march with the Solis Guard. He'd voiced the same concern, saying something was wrong with our land. It hadn't been as bad then. He hadn't said entire territories' crops were dead, but he'd grown up in a laboring family. He knew what healthy crops should look like, and he'd suspected that something was amiss.

Opening my eyes, I curled my fingers into my palms. "Why don't more fae know of this? Why is it being hushed?"

The prince and his brother shared another look.

"It's a delicate situation," Nuwin finally replied.

But my attention didn't leave the crown prince. He held my stare, unflinching, but then his eye twitched slightly, as though he could feel the rage that was burning through me.

Gritting my teeth, I bit out, "Yet you now think that I can create *orem*, and therefore, I can solve the problem of our continent's dying crops?"

The prince's expression was impossible to read as he gave a barely perceptible nod.

I scoffed. "How ironic. My own brother came to this court a full season ago, feeling it was his duty to ensure the court knew of the dire situation of our continent's food source, and do you know what was done to him for it?"

The prince stilled.

"He was murdered." I took a step closer to the crown prince as my face twisted into something ugly. I could feel it, growing and thriving in my expression. All of my anger, hurt, betrayal, lost hope, and aching sadness morphed my face until I was no longer Ilara Seary, daughter of Mervalee Territory. No. I'd turned into a creature consumed with wrath and hatred, of betrayal and retribution.

My lips peeled back as I pointed an accusing finger at him. "You murdered my brother. You *killed* him when he came here, asking for the court's help. And why? To apparently stop him from talking. And do you know what you then did?" Tears pricked my eyes as I glared up at the Death Master.

He didn't move. Didn't even blink.

"You murdered my parents next. They came here, in my brother's name, wanting to know why he'd been killed for voicing his concerns, and do you know what you did to them? You murdered them too." A shrill laugh escaped me. "So imagine my surprise now at the irony of all of this. You killed my family, and in return, you want me to save you. And what if I say no, Prince Norivun? What if I refuse the great crown prince of the Court of Winter? Will you kill me too?"

The prince continued to stare at me. Unmoving. Maybe not even breathing.

Nuwin stepped forward. "Nori, maybe we should—"

But the prince raised a hand. "No, I want to hear her accusations. I want to hear her condemnation for everything that I am. Let her get it all out now and be done with it, because at the end of the day, she'll still do as I say."

My hand shot out so fast that I didn't even know I was going to strike him until my palm met his cheek. A great ringing *slap* reverberated through the courtyard as the prince's head whipped to the side.

"No, I won't." I seethed. "I refuse to help you or your damned court or anyone else in this castle. I don't have magic. I can't create *orem*, and you're nothing but a fool and a murderer."

I turned my back on him, and neither he nor his brother tried to stop me when I stalked back into my chambers and slammed the door behind me, yet I could have sworn that when the door shuddered, it wasn't just from the strength of my swing.

It also felt as though the Bringer of Darkness was rumbling the entire castle.

I LOCKED myself in the bathing room.

And as the minutes ticked by and nobody came to the door, or murdered me through the window, or called for me to come out, I eventually came to the conclusion that they'd both left.

I stayed where I was though. My entire body was shaking, so I sat on the cold stone floor, wrapped my arms around my knees, and rocked back and forth.

The crown prince believed that I had magic. Magic strong enough to create *orem*. And he wanted to use my supposed magic to heal our land.

My brother had been right all along. Our land was dying. The crops really were withering, and we would all starve unless something was done to make our crops thrive again.

But how could that answer possibly be me? I didn't have magic. I didn't have wings. I was defective, wingless, magicless . . . And nobody could create *orem*. That came from the gods and was only replenished by our universe's celestial events. The gods decided those fates too. Not me.

It was so preposterous that I threw my hands up and pushed to an abrupt stand.

I paced back and forth as the prince's face burned into my mind. If this was why he'd taken me, why hadn't he just told me so from the beginning? Why had he kept it such a big secret?

He probably did it just to torment you, just because he could.

My lip curled as my hatred unfurled like a poisoned rose within me.

Prince Norivun was evil. Everyone was right about him, and his expression when I'd revealed to him what he'd done to my family hadn't been that of shock, regret, or surprise. Oh no. He hadn't worn any expression at all. He'd simply let me scream and rail at him while he probably counted the seconds until I was done.

I paused by the mirror, my chest heaving. Flushed cheeks, too-bright eyes, and dark hair that hung in curling waves past my shoulders reflected back at me. My eyes looked as blue as the gems mined in Harrivee. I brought a hand to my mouth when a sudden nearly hysterical laugh escaped me. I'd *slapped* the crown prince of the Court of Winter, and he hadn't murdered me. Yet.

That thought sobered me instantly, and I resumed my pacing.

I'd gone too far. I knew that, but I hadn't been able to contain my fury any longer. For a *month*, the prince had held me prisoner, and he hadn't told me any of his beliefs or his plans.

Quite simply—I'd snapped.

I padded to the door, my heart thrumming in my chest as I debated what he would do from here. If he truly thought I was the key to saving our lands, then I doubted he would kill me— even if *I* knew I couldn't save anything.

So then the next question became, just what exactly did he have planned for me?

I finally disengaged the lock to the bathing room and swung the door open. I was so lost in my thoughts that I almost stumbled into a dark figure standing by the glass doors.

I hastily backpedaled, a shriek caught in my throat.

The crown prince stood silently, hands clasped behind his back as he gazed at the garden. It was dark out since only one of the moons was alight.

I gasped as my heart turned into a galloping beast in my chest.

He's been here the entire time?

"I remember your brother," he said, without turning to face me. "His features were similar to yours."

A soft mewl worked up my throat, but I quickly swallowed it down. Tormesh, Cailis, and I all had similar features. Our father's nose, our mother's mouth, a combination of their eye shapes.

"He seemed intent on alerting the entire continent to our plight, but I couldn't allow it. To do so would cause panic and chaos. We'd been trying to find a solution to save our land quietly and discreetly even though some fae had begun to notice the decline in our continent's *orem*, so I did what was expected of me when your brother came to the court. As the Death Master, I did my duty."

He turned to face me. In the dim light, his eyes burned like sapphires. "I understand you hate me for killing him. Even more so because your parents presented themselves several weeks later and suffered the same plight."

"But why?" A sob shook my chest. "Why did they have to die? They would have remained quiet if ordered to do so."

His jaw tightened, so slightly that it could have been a shadow—a trick of the light. "I had to."

"You didn't." I shook my head back and forth rapidly. "You didn't have to. You *chose* to."

He turned back to the window, the aura around him pulsing so high that it threatened to swallow me, yet his face remained impassive. Completely blank. "It doesn't detract from what is expected of you. We need you to save our land, Ilara. Your parents' and brother's deaths don't change that."

He said it all so matter of fact, so businesslike, as though sucking souls from my family was part of his daily duties, and that was that.

"How can you be so cold?" Nausea rolled through me, and I collapsed onto the nearest chair. "Do you feel nothing?" I asked quietly as all of the fight went out of me. How did one fight a fairy who was as hard and immobile as stone? "Do you feel *anything* at all when you take a life?"

I blinked, and he was sitting on the couch across from me. He'd moved silently, like a phantom.

"What I feel is irrelevant." He sat as still as a statue, not one muscle moving or twitching.

Such control. Such *perfect* control of any outward expression.

My shoulders slumped. He would never care what he'd done to me or my family. And even worse, as the crown prince of the Solis continent, he controlled anyone his heart desired, so unless I played the game and danced the dance, I would never be free of him. I would never be free to return home. To Cailis. To my friends. To my small, meager life but a life that was *mine*.

Rivers of ice slid through my veins as I balled up that aching chasm of pain that had existed within my chest since the death of my parents and brother. I wrapped it into a ball. Wound it so tightly that it couldn't loosen again and make me do something stupid. I couldn't snap again.

I had to stay alive, return home, and be smart so I could see my sister once more.

Which meant that I had to play the Death Master's game, even if I wanted to end the gamemaster himself.

Leveling the crown prince of the Court of Winter with a weighted stare, I said, "What is it that you want me to do, my prince?"

CHAPTER 16

"It's really quite simple," the prince replied. "You need to learn how to control your affinity and replenish our continent again with *orem*."

I stared at him unblinking. "Our continent is *millions* of square millees."

"It is."

"And you want me to create *orem* to replenish all of it?"

"Correct."

I wrapped my arms around myself. "You're insane."

"I've been called worse." His lips kicked up in a humorless smile.

I stood and began pacing. "What if you're wrong? What if I don't hold strong magic, and I'm unable to do as you request?"

"You *do* have immensely strong magic, and you *can* do what I'm requesting."

I whipped back to him, my long hair flying over my shoulder. The prince had leaned back on the couch, his arm propped over the back. One leg was kicked across the table, the other crossed at the ankle on it. He looked relaxed, powerful, and so very sure of himself.

Something stirred inside of me at his image. He was so beautiful that I wanted to soak up his appearance, but then anger at myself kicked in, and I whirled away. *The beautiful Death Master*. It was such a waste of male perfection.

He inhaled, then said quietly, "You're angry again."

"I will always be angry with you. You murdered my family."

"And you hate me for it, just as many others do."

I paused by the bar, grabbed a bottle of alcohol, and poured myself a generous drink. "Does it bother you to be hated so much?"

"Would it matter if it did?" He stood and glided to my side, his walk so smooth and easy that I had a feeling he was often asked by angry family members if he had a heart at all.

When he reached me, he took the bottle, and I thought he was going to pick up my drink next and dump it down the sink, but instead he grabbed a second glass and poured himself a dose, just as full.

"Solls." He clinked his glass to mine before I could say anything and downed the entire cup in one swallow.

His throat worked, the muscles in the column of his neck as sculpted as the rest of him. When he finished, he set his cup beside mine. "Is there anything else you would like to get off your chest? Any other words of hatred or anger for me?"

My throat bobbed, my lips dry from his matter-of-fact persona. "No," I finally said. "I think I've made my point. For now."

"Then we'll need you to begin training your magic first thing tomorrow. We can start—"

"Wait." I held a hand up, then brought my glass to my mouth and drained half of it. The liquid burned in my throat, cutting a path like fire. Wincing, I set it back down. "How long will training take?"

He shrugged. "That, Ilara, is up to you. Affinities can take weeks, months, or full seasons to train. All fae are different, and each fairy dedicates themselves to mastering their affinities in different ways, but I suggest you devote yourself to this. We don't have full seasons."

"Do we have months?"

"We do. For now."

"What does that mean?"

"That means that at the rate our continent's *orem* has been dying, we have approximately one full season until it's completely vanished."

"Really? It's that bad?"

"It is."

"So I have twelve months." Blessed Mother, that would be the biggest undertaking of my life.

"Correct, unless our *orem* dies at an increasing rate. At the territories' current stores, there's enough food to last the continent until next winter."

I drained the rest of my glass, and flames burned down my throat so vehemently that I coughed. Suppressing another cough, I said hoarsely, "I hope I can actually do what you're asking." If I couldn't, we would all starve.

"You'll be able to."

"You sound so certain of that."

"Because you can. This realm has never seen an affinity like yours. I imagine its bounds have no limits."

"But you said your mother's like me."

His eyes shuttered. "She is. Her magic is as powerful as yours, but her affinities are different. She can't create *orem*."

"Where is she now? Does she really have black hair too?"

"I imagine she's in her wing, and yes, her hair's also black."

For the briefest moment, I pictured Prince Norivun as a toddler standing by a female with hair the color of onyx. "What are her affinities?"

"That, Ilara, is for her to share. But while your coloring is identical, that genetic anomaly doesn't extend to your affinities, merely the rareness and strength of them."

I quickly poured myself another glass and took a heavy drink. The room spun slightly when I set it back down, but at least I didn't cough again.

"You're nervous."

I gave him a side-eye. "You seem to be in the habit of reading my emotions."

"It's something I do with everyone."

I studied him, frowning. He had a beautiful face—firm lips yet full. A strong nose. Deep-set eyes that were so piercing and such a million shades of blue that I was reminded of glittering sapphires. And his chin with that cleft in the middle—it gave him such a rugged appeal.

His face was utter perfection, yet it was entirely blank.

My forehead scrunched together when I remembered our conversation about empathy. That had been weeks ago, on my flight into the capital. Somehow, someway, the prince *did* have empathy within him. His comment about my anger confirmed that since he was so in tune with others' emotions.

Yet, he still killed so easily. Even knowing how it ripped families apart.

So what exactly did that make him? A true monster? Since he understood the pain he was causing others? Or did he live with regret daily that he hid behind a mask of slate?

I hastily took another drink. "I can't say that I can read your expressions. Your face is about as expressive as a blank wall."

"Thank you."

"It wasn't a compliment."

"To you maybe not, but to me it is. It's preferable if you don't know what I'm thinking."

"Why?"

"It's not of your concern. But what *is* of your concern is training your affinity."

I frowned, then took another drink. Blessed Mother, there wasn't enough alcohol in the realm for this discussion. How could I be having a conversation with the fairy who'd murdered my family, while said fairy was also telling me I needed to save the continent, all while I was contemplating—in a quickly-growing-drunken state—if said male felt regret for all that he'd destroyed?

My fingers shook when I relinquished my glass. "I'm going to disappoint you. You might as well know that now. I'm not strong enough to do what you're asking, and I'm still entirely doubtful that I have an affinity that can create *orem*. Only the gods can do that."

"The gods and *you*. That courtyard"—he pointed to the glass doors—"was completely without *orem* when I brought you to this room. I've had it evaluated numerous times by very powerful scholars, and they all reached the same conclusion. No *orem* existed anymore in that soil. Not for millees beneath the surface.

Not even a trace. That land was dead, yet within a matter of weeks, you've brought it back to life."

"But I didn't do anything."

"You *did*. Your affinity created it."

"Maybe your scholars are wrong. The *orem* could have been there and just needed coaxing to the surface."

"I'm not wrong, and my scholars weren't wrong."

My hand shook when I picked up the glass again and drained the last of it. A dizzying feeling swept through me. It didn't help that it'd been hours since I'd eaten. I gripped the ice bar harder, the counter cool yet not cold. The magic swimming through it didn't allow the surface to actually freeze a fairy.

I thought about the garden here, then my garden back home and the bounty that it'd produced this summer. I'd pulled an endless vine of acorlis just last month. I thought it'd been luck, but what if it hadn't been?

Blessed Mother. I was actually considering what he was saying.

"I suppose it's . . . possible," I finally said.

A small smile ghosted the prince's lips. "You're coming to accept what you are."

I glowered. "I didn't say that. I simply said you could be right that the garden didn't have *orem*. I didn't sense any either when I first arrived."

His smile broadened.

Not liking how smug he was looking, I bit out, "Why didn't you just tell me that you thought I could create *orem* when we first met? Why did you keep it a secret and let me worry about what was being done to me?"

His smile vanished. "I'm sorry, for what I made you feel, but I couldn't tell you. It was too risky."

I reeled for a moment. He'd just apologized to me. Shaking that off, I asked, "What do you mean?"

"You're too powerful."

"Now I know you're full of it."

His lips quirked. "I'm not. When a powerful fairy's affinity first begins to manifest, it's quite malleable. If a fairy attempts to force it, alter it, or in any way manipulate it too early, it can shatter the potential of one's affinity."

"What are you talking about? I've never heard of that."

"It's because it's not common. Most affinities manifest, and their power level is set from the moment of its first appearance. It can still take time for the fairy to learn how to wield their affinity, but their power won't diminish. But with very powerful fae, that's not the case. One's affinity can only reach its true potential if it isn't manipulated too early, too quickly."

I scoffed. "And you think I'm one of those powerful fae."

"I do, which is why I haven't intervened or told you what I suspected. When we first met, I could tell that you had no idea what was happening to you, nor did anyone else. But when I saw your garden, and then I saw your black hair, I knew that it was possible you could create *orem* given how prolific your garden was, but I needed your magic to grow on its own without interference. That's why I brought you here, locked you away, and didn't tell you my plans. You needed to fully manifest independently in order to reach your full potential." His voice gentled, and a shiver ran down my spine when it turned slightly husky. "Our land needs you, Ilara. The magnitude of that need was too important to jeopardize, but now your affinity has truly been born, and you're past the initial stage when it could have been stilted. It will only grow from here, and with proper training, it could be immense."

I nibbled on my lip and avoided the urge to fidget. "If I can actually create *orem*, and if I can somehow replenish the crops on our continent, what's in it for me?"

He quirked an eyebrow. "Saving our race isn't enough?"

"Not to sound cold, but no. I want something in return if I'm to devote my life to this."

He stroked his chin. "Are you trying to bargain with me?"

"I am."

His lips pressed together, and for a moment, I thought he was going to laugh. "What makes you think you have any authority?"

I crossed my arms and scowled. "I don't, but I also know that you're quite desperate to have me help you, and I think getting something in return for saving the continent isn't asking too much."

He crossed his arms too. "Very well. What is it that you want?"

"To return home. To be allowed to live in peace."

His expression flattened. "You wish to be free of me and the court."

"Yes."

"Would you be more willing to cooperate if I agreed to this?"

"I would."

"In that case—" He started to hold out his arm, but I held up a hand.

"Wait. I'd also like to be allowed to come and go from my room freely. I don't want to ever be locked in the Exorbiant Chamber or any chamber, room, cage, lodge, or confinement ever again. And I want to see my sister."

His lips twitched. "Have you bargained before?"

"No."

"You should consider joining the courts as a magistrate."

I rolled my eyes but couldn't stop my reluctant smile. "You're very funny."

"Am I?" The corner of his mouth kicked up. "I don't often get told that."

"And sarcastic."

"Now, *that*, I've been told a time or two."

"You're stalling."

"I'm not. I'm merely considering what you're requesting."

"They're not requests. They're demands."

"Everything with me is a request. You cannot make demands of your crown prince."

"Really? Because I think I just did."

He sighed. "I've killed fae for such insolence before."

Since his tone was teasing, I didn't know if he was serious or not, but I still replied, "I'm sure you have."

"Yet you don't even flinch when you make such remarks."

"Maybe I'm not as weak as everyone thinks I am."

He studied me quietly. "I think you're right. In fact, I don't think you're weak at all." Before I could really contemplate that response, he added, "But I can't agree to you leaving your chambers freely. It would be too dangerous considering the unrest that's currently taking place within the court."

I shivered. Given the rumblings I'd heard, he wasn't wrong. "Then assign me a guard."

He grunted. "I don't trust any of the guards enough to entrust them with your life."

"Then assign me one of your personal guards. You seem to

trust them."

"True." He tilted his head. "All right, fine. I'll assign Nish to you."

I scoffed. "You must hate me if you're going to force Nish on me. How about Haxil?"

His eyes shuttered. "No."

"Why not? I like Haxil."

The muscle in his jaw ticked. "As I'm aware, but my answer remains. No."

I blew forcefully through my nose. "Then Sandus or Ryder?"

"Fine. Sandus."

"Do we have a deal then?"

He shook his head in amusement or annoyance, I couldn't tell. "You drive a hard bargain."

"Is that so? Do you make bargains often?"

"No, in fact, I try to avoid them, and come to think of it, you're the first female I've ever done this with."

"Are you saying I'm deflowering you?"

His eyes twinkled. "You are."

My cheeks reddened, and I cursed the alcohol for loosening my tongue and making me say such brazen things. Flustered, I held out my arm so we could seal our bargain, but he didn't take it. "Why do I get the impression again that you're stalling?"

"Because I am."

I waved my arm at him. "Quit stalling. I won't save the continent until you agree to this."

His curved lips turned into a grin. "Why, Ilara Seary, you're positively turning me on. I've never had a female speak so plainly with me before, and I have to say, it's quite arousing."

My eyes bugged out. I couldn't tell if he was messing with me or not. My heart beat harder, and I wasn't sure I wanted to know.

His strong fingers finally wrapped around my forearm, his large hand completely encircling my elbow. I did the same to him, or tried to, but his forearm was so thick with muscle that I could only get my fingers around half of it.

A spark of pleasure spiraled up my arm when our contact sealed. I tried not to flinch. *What in the realm was that?* I knew bargains elicited our realm's magic, but I'd never heard of them feeling palpable before any words had been uttered.

The prince's brow furrowed, and I couldn't help but wonder if he'd felt it too.

Raising his eyes to mine, he said, "Ilara Seary, daughter of Mervalee Territory, I hereby agree to a bargain that ensures you're returned to your home to live in peace after you replenish the Solis continent's dying *orem*, and while you're staying under my care at the Court of Winter, you shall be allowed to leave your chambers and all other chambers, freely as you wish under the accompaniment of one of the guards of my choosing, and your sister shall also be allowed to visit you while you're replenishing our continent's *orem*. I hereby end the terms of our agreement. Do you accept this bargain?"

I licked my lips, my heart still pounding. "Prince Norivun Deema Melustral Achul, first son of the king, Bringer of Darkness, Death Master of the continent, son of Prinavee Territory, and crown prince and heir to the Winter Court's throne, I hereby accept your bargain."

A clash of magic billowed around us, and I hissed when the bargain's mark seared into my skin like a hot brand before it abruptly released.

I pulled free of the prince's arm and rolled up my sleeve to see a single petal glowing on my skin before it disappeared. The prince rolled up his own sleeve. A shattering heart shone before it vanished.

I frowned. "That was an interesting mark."

His brow furrowed as he quickly rolled his sleeve back down. "The gods have a wicked sense of humor."

My frown grew, but then I smoothed my expression and remembered I'd had too much to drink, and that could be the cause of my confusion. And, *Blessed Mother*. I'd just made a sealed fairy bargain while drunk. With the crown prince of the Winter Court nonetheless. And if I failed to uphold the bargain, I would be subject to the gods' wrath, whatever hellish consequences those tricky bastards chose to bestow upon me. A horrified laugh bubbled out of me. Cailis would give me a tongue-lashing if she knew what I'd just done.

"Is something funny?" the prince asked.

"No, not at all." I poured myself another cup of leminai and ruminated over our bargain as I downed it.

I was fairly certain I'd covered all of the important bits, which meant the sooner I got my end of our bargain completed, the better. My head spun slightly as the leminai settled in my belly.

I gripped the bar top, then asked, "So now what, my prince? What do we do from here?"

"From here"—he gave my glass a pointed look—"you stop drinking and go to bed so you can begin training tomorrow."

"I don't think I'm ready for that yet." I poured another glass of alcohol and drank half of it in one swallow, suddenly needing it as the impossibility of fulfilling our bargain hit me. I had to replace our continent's *orem*. Every square millee of it. *Blessed Mother, what have I done?*

I finished the glass, and the room spun even more. I lifted the bottle of leminai for a second time. "Just one more drink. Or two. Or maybe three. Yes, definitely three."

Prince Norivun crossed his arms, but I didn't let him deter me. I drank another glass and then another. The room began swaying in earnest, but a blessedly numb feeling swept through me.

So I'd made a bargain to replenish our continent's *orem*. It wasn't *that* big of an undertaking. Surely. Sighing, I attempted to pour another drink from the mostly empty bottle, but I couldn't line up my glass with the lip.

A low growl came from the prince when I finally managed on my third attempt, although half of the leminai sloshed over the side.

"Oops." I brought the glass to my lips and stumbled into him when I tried to set the bottle down. "This leminai is positively divine."

"That's enough." The prince righted me, then took my glass and nodded toward the bed. "You need to sleep this off."

I hiccupped. "I don't want to sleep." I swayed away from him and nearly fell onto the couch when I attempted to swirl toward it. "I'm hungry. Oh! I have an idea. Wouldn't it be fun to go out? Perhaps an eating establishment? Or a fun salopas? Or somewhere to dance? Are there any enjoyable clubs in Solisarium? I've been cooped up for so long. I want to go somewhere."

"Blessed Mother," he muttered under his breath, then caught my arm before I could reach my chamber's door. "You're not going anywhere like this."

"Why not?"

He scowled. "Because you're drunk, and I don't trust you to keep yourself safe."

"But your guard will. Remember?" I waggled my eyebrows at him. "Sandus? Or was it Nish? I can't remember who's been assigned to me. Please tell me it's Sandus."

Prince Norivun steered me back to the sofa. "On second thought, you're right. You should eat something before you sleep. I'll ring for food."

I sat in a heap on the couch and began to hum a tune as the prince pulled the cord near my bed. But when I tried to stand up and begin dancing to the rhythm in my head, my foot caught on the couch.

The prince caught me a split second before my face hit the table.

I had the most ridiculous urge to giggle. "You're very fast."

He picked me up, as though I weighed nothing at all, and set me back on the sofa. "And you're very drunk."

"I think you may be right," I whisper hissed.

A reluctant smile tugged at his lips, and then the food arrived, and mouthwatering scents drifted through the room. But for some reason, my fork wouldn't line up with my mouth when I tried to eat.

The prince sighed. "You're going to be the death of me, female." He took my fork and proceeded to feed me. Actually feed me.

I opened my mouth dutifully as his expression turned serious. Smiling, I chewed the bite and swallowed. "You know, you're very handsome when you're so stern."

He forked another bite of grilled acorlis. "Is that so?"

"Indeed. In fact, I think you're the most beautiful male I've ever seen."

His hand paused from spooning my next bite. "I thought you hated me."

"Oh, I do, but that doesn't mean that I haven't noticed how attractive you are."

A smile tugged at his lips. "And you're the most beautiful female I've ever seen."

"Really?" I brought a hand to my chest, but another wave of dizziness swirled through me from the movement.

His nostrils flared. "Indeed, you are. I could ravish you right now and thoroughly enjoy every second of it."

My mouth dropped, and I laughed, because there was no way he was serious. "Then why don't you?"

"Because you're drunk."

"But you're not a gentlefae, remember?"

"Even I wouldn't take you in a state like this."

"Even if I wanted it?" I playfully inched my hand along his thigh toward his cock, that . . . *Blessed Mother*. Toward his cock that was *incredibly* hard. His thick length bulged against his leggings. The size of him was . . . My eyes widened. "Are you aroused by me?"

The next thing I knew, I was in his arms as he strode toward the bed. My heart pounded. *Is he taking me to bed?* Mother Below, the murderer of my family was carrying me to my bed to probably enact this ravishing he'd spoken of, and instead of being repulsed by that thought, a strange thrill ran through me.

I ran a hand up his chest, wondering how in the realm I could get his tunic off fast enough. He truly was a beautiful male, so thick and large, and I hadn't been pleasured in so very long. I suddenly ached for it. I wrapped my arms around his wide shoulders, then my mouth found his neck. I kissed his smooth skin, then nipped at him.

"Do you promise to pleasure me?"

His nostrils flared, and he inhaled deeply. Another low growl rumbled in his chest. "*Fuck.*"

Maneuvering in his arms, I wrapped my legs around his waist. He hissed when I rubbed myself on him. I sighed and kissed his neck again. Blessed Mother, this was so nice. I hadn't been touched like this in ages.

The prince finally reached my bed, and I arched into him until my breasts were straining against my tunic.

"Touch me. All of me," I whispered.

His hands gripped my thighs tightly, every line of him straining, but then he dropped me onto the covers. I bounced, a shock of surprise releasing from me.

"Go to sleep, Ilara," he said gruffly. "Before I do something we both regret."

The next thing I knew, covers were pulled over me, the light was extinguished, and then I was alone in my chambers as my core ached.

For a moment, I lay in stunned silence. *What just happened?*

The quiet reigned. Only the sound of my deep, rapid breaths filled the room. But I was alone now. I was pretty certain of that fact. *Did I just imagine all of that?*

Fuzzy thoughts crept into my mind, but then the room began spinning again. Minutes ticked by as I spun and spun and spun.

It was a dizzying, pleasant feeling as the soft mattress cocooned me, and even though that strange need still pulsed in my core, my eyes fluttered closed, and then the realm disappeared in a rocking motion of silence.

CHAPTER 17

Sunshine blazed brightly through the windows as someone
shook me.

"Ilara, *please*, you must get out of bed. The prince is
on his way, and he insisted you be ready."

Throbbing in my head threatened to split my skull. *For the
love of all the gods, somebody needs to stop banging against drums.*

"Ilara!" a female hissed again.

I tried to swat the hands away, but someone grabbed my
wrists and tugged. "You must get out of bed. The prince is
expecting you to be ready."

"Go away," I croaked.

The female sighed. "He said you'd be in a state. Blessed
Mother, how right he was."

Someone forced me to sitting, then pried my eyes open. I
winced when the blasted sunlight burned into my irises, and now
I was *certain* someone was pounding drums.

"What is that racket?"

"Most likely the blood rushing through your ears." The

❄ 199 ❄

KRISTA STREET

female cupped my jaw, prying my lips open. "I've brought a tonic, courtesy of Murl. Drink. Now. We don't have much time."

I frowned as I finally recognized Daiseeum standing beside me and holding a vial up. My stomach heaved, but she forced the vial to my lips and tipped the contents into my mouth, then closed my jaw.

I downed it in one swallow since I couldn't breathe properly with how she was holding me. Working free of her grip, I coughed. "Blessed Mother, that's *foul*."

"Yes, it is, but Murl is a gifted healer. You should be right as the northern winds within a few minutes, believe it or not. Now, up you go. Up!"

I stumbled when I stood but managed to follow her to the wardrobe. But even though Daiseeum paused to pick out clothing for me, I didn't stop. I carried on to the bathing chamber.

In the mirror, my appearance was a fright. Hair everywhere. Eyes bloodshot. Dried spit on my cheek. I was truly looking my finest.

I blinked, and my surprise increased when I realized *silver* hair stared back at me. Not black.

My head finally began to clear, and my bloodshot eyes turned white as the potion at last kicked in. I grabbed my toothbrush and cleaned my teeth, then picked up my comb to work through my snarls. I didn't remember the prince casting another illusion over me, but he must have. *Mother Below, what else did we do last night that I don't remember?*

My cheeks burned when I recalled how alluring he'd looked during our conversation about him believing my affinity created *orem*. And we'd made a fairy bargain. An actual fairy bargain.

My hand slapped over my mouth when it came rushing back to me. I had to replenish the entire continent with *orem*.

Fuck. Fuck. Fuck.

What else had I agreed to? After the bargain, everything got fuzzy. I faintly recalled him carrying me to the couch. Or . . . wait, was it the bed?

And there was dancing. No, there wasn't dancing. But I'd wanted to dance?

Blessed Mother. The entire evening was one giant blur.

"Ilara?" Daiseeum knocked on the door. "We only have *minutes* until he arrives."

I hurriedly set the comb down and joined her by the wardrobe. She waved a hand over me, casting me in rushed magic as her cleansing spell fell over my frame, cleaning the spit from my cheek and ridding my body of all dirt, sweat, and grime.

"Thank you," I said, my cheeks reddening. I really needed to learn self-cleansing if I actually had magic now.

She held up leggings and a fitted tunic. "You're to wear training clothes." Her lips pursed in a sour frown.

"You don't like them?" I felt the soft material. The tunic and leggings had been spun from soft wool. Warm yet dry, and practical for our northern climate.

"Ladies should wear gowns. Not *this*."

"You're forgetting, once again, that I'm not a lady."

Daiseeum and I had been through this multiple times during the past month. She kept insisting that I wear one of the many dresses that had been crafted for me, but unless I was simply trying on the garments as a way to pass time, I kept demanding pants and woven tops. Dresses and gardens didn't mix, yet

Daiseeum seemed aghast each time I refused her silks and brocades.

"You *should* dress like a lady. He certainly treats you as such," she muttered under her breath.

I frowned, not knowing what she meant by that, but before I could ask, she was pulling my nightclothes off and demanding that I slip my limbs into the garments she held. In seconds, I was dressed.

"Your bosom has grown since these were crafted for you." Daiseeum clucked her tongue as she surveyed my breasts. "I shall have the tailor return tomorrow to adjust your garments. And your hips . . ." She placed her hands just below my waist and smoothed my leggings down. "Who would have known you had such a female figure. You were skin and bones when you arrived."

I lifted my chin proudly. "I've gained two stone."

"And it was two stone you needed. Skin and bones won't do." Daiseeum clucked her tongue again and began picking up my discarded clothes just as a knock came on my door.

The doorknob turned, and the prince appeared. Since he hadn't waited for me to let him know he could enter, I placed my hands on my hips.

"You're lucky I'm not naked. If you'd come two minutes earlier, I would have been."

He stopped dead in his tracks.

I instantly regretted my words. I'd meant it as an admonishment, but when his lips curved in a smile, I wondered again what had transpired between us last night.

"Noted." His husky voice rolled toward me like a gentle wave caressing my soul. "I shall endeavor to arrive earlier next time."

My jaw dropped just as Daiseeum let out a shrill giggle and traipsed from the room.

"I thought princes were supposed to have manners," I said as my stomach began flipping with a vengeance.

"I'm sure some princes do."

"But you don't, obviously."

"Oh, I do when it suits me."

He sauntered toward me, inhaling deeply, and my heart beat harder.

Flustered, I waved my hands at my training clothes. "Well, I'm up. Daiseeum was insistent that I be ready. So what am I ready for?"

"You're to begin training today. Do you not remember?"

"Yes, I remember that, but I didn't know if that was why you were here."

"It is." Every particle of my body was acutely aware of how closely he stood. It was like a buzzing energy vibrated between us.

Blessed Mother, am I still drunk? I admonished myself internally and wondered if the tonic Daiseeum had given me had also messed with my brain function. I hated this male. Truly hated him. So why was my belly suddenly coiling in anticipation?

I had to still be drunk. It was the only rational explanation.

The prince peered down at me, his eyes piercing. His hair was pulled back into a low ponytail that settled between his wings. Shoulders so broad they looked as though they would rip his shirt stretched past my peripheral vision.

The corner of his mouth kicked up as he inhaled. "Are you feeling okay?"

My head snapped back. "Yes, I'm fine. Why do you ask?"

He inhaled again, the movement slow as though he was savoring something. "No reason."

That smile stayed on his face, and I suddenly had the urge to wipe him clean of it. He looked so . . . smug.

But I hadn't done anything to make him appear so arrogant, so I crossed my arms and arched a questioning eyebrow.

He stroked his chin. "Do you remember last night?"

My cheeks reddened when it occurred to me that he'd seen me completely intoxicated. "I remember that we made a bargain."

"And do you remember anything after that?"

My heart thrummed harder. "No," I said cautiously. "Should I?"

His eyes shuttered, and his strange small smile disappeared. "No, as long as you remember the bargain, that's all that matters. You're to replenish the continent with *orem*."

I groaned. "So I did agree to that."

"Correct, which is why your training begins today. And the first thing we're doing is getting you away from the castle's prying eyes and going somewhere discreet so you may practice your affinity without anyone judging you."

"Oh." Some of the nerves in my stomach loosened. If I actually had an affinity, he was right that I didn't want to begin practicing it only to fail while others watched me. "Thank you . . . for that."

He shrugged, and for a moment, it felt as though I was conversing with any other male. Not the male who'd murdered my family.

I shook myself. I was definitely still drunk.

"So where are you taking me?" I asked.

"Harrivee Territory. I need to do some business there

anyway, and the fields outside of Barvilum have been dead for six months."

"And what am I to do?"

"You're to restore the *orem* in the fields."

"You act like I know how to."

He waved toward the courtyard. "You do, although you might not be consciously aware of it yet, so this week, I'll be taking you to Harrivee daily so you may practice your affinity. I would like to see for myself where it's currently at before you begin training with the castle's most prestigious tutor next week."

I twisted my hands. "But what if I can't do any of what you're asking?"

"You'll be able to."

He sounded so confident. Much more than I felt.

CHAPTER 18

The prince led me from my bedroom chambers to the courtyard's garden. When I cocked my head at him amidst the warm air, budding flowers, and bright leaves, he pointed upward. "We're flying out."

"Under one of your illusions?" I figured if he was still trying to hide my imprisonment, then that would be the only way to conceal our departure. I just thanked the Mother that I remembered the details of our bargain, because I had a feeling the prince would have been fine with me forgetting the fact that I could now freely leave the Exorbiant Chamber.

Prince Norivun nodded, and in the same breath, a cloak of magic fell over me. This time I felt it, unlike when he'd cloaked me on the flight into Solisarium or last night when he'd hidden my hair again. Both times I'd been too distracted to sense it.

His illusion was subtle, like a light cloth settling over my skin, before it disappeared. Nothing like the heavy magic that Vorl's illusions created.

But before I could ready myself for what was to come, the prince's arms were around me, and we were shooting into the sky.

I swallowed a squeal, and my eyes closed automatically as a rush of wind blew over my skin. We climbed fast, and the prince's tight hold had my belly quickening. Reflexively, I gripped his neck with both arms.

He chuckled. "Are you still worried I'll drop you?"

I forced my limbs to loosen as I opened my eyes to peer up at him. "Well, I don't know. You did threaten me with that last time."

His chuckle deepened, and since he didn't tease me further, I pried my attention away from his square jaw and that cleft between his chin.

Around us, the castle grounds sprawled in a complex array of connected buildings, open courtyards, jutting turrets, and soaring towers.

The prince flew us right past the highest tower, passing only feet from its balcony.

I caught sight of a figure sitting in a chair, just the briefest flash of a female with long black hair, wings hanging limply, and a green gown.

"Was that your mother?" I asked, my heart beating harder. I'd never met another Solis with hair like mine.

For a moment, he didn't respond as his giant wings flapped, but then he said quietly, "It was. That's her tower."

"But her hair isn't hidden."

"That's because the wards around her tower only allow a few of us within viewing range. When she's alone, she doesn't like to hide who she is."

I wondered if I'd imagined the pained ache in his voice or the way the queen's wings had hung so limply.

"Is she unwell?" As soon as the question left my mouth, I wondered why I'd asked it. It was nothing to me if his mother wasn't of good health.

His hold on me tightened. "She lives in peace."

"That's a rather . . . strange response."

He didn't reply as we crested the castle's walls and pierced the outer ward. The ward's magic prickled my skin before it released us, and then the sprawling capital lay all around. Wind whipped through my hair since the prince obviously hadn't used his air affinity to suppress it.

Movement behind us caught my attention, and a smile spread across my face when I saw the prince's four guards racing to catch up with us.

"Are your guards following us?" My grin grew, not because I was looking forward to seeing Nish, but I welcomed Haxil's company, and since Sandus was to be my new guard, I figured I better get to know him.

"They are."

"You need their protection while I'm—" I couldn't bring myself to say *creating orem.*

"No, not for your training, but for the business I need to attend to. There's unrest in Harrivee right now. I may need their assistance in Barvilum."

It only took his guards moments to reach us, and then they were right beside us. Black wings flexed as they glided, and their wings brushed tips on occasion they flew so closely, but nobody seemed to mind. Instead, the four guards flanked the prince's side as though they were the God Seemus's warrior hounds guarding his back.

"Ilara Seary, daughter of Mervalee Territory." Haxil dipped his head as his round cheeks lifted while his voice carried to me on the wind. "Nice to see you again."

I returned his smile. "It's lovely to see you too, Haxil Hubberline, guard to the crown prince and son of Isalee Territory."

The guard's smile turned wolfish, and a low growl rumbled in the prince's chest. Nish gave me a side-eye, then a barely suppressed sneer, while Ryder and Sandus both nodded hello.

"And where are we off to today, Nori?" Sandus asked as his large wings flapped.

The prince pointed south. "Back to Barvilum in Harrivee Territory. The Lochen fae have stolen more goods from their wharf, and there's a field I want Ilara to see."

"Ah, another diplomatic mission." Ryder's braid trailed down his back. "Along with . . ." His words trailed off with a glance in my direction.

Exactly. Whatever I was to the prince. His protégé? His savior? I nearly snorted at that thought.

With each flap of their wings, we grew closer to the edge of the capital. Similar to when we'd entered Solisarium a month ago, the skies were busy and congested outside of the castle's protective barrier, but none of the capital's residents dared travel in the prince's path. He once again flew in a straight line, everyone moving out of the way for him.

Eventually, the capital disappeared behind us until nothing but rolling hills of snow and small cities dotted the landscape.

Abruptly, the prince spiraled downward. I clung to him, the movement taking me by surprise.

His arms tightened, and then his lips met my ear. "I won't let you fall."

The vibration of his words and flutter of his lips against my skin made tingles race down my spine. I jerked away, my heart hammering in staccato beats as I cursed my body's response.

Light puffs of snow drifted into the air when the prince's feet touched the ground. He set me down, and his hand settled on my waist until my footing was secure. My heart pattered harder as I lurched from his grip.

Prince Norivun dropped his hand, his jaw working, as his four guards raised questioning eyebrows.

"Is there a reason we've landed, my prince?" Sandus asked as he smoothed his beard.

The prince eyed me again. "I'm going to mistphase with Ilara. Her magic has manifested. She should be able to now, and it'll make traveling faster."

My eyes bugged out. "You're going to . . . *what?* Wait. I can't. I mean, I've never—" I swallowed my sputtering because surely I hadn't heard the prince correctly. I couldn't mistphase. That required power I didn't possess.

"You're magical, Lara." The prince's irises sparkled like sapphire gemstones, and damn my traitorous body for noticing. "You can mistphase with me. I have enough power to cross both of us."

"But what if I'm not magical?" I picked nervously at my fingernails. "What if you're completely wrong about me? A fairy must have enough magic to cross with a mistphaser. If one doesn't, it's too dangerous."

At least that was what I remembered from my primary days. It was why children typically didn't mistphase with a magically-strong parent since a child's magic and affinity didn't appear until maturing age.

The prince's lips kicked up. "Then it's a good thing you have magic." He sounded so confident, as though he was certain that my affinity had indeed been born.

My lips thinned. "I'll die if you're wrong."

"I'm not wrong."

"Ock, just get it done with already," Nish grumbled.

The other three guards all watched us. Only Haxil looked concerned. Indeed, that male knew I could end up splat on the snow, like a gelatinous mush of flesh and blood, when I emerged from the crossing if the prince was mistaken.

Haxil's frown deepened. "My prince, are you sure—"

"Do you really think I'd put her in harm's way?" the prince snapped.

Haxil immediately lowered his chin. "Of course not."

"Ilara?" The prince's tone dropped until it was so deep and rich that it melted all over me. "Trust me."

"Says the fairy who murdered my parents," I muttered under my breath.

His jaw clenched, the muscle like a marble, but his hands remained extended, and I knew he wasn't going to relent.

My shoulders sagged. "Tell Cailis I love her if I don't make it."

His lips twitched. "You'll make it. Now come here." He clasped both of my hands and pulled me toward him.

My breath sucked in at the feel of his hard abs pressed against me. A pulse of sparks ran through my veins, and the feel of his body touching mine created a gridwork of unrest among my nerve endings.

His nostrils flared, and that hooded look befell him again, his expression turning carnal, but then a rush of magic stole over me that was so potent, so raw, that it *consumed* me.

The ground dropped out from beneath me, and then I was nothing more than mist and shadows, air and wind. The world turned into a blur of colorless sound, and then—

Waves crashed. Shores of sandy beaches stretched along the edge of a snowy field. Rolls and rolls of water waited before me.

My jaw dropped as I felt my arms, chest, and legs. I was solid. Whole. I hadn't been obliterated into a million pieces.

"I made it," I whispered.

"Of course, you did." The prince's husky words brushed my ear. "Do you still doubt that you're magical?"

I hastily stepped away. "I . . . it could have been a fluke."

"It's not. You have power, Ilara."

My stomach became a jittery mess because the prince was right. If I didn't, I wouldn't have survived the crossing, which meant the prince could be right about everything else. My affinity. My ability to create *orem*.

I wrapped my arms protectively around myself and fixated on the ocean again. The sound of the surf hitting the land was strangely peaceful, hypnotic almost.

Prince Norivun cocked his head. "Have you never seen the sea?"

"No. Never."

A wink of magic flashed around us, and then the prince's four guards appeared.

Haxil cast a relieved look my way. "Made it in one piece, I see."

I gave him a shaky smile and stepped closer to him. The pounding aura from the prince warmed my back, basking me in its strength, and it felt . . .

I shook myself. His power was too much, but the fairy

guard was open and soft. He'd been nothing but kind to me since we'd met, and he was the only one I trusted at the moment.

The prince's eyes darkened when Haxil reached out a steadying hand to me.

I gratefully accepted it just as the prince said tightly, "Haxil, report to Lord Sillivul and the Barvilum Council, and only return when you've thoroughly assessed the situation."

Haxil's hand lingered on mine before he gave me a comforting pat.

"Haxil," the prince growled.

"Yes, my prince." Haxil offered me a reassuring smile before he shot into the sky and flapped west. Down the hill beside us, the town of Barvilum waited, but around us there was nothing but a snowy field and crashing ocean.

"Nish, Sandus, and Ryder watch the perimeter. Alert me if any fae draw near. I'll cloak her, but I don't want anyone near this area."

"Yes, my prince." They all dipped their heads.

When they took to the skies and retreated to the edges of the field, I planted my hands akimbo. "Do you ever grow tired of bossing fae around all day?"

"When it involves banishing a male who's looking at you in a way I don't particularly care for? No." He gave me his back, and I got an eyeful of his wings tucked in tight just as his statement struck me.

"What in all the realm does that mean?"

He stalked away, then crouched near something black in the snow.

I approached him and rubbed my arms. My tunic was thick,

but it didn't fully alleviate the chill. "Who were you referring to?"

"Never mind," he said gruffly. He waved toward the black item, and when I joined him, I realized it was the withered remains of a wheat stalk. A very *dead* wheat stalk. "This is all that remains of what once grew here. This entire hillside used to be cropland. Some of our finest wheat came from this area. Now, it produces nothing."

My fingers encircled the plant as my other hand drifted to the soil beneath the layers of snow. I had to burrow under a thin coating of ice at the bottom, and when my palm met frozen dirt, I searched for a hum that *orem* existed within this land. Nothing greeted me. I closed my eyes, searching for that pulse that always accompanied the fields.

Silence.

"There's no *orem* here," the prince said quietly.

My lips parted as the implication of what that truly meant took hold of me.

The prince was right.

We would all starve.

I withdrew my hand, shaking. "What you're asking of me is impossible."

"It's not. I know you can do this."

His eyes were so vivid, so blue, and such stark honesty shone from them that for a moment, I ached for his words to be true. I wished I could be who he wanted me to be. I wished I knew *how*.

"I have no idea how to make this field thrive again."

"What did you do in the courtyard?"

"That's just it. I didn't do anything, not really. I just cleaned the snow from the plants, fingered the dead stalks, felt the dried bark. The *orem* appeared on its own on day three, just a tiny flutter of it, and then it grew."

"Perhaps your presence alone creates it. Or your touch."

"Is that how affinities work?"

"Affinities can work in many ways. Some are entirely unique."

"But how do I learn mine?"

His eyes softened. "The first thing you need to do is trust yourself. Believe that you're capable. Once you do that, you'll start to become more aware of the subtle nuances that accompany your magic. Self-awareness is key to mastering one's affinity."

"Is that what you did?"

He sat down, crossing his legs in the snow as though the cold didn't bother him. "I did. When I first manifested, I was like you —powerful, but my tutors had expected as much given my lineage, and I'd been prepared not to meddle with it until I was past the initial stage." He shook his head. "Telling a fairy of thirteen not to test his limits is one thing, but to actually hold myself back . . . That was something else entirely."

I sat on the ground too, but far enough away from him that our knees wouldn't bump. "So you always knew you were going to be strong?"

He shrugged. "I'd been told my entire life that I would be. I was born on the triple lunar eclipse, at the cusp of that great and rare event. A powerful seer said it was a sign of what I was to become."

I frowned. "Wasn't that the event that unleashed a magical shockwave that killed thousands of fae?"

"It was. Fitting, I suppose, considering what my strongest affinity became."

The ability to suck souls. Nobody had ever heard of the prince's affinity prior to him. It was well known that his ability was unrivaled on the continent simply because there was no one else who could do it.

"And how did you grow your affinity?"

He pointed toward the soil. "I started with believing that I could."

THE PRINCE STAYED at my side throughout the morning, his presence steady and strong. Gentle pushes of his aura frequently drifted around me—as if his power was constantly releasing from his body.

As the day passed, I cleared snow from the dead plants, touched the withered leaves, sank my fingers into the dirt, and let myself drift to that soft place that I always traveled to when I was working in my garden or laboring in the fields.

Breathe. Touch. Feel. Give. The dirt was dry, cold, and hard, but I'd spent full seasons feeling the soil between my fingers, and I knew with the right amount of tending, it would loosen and soak in moisture.

I hummed as I worked, and even though I didn't have my tools and was unable to churn the crops or turn over the lifeless vegetation, I didn't worry about that.

At the prince's insistence, I allowed my mind to wander. Before long, I was singing as I swept snow to the side and wiggled my fingers around lifeless roots. I had no idea if what I was doing would help, but I treated the dead field as I would any other, with loving touches and soothing words.

I grew so lost in the aura of the land around me that it wasn't until the prince touched my shoulder that I stopped.

"We must go, Ilara." His tone was soft, and when I met his stare, raw emotion was in his eyes. With a blink, it was gone, but I only grew more flustered when I saw that all four of his guards surrounded us.

"What time is it?" I asked.

"Near evening."

"I've been doing this all day?"

"You have."

My heart beat harder since the time felt as though it'd vanished in the blink of an eye. Around us, areas of the field were now bare as piles of snow sat to the side. Withered crops lay exposed to the elements, and footprints littered the land.

"Do you think my being here helped?"

His lips curved. "I think it did something."

I cocked my head, but he didn't allude further.

"I must meet with Barvilum's council before we return to Solisarium," he said. "We must go."

The sun hung low in the sky. It'd grown much later than I'd been aware.

The prince opened his arms, and I stepped into them. A surging jolt buzzed through me when we made contact, but it was only when he pushed from the ground and into the skies that I realized how easily I'd stepped into his embrace. As though I trusted him.

My brow furrowed as he flew us toward the town. I didn't trust him. There was no way I could possibly feel that for the male who'd taken so much from me.

CHAPTER 19

The small city of Barvilum sat at the edge of the Tala Sea. Homes lined in faded sea wood with thick glass windows overlooked the rolling ocean. Salt filled the air, and I inhaled the tangy fragrance as the prince landed us on the cobblestone streets of the small city center.

The city council's building sat near the wharf, and a crowd had gathered. A tall male fairy with exceptionally pointy ears and spindly legs stood at the building's front door, several steps up from the crowd. He kept waving his hands, and from a distance it looked as though he was trying to quiet the crowd.

"That's Lord Sillivul of the Barvilum Council," Haxil said under his breath.

"Do they know you're coming, my prince?" I asked as we began walking toward them.

The prince's aura darkened. "They know I can be coming at any time."

"It's what keeps the streets in order here," Nish added with a wink. "It's the only thing that's kept this town from burning itself to the ground in recent months."

My brows furrowed. "Because of what's happened to the crops?"

"The crops are only one small problem in this city," the prince replied, his deep voice carrying through the night. "As a seaside town on the southern end of our continent, they also regularly deal with the Lochen fae." He jutted his chin toward the sea. "There's a series of islands called the Glassen Barrier Islands, just thirty millees off the coast here, that the Lochen claimed centuries ago. Unfortunately, the short distance also allows the Lochen easy access to our shores."

"The Glassen Barrier Islands," I repeated and felt so stupid that I didn't know what he was talking about.

The prince pointed toward the sea. I squinted and was able to make out a rising mound, still visible in the dying light if one knew where to look for it.

"It's an island chain far away from the main series of islands that the Lochen call home," the prince explained, "but centuries ago in a sea and air battle among our kind and theirs, they claimed them in their victory."

I ducked my head, feeling uneducated and stupid, but my learning had halted at primary school. I'd been sent to help part-time in the fields when my affinity never manifested, and further learning wasn't required, so my education had stopped once I'd read all of the books in my village's small library. I'd always liked to read. I just hadn't had books available to learn from. Well, until a month ago. I'd read a number of books from the castle's library when I'd been locked in the Exorbiant Chamber, and the prince had been away, but I hadn't read any geography books. Perhaps I needed to change that.

"Can you tell me more about the Lochen fae, my prince?"

He inclined his head. "Since the Lochen fae are a seafaring race, they only occasionally come on land. Unlike the Solis, Lochen can breathe underwater and are adept swimmers whose magic allows them to morph into fish-like creatures when they stay submerged for months on end. But even in their fae forms, they can still move much faster than us in water."

I frowned, trying to remember what I could from my primary days. "But they can also reside on land, right?"

"Correct, which makes them difficult to contend with when they choose to raid our coastal cities. It's not unheard of for Lochen fae to sneak ashore at night, pillage an unsuspecting village, and then escape to the sea. And once they're in the water, it's near impossible to track them."

We reached the edge of the crowd, and those in the back shuffled away as soon as they saw who stood in their midst. Those closest to the pulpit continued grumbling and bemoaning.

"Please, I beseech you," Lord Sillivul called, his words carrying to us. "We are doing what we can to stop the Lochen from stealing our wares."

"But they took four of my chests of rulibs!" a male yelled from the crowd. "They snuck aboard my vessel in the middle of the night just after we docked. I had to sail all the way to Guxbee to sell my silks, and all I have to show for it are a broken lock and a damaged ship railing. How am I to feed my family now?"

More shouts rang from the crowd, and my ears pricked toward the angry curses and muttered comments.

"What's the Death Master going to do about it?" a female yelled.

"Yes, what will the prince do?" another agreed.

"Why don't you ask him yourself?" Lord Sillivul gestured in our direction. "I see that he's arrived."

The crowd turned, some of the ire floating through the air quietening as the fae closest to us stepped farther away.

The prince crossed his arms. "I've been told that the Lochen's raids have increased of late."

"They have, my prince," a male near us replied. He stood a few inches shorter than Nish and wore homespun pants and a thick, durable top. A field hand. I'd recognize another laborer anywhere. "Between their raids, which are destroying the few items our shops have, and the crops withered to nothing, we're all going to starve."

"You won't starve," the prince replied. "We're sending stores from Mervalee to keep you fed for the winter."

"But what about next season and the one after that?" a female called.

"The king must do more!" another screeched.

The prince's jaw flexed, but if I hadn't been standing so close, I wouldn't have seen it.

"Prince Norivun?" Lord Sillivul gave him a tight smile. "Perhaps you could assist us and pay the Lochen a visit? Perhaps a show of our strength is needed?"

"If it would appease you."

The crowd cheered, and Lord Sillivul inclined his head. "Very much so."

"Ilara?" Before I could respond, the prince wrapped his arms around me, and then we were launching into the sky as continued cheers roared from the crowd.

"Where are we going, my prince?" I asked as he flew over the sea.

"To the Glassen Barrier Islands. If the Lochen have been raiding, their leader will be close by. It's time I paid Drachu a visit."

❄

WE TOUCHED down at the base of the most northern island. In the distance, the moonlight illuminated the entire island chain, making each drop of land look like a black pearl jutting up from the sea.

Ryder, Sandus, Nish, and Haxil touched down a second later, and all four drew their swords, one in each hand as a swell of their affinities rippled around me.

"Is this safe, my prince?" I whispered.

Around us the sea crashed on the black sand shores as jutting fjords rose steeply on each side of the island. Tall trees and thick vegetation covered in frost obscured most of the land.

"As safe as anything I do." The prince's cocky response did little to put me at ease, especially when he placed a hand on my lower back. "Stay close."

My spine straightened as warmth from his palm coasted over my skin, but then a rush of ice prickled my veins when a shrill call came in the distance. Then another.

I inched closer to the prince. "Please tell me those are birds."

"Those are birds." Nish snickered.

"You shall be safe, Ilara." Haxil drew closer to my side. "But be wise and do as Prince Norivun commands. Don't drift away from us."

I swallowed the dryness in my throat as my eyes adjusted more to the night. Unlike in Barvilum, there were no fae lights illuminating the way. Here, inky darkness and dim moonlight fogged my vision despite the stars twinkling brightly in the galaxy.

"I know you're there!" the prince called out. "Show yourself, Drachu."

I nearly shrieked when a Lochen fairy appeared from behind a tree. He glided toward us, curving around the rocks nearest to where we stood. Four more Lochen emerged from the forest, then a dozen more until they surrounded us. All moved fluidly even though they walked on two legs, and their skin shades varied from the palest of white to the blackest of night and everything in between.

My eyes widened at how closely they stood before us. I instinctively took a step back and bumped into the prince's chest. His arm locked around me protectively.

As soon as I realized that, I forced myself to put several inches of distance between us, but even my hatred for the prince wouldn't allow me to do anything stupid. I was definitely staying close to his side as the bright-green eyes of the Lochen fae shone from the darkness.

"Prince Norivun," the one in the front said in a deep, commanding voice. An intricate necklace hung from around his neck that held shells, gems, and teeth from predators in the Tala Sea. A large center stone throbbed with an emerald light, illuminating his brown skin. "Why have you come to my shores this time?"

"I think you know exactly why I'm here, Drachu. Your raids have become too often. The Solis grow weary of your thievery."

Drachu shrugged as his lips peeled back in a smile. Rows of straight teeth and two pointy incisors appeared in the moonlight. "It's not my fault if the Solis are too weak to guard their shores."

"I think you know we're anything but weak." A rush of the prince's affinity undulated from him, just enough for everyone in the vicinity to feel the depths of his power latch onto our souls and give a slight tug before he released us.

I gasped as all of the Lochen hissed and crouched. The prince's four guards bent their knees and widened their stances as their swords raised. Nish's wings flexed as Prince Norivun's hand again brushed against my back when he moved closer to me.

Drachu made a clicking noise in his throat, and the Lochen around him all fell back a step. "You dare try to intimidate me on my shores?"

"It's only a reminder of what I'm capable of."

Drachu's gaze drifted to me, then to the close way the prince hovered beside me. He cocked his head and took a step closer.

I tensed, and a low growl rumbled in the prince's chest when Drachu stopped right in front of me.

The Lochen leader straightened more. His chest was bare save for the necklace, and like the prince, he was heavily muscled and had the build of a male seasoned to fighting. A strip of fabric covered his legs. It was all he wore as his hair fell in artful tangles to his shoulders. He looked fierce and proud. He looked like a king.

"Who is this female?" Drachu asked.

Another rumbling warning filled the prince's chest, and he

stepped around me, putting himself between me and the Lochen leader. "She is not of your concern."

"She carries power." Drachu cocked his head, and a flash of green light filled his eyes. An answering hum of light flared in the stone around his neck. "Power unlike I've felt in the Solis fae." He sidestepped the prince, but Prince Norivun moved just as fast.

"As I said," the prince replied on a low growl. "She's not of your concern."

Drachu's lips ghosted in a smile as he fixed his attention on my face, his gaze skimming over my features. "A wingless Solis with strange power and unrivaled beauty. A true treasure."

The prince snarled. "She's *mine*, Drachu."

My heart jolted at that fierce declaration. *His?*

But I didn't have time to show my surprise before Drachu inclined his head at me. "Should you tire of the death warlord, my shores are open to you."

My chest rose and fell as his strange declaration left a whispering confusion swimming through my veins.

"Sandus?" the prince seethed. "Get her out of here. Now."

Before I could protest, Sandus's arms were around me, and we were shooting into the sky. I let out a breath of shock, but the guard didn't stop.

Sandus ascended quickly, and the ground disappeared until only rolling ocean waves were beneath us.

I clung to the guard. "What's going on? What did Drachu mean, and why did he say those things to me?"

Sandus's grip tightened. "I don't know, Ilara. I don't know."

CHAPTER 20

Sandus flew fast and hard as his affinity magic heated his muscles until his wings flapped faster than the eye could see. Night had fully set in, and clouds drifted in front of the moons. Wind pummeled my face as the guard's beard tickled my forehead.

A million questions swirled through my mind as salty air whipped around us, but I didn't have time to voice any of them. Only minutes later, we landed on the cobblestone streets of Barvilum. The crowd parted for us, everyone backing up. I brought a hand to my head, my heart racing, just as a gasp came from the crowd, and then another.

Lord Sillivul crossed his arms and nodded in approval, a smug smile streaking across his face.

A female fairy pointed toward the sea as a hand covered her mouth. Another shrieked as her eyes grew wide.

I turned to the ocean, and my stomach plummeted when I saw what all of them were gaping at. Just off the shore, floating shapes appeared on the water's surface, but I still didn't want to accept what they were.

Bodies.

Dead Lochen fae floated in the sea's waves just beyond the council building's shores. Dozens and dozens of them appeared, face down. Lifeless. Dead.

"The prince killed them?" I whispered. Horror seized my insides.

"He was doing his duty, as is expected of him," a male called from behind us.

Sandus whipped around. "Lord Crimsonale?"

An older fae male stepped through the crowd.

"What are you doing here?" Sandus asked in a deadly quiet voice, his words as cold as ice.

A pit formed in my stomach as nausea rolled through me. So much death, but when Lord Crimsonale took another step closer to us I shifted my attention away from the dead Lochen because Lord Crimsonale was staring right at me.

He looked as I remembered him in the brief encounter we'd shared on my first day arriving to the castle—a portly figure, a balding head, and gray hairs lining his temples.

A perverse smile twisted the Osaravee Territory archon's lips, and my skin crawled. There was something about the older male, something in his eyes that caused my insides to wither.

"Here you are at last." Lord Crimsonale crossed his arms as he assessed me. "I told the council that the prince was keeping a female confined in his wing, but the king thought I was speaking nonsense. Yet, you're exactly as I remember you." He cocked his head. "Tell me, what have you been doing in the prince's private wing during the weeks he's been gone?"

"You don't have to answer that, Ilara." Sandus's nostrils flared.

"No?" Lord Crimsonale cocked his head. "I am a council member and the archon of Osaravee Territory. I hold more authority than *you*." He sneered at the guard, and even though Sandus was taller than him, it was as though he gazed at the guard down his nose. "So tell me, Ilara, was it? What have you been doing in the prince's wing?"

I licked my dry lips "I—"

"How did you know we were here?" Sandus cut in. "Did you follow us? Prince Norivun won't take kindly to that."

Lord Crimsonale shrugged. "I was merely investigating. I knew sooner or later she would have to leave his walls, and considering the prince is being quite secretive about it all, I figured eventually she'd have to join you when you left." He smiled, but it didn't reach his eyes, and then he made a flourishing bow in my direction, bringing a fist to his chest in traditional greeting. "How do you do? Lord Crimsonale, baron of Highsteer Castle, councilor on the king's council, and son and archon of Osaravee Territory."

As a territory archon, he would automatically sit on the king's council, which meant he was right. He had more authority than Sandus. If Lord Crimsonale ordered me to go with him, I would have to.

A shiver danced down my spine as I nodded in response and brought a fist to my chest, but I was loathed to give him my full name. "How do you do?"

Lord Crimsonale eyed me curiously. "I'm sorry we haven't become acquainted. I'm sure the king would also be curious why he's unaware of your stay in his castle." He cast a shrewd look at Sandus just as the crowd pointed toward the sky. My heartbeat skyrocketed when I spotted the prince and his guards flapping toward us. "But I'm sure he will look forward to introductions at the much-anticipated ball this weekend. Do come, Ilara. After all, once I tell the king of you, that you're real and of flesh and blood, he'll insist you attend."

"The ball?" I asked dumbly.

Before he could clarify, the prince landed right beside me, and positioned himself between me and Lord Crimsonale, as a snarl cut loose from his throat. "What are you doing here?"

"He followed us," Sandus answered. "He's curious about Ilara."

Prince Norivun's power rumbled the cobblestone street as he took a step closer to the lord.

Lord Crimsonale's throat bobbed as he took a step back.

The prince's aura rose as his eyes narrowed to slits. "You followed me?" he asked with barely leashed violence in his voice.

My heart was beating so fast now I gripped Sandus to steady myself.

"I do apologize if I've overstepped, my prince." Lord Crimsonale's lips thinned. "I was merely acting in the best interest of the court. When it had come to my attention that the king wasn't aware of a female's habitation in your wing, I thought it was best to seek clarification, especially considering what's happening this coming weekend."

Blue ice shone like fire in the prince's eyes. "You've more than overstepped, and you know it."

The lord's eyes shuttered, growing colder than the snow in

the Gielis Mountains. "As you wish, my prince. I shall be on my way then."

Magic swirled around the lord, and then in a wink, he vanished.

Blessed Mother, he can mistphase too.

Prince Norivun's hands fisted as a tremble shook my frame.

"Why are Drachu and Lord Crimsonale so interested in me?" I whispered. "And why did that lord just invite me to a ball this weekend?"

"Fuck," the prince whispered under his breath. He pinched the bridge of his nose, and I shivered when a wave of the prince's frosty magic kissed my skin. "I suppose I cannot hide you any longer, not if council members have taken to following me to get answers."

The prince's arms closed around me once more, and then a rush of magic stole over us as I fell into a void of mist and shadows, air and wind. Everything disappeared around us.

❄

THE PRINCE MISTPHASED us to the courtyard outside of the Exorbiant Chamber. The second my feet touched solid ground, I stumbled away from him as warmth from the courtyard's *orem* and the sweet fragrance of the juniper blossoms filled the air.

Thoughts of Lord Crimsonale and whatever ball was happening in a few days swirled through my mind, but I pushed those aside and focused on the more important matter.

The prince had just murdered dozens of Lochen fae, and nobody had batted an eye.

"How could you?" I said quietly, putting distance between us as soon as I could. "How could you murder all of them like that?"

"Ilara." He advanced on me, but I widened the distance between us.

"Stay away from me. I want all of you to stay away from me. You! Lord Crimsonale! All of you!" I was sickened by everything that I'd seen and heard tonight. Everything about the Court of Winter was filled with death, malice, games, and political intent.

Prince Norivun hissed and in a flash stood right in front of me, gripping my upper arms. I shrieked and tried to pull away, but he didn't let go. Dazzling blue eyes flashed fire as he stared at me.

"Everything is not as it seems." His aura pounded into my frame, and his grip was too strong for me to break free. His jaw pumped as the muscle bulged in the corner. "I *didn't* kill those fae."

My chest rose up and down so fast that I struggled to breathe. "Yes, you did. I saw them floating in the sea. Don't lie to me. You're a murderer. A vile, twisted *murderer.*"

His nostrils flared as his scent clouded around me, drawing me in. Snow and cedar, decadent and alluring, threatened to siphon his ugly affinity and masterful power from my mind. But I couldn't forget what he was. I wouldn't.

I tried to wrench away again, but he refused to let go.

"Blessed Mother," he said on a low growl. "Listen to me! It was an illusion, Ilara. I didn't kill anyone. I created that illusion to appease the citizens of Barvilum. Drachu and I reached an agreement, so I did *not* kill any Lochen tonight."

I flinched. "But the bodies—"

"They weren't real. It was all an illusion, a trick of the mind. The Lochen are still on their island or in the sea or wherever they've chosen to go, but none of them are dead and floating in that harbor."

My mouth opened, then closed, then opened again. "But it looked so real."

"Because I'm a master at illusions."

I paused, taking a moment to consider what he was saying. *Not real? Was that possible?* I inhaled the sweet scents of the garden's flowers, letting the warmth and peace of the small, beautiful courtyard soothe my frayed nerves. Shaking my head, I tried to wrap my head around what he was claiming.

His brow furrowed, and he took a deep breath. "Look, let's just forget about all of this. It's been a long day. We should both try to sleep."

He made to turn away, but I called out, "What was Lord Crimsonale talking about this weekend? A ball of some kind?"

He stilled, his entire body going rigid as his wings flexed. "Yes, there's a ball being held. Unfortunately."

I frowned. "Why unfortunately?"

But instead of answering, he gestured to my chambers and took a deep breath. "Not now. Sleep, Ilara. I'll come for you in the morning." And with that, he was gone.

I SLEPT FITFULLY, tossing and turning all night. I kept picturing the dead Lochen, the illusion the prince had created, and then the vile curiosity on Lord Crimsonale's face.

Everything about that encounter had left a sour taste in my mouth that permeated my dreams and made me want to vomit.

Not surprisingly, when I woke the next day I didn't feel rested. Dark circles lined my lower eyes when the prince came for me just as Daiseeum finished dressing me.

"Thank you," the prince said to the lady's servant, dismissing her.

She bobbed a curtsy as the prince frowned, taking in my appearance. "Did you eat?"

"I did. I'm ready to begin working again."

The prince clasped his hands behind his back, right beneath his wings before strolling toward the courtyard. His aura puffed out of him, bathing my chambers in his strength. "You're to attend the ball this weekend. My father insists."

My heart beat harder as I moved closer to him. "He does? Why?"

The prince growled low in his throat. "Apparently, Lord Crimsonale went straight to him yesterday, and now my father is curious to meet you."

I twisted my hands. "So the entire court now knows of me?"

"Yes, and your presence has caused quite a stir."

"But I thought my only purpose here was to heal the fields, not go to balls."

"I had hoped to contain your activities to that only, but—" His nostrils flared. "It's now out of my control." He held out his hand. "Come. Let us continue in Barvilum."

We mistphased from my chambers and spent the morning and afternoon similar to the day prior. At least I found some solace in the field despite its dead stalks and gray dirt, but even with that distraction, in the back of my mind, I kept picturing Lord Crimsonale's interest in me, and now the king's curiosity.

But that didn't impede why I'd become the prince's prisoner. Despite what loomed, the crown prince returned for me each morning before whisking me away in a blur of mist and shadows, air and wind.

He took me to the same field in Harrivee over and over.

The morning sun hid behind pastel-colored clouds on our fourth day in the field. Salty, cool air whipped around me as I knelt to the ground while Prince Norivun sat at my side. Piles of snow lay around us, the only evidence we left behind of what we were doing, but the residents of Barvilum seemed to have given up on this field. Nobody came up here.

I dug into the frosty dirt with my spade, then sank my fingers into it.

Unlike in the courtyard, I still didn't detect any *orem*.

Straightening, I flung my spade to the side. "It's not working. The *orem* should have appeared by now. I can't do this."

It didn't help that the ball was tomorrow. All week Daiseeum had been gushing about it. I knew it was being held in honor of the prince. She kept talking about the young females that would also be attending, but ballgowns and parties were the furthest things from my mind, even if I was to meet the king at it, so I never listened to half of what she was saying.

All I wanted was to fulfill the bargain Prince Norivun and I had made so I could return home and be done with the prince and the Winter Court.

Prince Norivun settled more beside me. "You're frustrated."

"Obviously."

"You *can* do this, Ilara."

I blew a strand of silver hair from my forehead. "How can you be so sure?" I swept my arm out. "This field is huge. What you're asking of me is impossible, and there's no life here. No *orem*. Four days I've been at this, and I have nothing to show for it."

He gently encircled my wrist with one of his large hands. A shiver ran through me. His hand tightened around me more, as though he felt it too.

He placed my fingers back into the dry, cold dirt. "Channel that energy into the field. I have no doubt it's helping, and remember, next week you'll also begin working with a tutor. You'll learn how to do this."

I scowled as a tingle of awareness slid up my arm. Every time he'd touched me this week that had happened, as though my body recognized something in him.

His palm lingered, his touch so warm in the frigid air. My breathing sped up, and I wondered why I wasn't snatching my hand away. Perhaps it was because I was tired. Working in the fields each day had left me fatigued every night.

"Keep trying," he finally said, then slowly withdrew.

I felt every inch of his fingers slide along my skin, the tingles and shivers increasing within my arm until he severed our connection.

I could have sworn that his eyes darkened in the overcast sun. Energy charged the air around us. *Blessed Mother.* My life had truly become pure madness.

I ran a hand through my hair. "Why are you here with me every day?" I asked, anything to break the current flowing between us. "Why not just leave me with your guards to work on this alone?"

He arched an eyebrow. "Is my company so abhorrent?"

It was on the tip of my tongue to say that yes, it was, but . . . That would be a lie. Like it or not, the murderer of my family had become the one constant in my unpredictable life. He was also the only fairy who had the power to keep me safe and shield me from the court's perverse curiosity. I hated that, but whenever Prince Norivun appeared, a strange feeling of relief flowed through me. It was as though I was worried the prince would one day disappear and leave me to fulfill our bargain on my own while trying to fend off the court's growing interest.

How had my life descended into this? Not for the first time this week, I realized that I needed to put a stop to whatever strange bond was growing between the prince and me.

I resisted the urge to pick at my fingernails. "Don't you have other things you should be doing?"

"I have a million other things I should be doing."

"Then why not tend to them?"

He eyed me, his expression impossible to decipher. "Next week you'll start training with your new tutor and be done with me, although I'll still have to mistphase you to the fields when you're not training with her, but I won't be staying at your side indefinitely. So rest easy, Lara."

I started at the sound of my nickname. To hear that name roll off his lips was so intimate, somehow. And I didn't like the shiver it provoked.

I studied the squareness of his jaw and the cleft on his chin, then forced myself to focus on the task at hand. "What happens if I fail? What happens if all of us begin to starve?"

"I think you already know the answer to that. Nothing good comes from an entire continent of fae going hungry."

He was right. Obviously. Images of burning cities, pillaging, crime, unrest, and violence swirled through my thoughts. It would be a nightmare.

I fingered the dirt again. If our entire continent truly was going to starve, maybe it was best that my parents and brother were no longer here. Nobody wanted to suffer. It was bad enough that I'd have to watch Cailis starve if it came to that.

"Sometimes I forget that you killed my family. Maybe it's a blessing that they won't have to see what's to come if I fail." I rubbed more soil between my fingers. "I still have dreams about them and their final moments."

"I know."

My head whipped up. "You do?"

"You had a nightmare when we were in High Liss. You were calling for them in your sleep."

My lips parted as that night came crashing back to me. I recalled a nightmare that I'd experienced in that lodge, but the details were fuzzy. One thing surged to the center of my thoughts, though. I'd awoken the next morning in his bed. I still remembered that very clearly.

"Did you carry me from the floor to the bed in High Liss?"

"I did."

My heart fluttered more. "Because of my nightmare?"

"Yes."

I sat back on my haunches, my mind reeling. Breaths coming faster, I shook my head in disbelief. "So I didn't stumble there on my own? But when? When did you move me into the bed? Right before you left that morning?"

His jaw tightened, and he shook his head so slightly it was barely perceptible.

My heart beat harder. "During the middle of the night?"

"During your nightmare, you were thrashing and screaming, begging me not to kill them. I came to you and put you beside me in the bed. I tried to soothe you until you calmed. You were quite distraught, but you never woke. Eventually, you settled back into a deep sleep. I didn't have the heart to return you to the floor." He leaned back more on the ground as his giant wings splayed behind him while I processed that kind yet shockingly intimate gesture. "Do you want to talk about your family?"

"What? No," I replied too quickly. "That would be . . . weird."

He abruptly reached forward and tucked a strand of hair behind my ear. The second he made contact with my skin, my entire being buzzed with energy.

"I don't take what I do lightly." His comment was said so quietly, so genuinely, as though he actually meant it.

Tears threatened to fill my eyes. So much had happened this week. Too much, and now we were talking about my family. I didn't know how much more I could take, but I forced the tears back. "Do you regret killing them?"

"I regret a lot of things."

"But what about my family? My parents. My brother. Do you regret killing *them*?" I stared at him pleadingly.

"Yes." His eyes bore into me, the startling blueness of them like millions of twinkling stars. "I'm sorry for every life I've taken that wasn't from a vile murderer or pedophile, and I regret what taking your parents and brother from their lives did to them, you, and your sister."

More tears filled my eyes. "You do?"

He nodded.

My breath stuttered out of me. Never, not once, in the past season had I ever thought I'd get an apology from him, much less an apology that seemed sincere.

A flash of something coated my insides. Relief, maybe. Or, perhaps even the beginning of forgiveness. But it was all twisted up, all jumbled together as I struggled to keep the tears from falling. I didn't know what I was feeling, but I knew for the first time in a full season, the constant anger I felt over their deaths lessened.

Before I could process anything further, he stood. "Come. I can see that everything is wearing on you. This week has been difficult, so I propose we take a break."

Holding his hand out, he reached for me.

Dirt still lined my fingers, but he didn't seem to care when I slipped my hand into his.

With a tug, he lifted me to my feet. My heart hammered again as his snowy cedar scent hit me while I waited in front of him, only inches from his chest.

He smiled and tucked another stray lock of hair behind my ear.

I couldn't breathe. He stood so close, and his look was so . . .

He retreated a step, and some of the heaviness in his expression eased. "Have you ever been to the shores of Kroravee?"

I shook myself out of whatever fog was descending over me. "No, of course not. Prior to meeting you, I'd never left Mervalee."

Besides, Kroravee Territory had a reputation for being standoffish to fae from all other territories. They were a reclusive lot, preferring to keep to their own. Even though all of the territories had been under one reign since King Novakin united the continent over three hundred winters ago, it was said that Kroravee still held a grudge about it.

The prince raised an eyebrow. "So you haven't visited Pentlebim or the ice caves? Then I suppose that's where we're going."

His arms closed around me, and then in a whisper of mist and shadows, air and wind, the field vanished.

CHAPTER 21

We reappeared in the bustle of a market. Dozens of
fae walked and hurried to vendor stalls as they
searched for the goods they needed.

I peered around, taking in the stalls that were
similar to Firlim's harvest market but larger. A multitude of inter-
locking streets zigzagged every which way. Conversation drifted
in the air as a cool breeze caressed my cheeks.

"Where are we?"

"Pentlebim's midday market. It's open several hours each
afternoon."

I sniffed, catching the scent of salt on the wind. "Are we close
to the sea?"

"The Brashier Sea is only a millee north of here."

Since nobody was paying us any attention, I cocked my head.
"Can anyone see us?"

"Not yet. I've cloaked our arrival and haven't released my
illusion yet."

My lips curved as I fully relaxed in the secretiveness of our arrival. I took in the displays. Jewelry, enchantments, clothing, shoes, charms of every sort, and bottles of ale were only a few of the items visible. I'd never visited a market just to browse before, and even though I had no rulibs and wouldn't be able to purchase anything, it didn't mean it wouldn't be enjoyable.

Already, the weight of the responsibility that had been placed on my shoulders was lifting. Perhaps the prince was right. Maybe I needed a break. A few hours reprieve was bound to help before I attempted to revive the field in Harrivee again.

"Where should we start?" I asked excitedly.

He grinned. "We can start right here if—"

A commotion came from down the lane, then a scuffle of feet and a sharp whistle as the city's guard ran past us. The two guards—fae males with wings tucked in tight, clubs in their hands, and glowing cuffs snapped to their waistbands—ran down the lane. From the sounds of it, a fight had just broken out.

My heartbeat ticked up. "What's going on?" More yells and shouts reached my ears.

The prince's nostrils flared. "Probably more fighting over the food. It's been a common occurrence here of late."

I strained to see through the throng of fae, but already a crowd was forming at the end of the lane. The fight had erupted a dozen stalls down from where we stood. Another sharp whistle pierced the air. The sound of fists hitting flesh and sparks from magic being cast followed.

My stomach sank even more as a shiver ran through me. "They're fighting because they don't have enough to eat?"

"No, they *do* have enough, for the moment at least. We've been carefully rationing the stores in Kroravee for several months now, but some fae are trying to take more than their share. They're frightened, so they're hoarding, or trying to."

A male yelled out, cursing the guards, just as the crowd parted enough for me to see the guards wrestle a fairy to the ground.

"Do you need to intervene?" I asked the prince.

His lips pressed into a thin line. "I could if they need my help."

I studied his expression. "But you don't want to?"

He hesitated, then gave a rueful shrug, which made his giant wings lift and my attention snag to his broad shoulders. "It can be tiresome to always be working, but I suppose that's my problem to deal with. Not yours."

He made a move to join the guards, and I didn't know why, but I reached for him.

The second my hand made contact with his arm, a shiver ran through me. Everything in me locked up, as though I couldn't breathe, couldn't think, couldn't exist knowing he was unhappy, and—

What in all the realms?

I snatched my hand back as though I'd been burned, my breaths coming so fast that I feared I would hyperventilate.

The prince froze.

I wanted to ask him if he'd felt that too, but I didn't dare open my lips. Having any kind of reaction to him disturbed me to no bounds, and I couldn't even comprehend how something like *that* could happen.

I inwardly shook myself. *It must be his strange affinities or perhaps my new affinity. They're messing with my head.*

I ran a hand through my hair, still in disbelief that I'd tried to stop him from doing his duty, but he'd looked so . . . tired, but it wasn't like the crown prince needed my help.

I made a point to wrap my arms around my waist. "I can wait here if you need to assist."

Shouts still came from down the lane, but they were growing less frequent.

The prince stared down at me, his gaze so intense it was burning, as though he was waiting for—

He snapped upright. "I shouldn't leave you unattended."

I shook my head. "I'll be fine, especially if I'm still cloaked under your illusion. Nobody can see or hear me, and I know Kroravee has a reputation for being unfriendly, but surely nobody will bother me. They have no idea that we're connected. Right?"

His frown deepened, but then the fae guards who had passed us returned, towing a male behind them. The male's head hung as his wings drooped down his back. His hands were cuffed, and he dragged his feet, but whatever scuffle had been occurring seemed to have been contained to him and him alone.

The prince's lips curved up when they passed, and the market returned to its normal hustle. "I guess my services aren't needed after all."

A mist of magic descended over me, and then a fairy walking by jumped. "Ock, apologies, miss. Didn't see ya there."

He didn't say anything to the prince—he didn't even glance at him.

"Doesn't he know who you are?" I whispered, amazed that anybody in the realm would act so nonchalantly around their prince. Prince Norivun's aura alone commanded one's attention, and the *feel* of him . . . Even I'd known he was the prince when he'd stormed into my village's field kitchen all those weeks ago, and I'd never laid eyes on him before that.

The prince's lips twitched. "I'm wearing an illusion mask."

I arched an eyebrow as the prince held out the crook of his arm to me. "A what?"

"An illusion mask. It hides my true appearance, like a glamour when fae travel to other realms and don't want to be recognized as different."

"You look the same to me."

He smiled wickedly. "My mask is only for those outside of my Shield." He held out his arm again. "Stay close, and I'll look the same to you."

I shook my head, not taking his arm. Before he could stop me, I jumped away from him, then turned.

My breath caught.

The male staring back at me was shorter than the crown prince, with hair cut close to his head, a larger nose, and pointier ears. With widening eyes, I took a step closer to him and then another.

I didn't feel when I passed through his Shield, but I blinked, and the crown prince looked like himself again. "Unbelievable. Your magic truly created that?"

"It did."

"How are you so strong?"

"I told you. I was bred to be powerful." He held out his arm for a third time. "Now, shall we? I'm due back in court this evening. We don't want to waste what time we have."

Maybe it was his cheeky smile or the way he looked so boyishly playful, but I found myself slipping my hand around his elbow and settling my palm on his forearm.

That strange sensation washed through me again when our bodies connected. Something in me calmed, as though everything was now right.

Mother Below. I was truly losing my mind.

WE SPENT most of the afternoon strolling through Pentlebim's market. I quickly learned that it was much larger than Firlim's, with an entire section dedicated to luxury items and things I'd never seen before.

Fur cloaks. Fragrant perfumes. Delicious chocolates and sweets. Beautiful silk dresses. Butter-soft leather gloves. Large jewels and sparkling gems. Handcrafted daggers and swords. Intricate artwork and sculptures.

They were extravagant items. Decadence at its finest, yet I still marveled at the richness that our great continent had to offer. I'd never in my life owned anything close to the wares that Pentlebim's market sold.

"I didn't know such goods existed," I murmured for what felt like the hundredth time. My eyes widened as I studied everything that we passed. So many colors, textures, and fragrances. This market felt like a living and breathing entity. No wonder so many fae traveled from around the territory to visit it.

"It's why I brought you here." The prince casually strolled by my side. "I thought this may be a new experience for you."

"It certainly is." I fingered a pair of gloves. They were dyed a rich purple and were so soft they felt like silk. Thick fur lined their interior. They would likely keep one's hands warm and dry even on the coldest of winter nights.

Since the vendor didn't shoo me away—probably thanks to the expensive-looking tunic and slacks I wore courteous of the Court of Winter's tailor—I slipped a glove on, just to see if it was as soft and warm as it looked.

My fingers burrowed into the fur, the heat from the gloves already igniting my chilled fingers. I'd never owned anything even remotely as nice as them. With a sigh, I took them off.

"Would you like them?"

The prince's question had my head snapping toward his. "What?"

His hands were clasped behind his back, making his shoulders appear even broader than normal. "I could buy them for you. Would you like them?"

"Oh no, that's all right." I ran fluttering fingers through my hair. "You don't need to buy me anything."

"I insist." He picked up the gloves and held them out to the vendor. "It's the least I can do since I haven't properly paid you yet for your time and help, but I will. I've been meaning to set up a bank account in your name. I will back-pay you from the day you arrived at the castle."

My mouth opened and closed like a fish as the prince bought the gloves before I could stop him. The vendor held them out to me in a beautiful sack. Even the bags one received here were luxurious.

I took it automatically as I tried to comprehend what I'd just heard. "You're going to *pay me*?"

"Of course."

"But I thought I had to do as you said since you're"—I lowered my voice so I wouldn't blow his disguise—"the *crown prince*."

His lips twitched. "You do have to do as I say."

"Then why are you paying me?"

"Because it's the proper thing to do. Nobody works for free."

"But that's something a gentlefae would do. I thought you weren't a gentlefae."

He coughed, muffling a laugh. "That's not something a gentlefae would do. That's something an honest fae would do."

"So you're honest?"

"I try to be."

Blessed Mother. I truly was losing my mind because I actually found myself believing him. My frown deepened as we strolled to a food stall.

"What's changed between us?" I asked when he stopped to study the menu.

Fried pastries dipped in honey and sugar were visible in their display. Something that decadent couldn't be found in Firlim's harvest market. Of course, the prince purchased two of them, then held one out to me.

"Nothing's changed." He bit into his, his strong jaw working the pastry. "It's simply become apparent that you're going to be working at my side for the foreseeable future. Therefore, I need to put you on the court's payroll."

"But you're acting . . . nicer now."

He gave a wicked grin. "Shall I go back to being a bastard?"

I laughed, unable to help myself, then realized I was *laughing* with the male who'd murdered my family.

But even that realization didn't sober my enjoyment.

Ock. It was official. I was either certifiably insane, or his regret at what he'd done to my family was thawing my resolve to hate him.

The prince held out his arm. "Come. I'll show you the ice caves before it gets too dark."

THE PRINCE FLEW us north of Pentlebim, to the coast of the Brashier Sea. Tangy salt nipped the tip of my tongue as the rich air grew denser the lower the prince flew.

Icy waves crested the shores as ice caps floated in the frigid water. My new beautiful leather gloves covered my hands, and I didn't think my fingers had ever felt so warm.

"Thank you for the gloves," I said softly just as he touched down, his booted feet hitting the snow-covered sand. "I didn't properly thank you back at the market."

"You're welcome." He released me and held on to my waist until I was steady.

My breaths increased, but I made myself step away, anything to stop these strange reactions I was having to him.

Ahead, a looming mountain rose right at the coast's edge. Jagged ice crystals covered the entire base as snow blanketed its peak.

"It's so big." My head tilted back and back and back. It was as though the peak touched the stars.

"And unusual. This area is well known simply because a mountain of this size at the sea's surface is geographically rare. Some say the God Xerious built it as his temple, and the ice caves within it were his private chambers."

He gestured for me to walk at his side, and within minutes we reached the entrance to an enormous cave. Blue ice with veins of silver and white running through it made up the entire exterior.

As we walked inside, I shuffled my feet along the cave's slippery floor so I wouldn't fall.

A hum of magic washed over me the farther we went, and amazingly, it didn't grow dark—just dim—as we ventured more inside. When we rounded a corner, a light shone from farther in the cave's belly.

"What's that?"

The prince smiled, and with a start, I realized he'd been watching me the entire time we'd been walking in the cave. "You'll see."

When we rounded the next turn, I gasped.

Millions of sparkling gems poked out from the ice, not only above us but all around us. The cave's ceiling, sides, floor, continuing tunnel, *all* of it. It was as though light illuminated the precious gems from behind them. Like the sun itself lived in the belly of this mountain.

I gazed in awe, turning slowly in a circle as a grin stretched across my face. It looked as if a galaxy of stars lit up the cavern, and that I was suspended in the midst of it. But there were so many colors and shimmering textures here, even more so than one saw in our great universe's sky.

"So this is why fae believe this mountain belongs to the gods." Tears formed in my eyes, and my breathing stuttered. For a moment, I couldn't speak. Couldn't take a breath. I never thought I'd witness beauty like this. My life in Mervalee was so small. So insignificant compared to something like this.

An ache formed in my chest. If only my parents and brother were here. My mother had loved beautiful things. She had always kept a patch of our garden reserved for flowers—pretty little petals that in no way helped feed us—but their vibrant colors and enchanting fragrances had always made her smile even on our darkest days.

When I finally found my voice again, I whispered, "It's so beautiful. Possibly the most beautiful thing I've ever seen."

"I think so too," the prince replied, his voice so quiet that I almost didn't hear him.

When I shifted my tear-filled eyes to his, his comment pierced my soul, and the emotion strumming through me caught in my chest.

Not because he agreed with me that the cave's sight was extraordinary, but because when he said it was the most beautiful thing he'd ever seen, he hadn't been looking at the cave.

He'd been looking at me.

CHAPTER 22

Daiseeum held up a floor-length royal blue gown that looked to be made of the finest silk and was encrusted with thousands of tiny gems. It glittered and shimmered when she swayed it in the light.

The lady's servant gave a wistful sigh. "'Tis lovely, is it not?"

I eyed the silky material with the plunging neckline, cinched waist, and nearly bare back. The bareness would have suited any female with wings, but since I didn't have wings, my naked flesh would be exposed for all to see.

"It *is* beautiful," I agreed, even though my hands were clammy and my entire body stiff.

All day I'd been thinking about what the prince and I had experienced together yesterday, and it'd been hard to focus, even more so when Sandus had popped his head into my chambers a few hours ago with a ledger from the court's bank. More rulibs than I'd ever owned in my entire life had been transferred into my name in a newly opened account. It seemed as though the prince hadn't been jesting when he'd said that he would pay me for my time. Even though I hadn't accomplished anything aside from the flourishing garden in the courtyard, he'd still paid me for each day I'd been at court.

Daiseeum's smile grew. "Shall we put it on you?"

I began picking at my fingernails. I still couldn't believe I was going to the ball or that I was going to meet the king, but now that Lord Crimsonale was telling everyone of my existence and the prince's interest in me, the entire court knew of my month-long stay in his wing.

It didn't help that, apparently, the prince's behavior toward me was unusual. According to Daiseeum, no other female had ever captured his interest like I had.

I snorted at that thought. I supposed having the ability to save our continent would garner that kind of attention, even from a prince.

"Well?" Daiseeum asked with raised eyebrows when I remained quiet.

I plastered a smile on my face. "Um, I guess so?"

She *tsked*. "Your head's been in the clouds all day. Now, come, we must get you ready." She beckoned me forward and sighed in contentment. "I shall finally be able to dress you as a lady should."

After I slipped into the gown, which fell over my body like liquid silk, she smiled.

"Beautiful, just beautiful. Now, have a seat." She patted the stool in front of her. "My affinity shall have you ready in no time."

The minute I propped myself on the stool's plump cushion, she set to work on my hair and makeup.

The lady servant's affinity, as I'd come to learn in the

previous weeks, was that of beauty. She could make anything look beautiful, whether that be a decorative array of flowers in a vase, an arrangement of pillows on a bed, or the styling of one's hair and makeup.

Some fae considered superficial affinities such as Daiseeum's to be inadequate, since her magic didn't hold anything mighty or powerful, but I'd come to see just how talented she was. The lady's servant had a gift of making any fairy look their best, and for the first time since I'd met her, I didn't try to restrain her from wielding her magic.

I was meeting the king after all.

"Daiseeum?" I said as she twirled a hot iron through my hair. Strands of silver fell around me. The prince hadn't shattered his illusion again, not since he'd revealed to his brother what I was. "Do you know Lord Crimsonale?"

Daiseeum's fingers faltered, just for a moment, before she steadied her hand, and a soft curl twirled from the iron. "I know of him, my lady."

"Can you tell me what you know?"

Her lips pursed. "He's a very powerful lord from Osaravee Territory. He's the territory's archon, so he sits on the king's council. His father only stepped down from his title perhaps five winters ago, which allowed Lord Crimsonale to ascend, so he's a somewhat new ruler in his area. I've heard that he's very ambitious and is looking to stamp his mark. I also heard—" Her lips clamped closed.

"What else did you hear?"

"I shouldn't speak so."

"Please? I feel like I'm being thrown to the wolves tonight. I know nothing of the court."

Her fingers continued to move assuredly through my hair as she clucked her tongue. "Very well. I heard that he can also be cruel. Trillis, a servant who works in the kitchens, told me that he purposefully burned one of the young males who had tripped while helping the lord dress. The lord's shirt ripped, and Lord Crimsonale became angry."

"Burned him how?"

"With his magic. Lord Crimsonale's affinity is an element— fire. When he's displeased, it's been said he burns those who anger him."

I made a disgusted face. "That's horrible. Was the young male badly injured?"

"The entire layer of flesh on the back of his hand was burned through. Murl wasn't powerful enough to fully heal the wound. That young male now carries a rather ugly scar."

My stomach churned when I remembered the feeling I'd gotten from Lord Crimsonale when he'd appeared in Barvilum. I shuddered.

"And what else can you tell me of the court? Who do I need to be careful of? Who can I trust? Please tell me everything."

Daiseeum continued to work her magic but gave a slight nod. "Very well, my lady."

The minutes ticked by as her soft magic floated around me, and she filled me in on the court's gossip and hierarchy. She went through all of the lords and ladies, what their rankings were, their affinities that she knew of, and which territories they called home, but they were all faceless names and titles. I didn't know what kind of fae they were, if they were kind, cruel, noble, or mundane.

Daiseeum hummed in between divulging the court specifics, and her fingers moved with liquid grace as her magic grew in strength around me. "To be truly safe, simply steer clear of Lord Crimsonale and Arcane Woodsbury—the Isalee Archon's third son. He's been known to hurt animals and children, although he's clever, so nothing has ever been pinned on him, but rumors follow him wherever he goes. Oh, and give Taberitha Wormiful, the archon of Kroravee Territory, a wide berth. She's been known to eat young fae females for breakfast." When my eyes widened, Daiseeum bumped me playfully. "Not literally, Ilara, but she's a spiteful fairy who despises all females who climb higher than her on the social chain. She is from Kroravee after all, so it shouldn't be too surprising."

Holding still as Daiseeum did the finishing touches, I said, "All right. Stay away from Lord Crimsonale, Lord Woodsbury, and Lady Wormiful. Avoid those three at all costs, be wary of everyone else, and don't draw attention to myself, and all should be fine. Did I understand that correctly?"

When I picked at my fingernail, Daiseeum patted my shoulder. "You shall be fine. I doubt the prince will leave your side." She finished with the makeup she'd been wielding and gave a contented smile. "There, all done." Her eyes sparkled with pride as she looked me over. "Come see."

She led me to the floor-length mirror near the bathing chamber, and I gaped when I saw myself.

The silky dress shone like glass in the mirror, shiny and bright in the overhead fairy lights. A single pendant necklace dangled between my cleavage, drawing one's attention there. I had no idea if the jewelry was real, but the sapphire sparkled and twinkled, reminding me of the jewel that Drachu had worn around his neck.

Around my waist, Daiseeum had added a jeweled belt, highlighting the swell of my hips and hourglass figure. Now that I'd had over a month of daily meals, I'd developed curves that I'd never known existed.

"How did you do this to my hair?" I asked, bringing a hand up to the delicate design. Glimmering gems glistened in the half-up, half-down style. Beautiful diamonds interwove through my curls, shifting and sparkling as though suspended in the strands, and the loose curls swirling through my long locks swayed like gentle waves in the Tala Sea.

"Magic." Daiseeum smiled sweetly.

My makeup was also flawless, making my eyes look bigger and brighter, my lips fuller, and my cheekbones sharper. I still looked like me, but I'd never seen myself look so striking.

I pivoted, taking in the floor-length dress that moved like water. My entire back was exposed, and since the dress stopped in a V just above my backside, it drew attention to that area too. Since I'd gained weight, there was a definite curve to my bottom that hadn't been there a month ago either.

I laughed in delight. "You're amazing at this, Daiseeum. I never knew I could look so beautiful. Thank you."

Daiseeum's head bobbed, and her cheeks flushed as she curt-sied. "I do so enjoy it, and you are truly exquisite, Ilara. You were already a beautiful canvas who just needed the finishing touches to be a true masterpiece."

I grinned and clasped her hand before giving her a squeeze. Her cheeks pinked even more.

A soft knock came on my bedroom chamber door, and she hastily removed her hand. "That would be the prince. Right on time."

The door opened, and the prince strode in. "Ilara? Are you ready to—"

The prince stopped in his tracks when he saw me, his eyes widening.

He stood at the threshold, dressed in the royal colors and in full uniform. His fitted tunic was deep blue with the royal crest on the side of his chest. Beneath it were the medals of honor that only royalty could wear, each proudly displayed. The decadence of his attire highlighted his wide shoulders, muscled arms, and large palms. Black leggings and knee-high black boots drew my attention to his strong thighs. Of course, I'd seen the prince in fine clothing before but nothing like this.

He didn't say a word as his gaze swept over me, drinking me in as though I were a fine wine, and with each inch of his perusal, my heart beat harder and harder.

A tingling sensation began deep in my stomach when his eyes grew hooded, and heat flooded my core when that primal look entered his eyes. It was a look I'd been seeing more in him, ever since he'd returned from his month away. It was as though something was barely contained within the prince, like there was a predator prowling around inside him, just waiting to be unleashed.

He finally began walking toward me, and the air seemed to shudder, stretch, and bend between us. With each inch that passed, it felt as if the air around me caressed my skin and flowed over my bare flesh like a lover's kiss.

But surely the prince's air affinity wouldn't do *that*.

My heart was beating so fast it felt as though it would explode. I still felt anger, perhaps even hatred for this male, but I couldn't deny the attraction that sparked between us. I'd felt it previously, had known it existed, but I'd tried mightily to pretend that it was all an illusion.

But this? This I couldn't deny. The prince was looking at me like he wanted to *devour* me.

His wings snapped in tight to his back when he reached me. Lifting a finger, he touched one of the gems swirling in my hair, and I could have sworn that a stroke of air also trailed down my neck.

"You look lovely," he finally said, his tone husky. "No, you're beautiful, exquisite, beyond anything. I have no words." His tone was so deep. A shiver ran down my spine.

Daiseeum murmured something that I didn't hear due to the blood pounding through my ears before she glided from the room.

I barely noticed her departure. *Ock, this is insane.* This male had murdered half my family, yet my stomach was flipping like a female fairy in the midst of maturity.

The prince held out his arm to me, and I automatically slipped my hand through the crook of it. His heat warmed my palm when I settled my hand lightly on his forearm, and a sizzle of desire coursed through me. *Blessed Mother.* It seemed every time we made contact, that happened.

Something gleamed in his eyes, something entirely carnal.

I shook myself internally, wondering if Daiseeum's magic was also messing with my mind as the prince led me toward the door.

My feet followed of their own accord, and when he opened it wide and we slipped through it, it struck me that it was the first time since I'd arrived at the castle that I'd walked out of that door. We'd been so busy this week that I hadn't had time to leave on my own, and the prince always flew us out of the courtyard, or we mistphased when we left.

"Where's Sandus?" I asked. The hall lay empty.

"I dismissed him when I arrived."

The prince's strides were purposeful as a slight tightening appeared around his mouth. "Are you ready to meet the court?"

"As ready as I'll ever be."

"I'll help you with the names and matching them to faces. Stay by my side, and all shall be fine."

"Yes, my prince."

Prince Norivun led me down the hallways and staircases in his private wing. I barely noticed where we were going and hardly observed anything at all. All I could feel was the warmth of his skin searing through his jacket, the effortless way his large body maneuvered the halls, and the way he held every door open for me, as though without a thought to his chivalrous behavior.

But more than that was commanding my attention. The prince's aura was potent tonight, as though it had ratcheted up even higher from its usual state. He felt like a tightly coiled spring at my side, as if one flick in his direction would result in his deadly affinity being unleashed.

Strangely though, that sensation didn't frighten me. The first day I'd met the prince, I'd been convinced that he'd eventually murder me, just as he had my family, but in the past weeks my perception had changed. If anything, the prince seemed intent on keeping me alive. I did have an enormous promise to fulfill for him after all, since he truly believed I was needed to save the continent.

The twists and turns eventually gave way to an arched doorway swimming in a strong ward. When we passed through, it exited into a dark tunnel. Ahead something billowed as though air rustled it.

"Did we just leave your private wing?"

"We did." The prince strode forward and pushed a hanging tapestry aside for me to step around. On the other side of it, another stone hallway waited. Once the prince joined me and the tapestry settled, I would have never known that it hid a tunnel to his wing, and I marveled at how secretive the entrance was.

"This way." The prince gestured to the right.

We left the hallway and walked into a large great room with a ceiling at least thirty feet high. There wasn't any furniture. It seemed more like a convening area of various wings in the castle.

Servants hurried by. Some carried blankets, others buckets of wood, a few held piles of clothes, and one even held a dozen beheaded hens. They were a flurry of activity, no doubt because of the ball.

All of them looked at me wide-eyed when the prince led me past them, and I brought a hand self-consciously to my hair, hoping his illusion still held.

"It's still silver," the prince said softly, beneath his breath. "They're staring because you're a sight to behold."

My cheeks warmed.

His shoulders tightened when murmuring from dozens of voices carried to us. "The entrance to the court is just up ahead."

He led me to it, and when we rounded the final corner, a wide, grand walkway appeared. Silver-rimmed paintings of various winter scenes from all of the territories lined the hall. There were the Cliffs of Sarum, the Tala Sea, the plains of Harrivee, Osaravee's floating meadows, the Bay of Korl, the Bay of Nim, Kroravee's ice caves, Prinavee's resplendent capital, and the crops of Mervalee painted in a hundred vivid colors. Large mirrors and decadent sculptures intermixed with the paintings.

And the *snow*. It was actually snowing inside.

Across the domed ceiling, vines of ice flowers curled and writhed. Their delicate buds of blue, navy, and turquoise sparkled like gems, and every few seconds, tufts of snow puffed from the flowers and swirled with the magic in the room that kept it warm while snow rained from above. But the warmth of the magic kept any of the snow from reaching the floor. It all evaporated about ten feet above one's head.

I'd never seen anything like it.

"So beautiful," I whispered.

The prince's arm stiffened beneath mine. "My father does like to put on a good show."

My gaze fell on the double doors at the end of the hall. A guard stood at each side, their bodies stiff and ramrod straight. Each door was made of blue ice and was so clear it was nearly translucent. The door handles, black with veins of silver, looked as if crafted from Isalee steel.

The prince gestured toward the ice doors. "The entrance to the throne room of the Court of Winter."

CHAPTER 23

The prince's skin warmed even more beneath my palm, and for a moment, he just stood there as though warring with something within himself. His expression was impossible to decipher, but the pounding strength of his aura nearly took my breath away.

"My prince?" I asked, frowning.

His chest rose in a deep breath, and then his arm was slipping around my waist, drawing me closer.

A zinging sensation shot through me at the feel of his large hand on my hip. I forced myself to ignore it as the prince's powerful wing extended slightly to form a protective cage around me, and then he stepped forward and began leading me down the hall.

One of the ice doors abruptly opened, and a group of males spilled out.

There were four of them, and they were all talking and laughing as leminai in their goblets splashed over the sides. They grew silent when we neared.

Given their fine clothing and the casual way they held them-selves—as though they didn't have a care in the world—I knew they were members of the court.

"Prince Norivun?" one of them called. He looked young, perhaps my age, and had short white hair that curled slightly at the ends. Similar to the prince, he wore black leggings and boots, but his royal tunic was a deep red with embellishments—the color of the nobles from Osaravee Territory. Another male stood next to him with a trimmed beard and bright eyes. He also wore red.

"Who have you brought?" the bearded one asked with a sultry smile.

The prince's fingers curled into my flesh. "Not of your concern, Sirus." The prince didn't stop walking and strode past them, his expression icy.

All four males bowed when we passed, but the one with slightly curly hair gave a flirtatious and knowing wink in my direction. Despite their questions, I was fairly certain they knew who I was.

A low growl came from the prince just as the two guards at the ice doors opened them with a flourish. We didn't even slow as the prince breezed into the throne room.

A cool wind kissed my cheeks when we passed over the warded barrier, and my stomach dipped. Hundreds of nobles stood in the room, talking and laughing in small groups as music played and enchanted trays floated around the room carrying food and drink.

My breath sucked in at how beautiful everything was. Ribbons of silk draped across the ceiling as enchanted balls of ice hung suspended in the air. Puffs of snowflakes blew from the icy spheres even though the room was warm and dry. Similar to the grand walkway, all of the snow evaporated before it could touch any surface.

Ice sculptures decorated every corner, jewels sparkled from all of the females' necks, and the males' attire was just as dashing as Prince Norivun's. And the music . . .

A symphony of sound strummed through the room in a haunting melody that made me want to dance and sway.

But before I could get too caught up in the atmosphere, a vibration of the prince's power shot out of him. It washed over me, like a breeze that caressed my skin but didn't chill. Even though his aura moved around me, the strength of it felt *powerful*.

Everyone standing in our direct path to the throne scattered out of the way, and a hush fell over the room as all eyes fell on the prince and then me. Only the haunting music continued, as enchanted harps, violins, and woodwinds played under magical fingers.

My heartbeat ticked faster and faster with each step that passed, but the prince didn't slow. His strides ate up the room as the silence grew. Ahead, the king and queen waited.

Everyone watched us, as though we were puppets in a circus, and despite my hair color being hidden under the prince's illusion, my wingless back wasn't concealed. Whispers immediately erupted, from both the males and females, and a flush worked up my spine.

"That must be her." A low tone from a female reached my ears. "They say he's keeping her in his wing."

"I heard she's his courtesan." A trill laugh followed.

"She's certainly mouthwatering," a male replied. "Despite her shaved wings."

Another male snickered. "I'd hide her away too with a body like that."

A warning growl came from the prince, low in his throat, and his eyes shot daggers at everyone talking behind fans and cupped hands. Those at the receiving end of his ire immediately quieted.

Ahead, King Novakin waited on his throne. Beside him, the prince's mother, Queen Lissandra, sat silently.

My breath sucked in when I beheld the queen of the Winter Court. Silvery-white hair cascaded around her shoulders and down her back. Her hair was perfectly straight and entirely smooth, and I couldn't help but wonder what her hair looked like without her illusion. But unlike me, wings stretched behind her and were carefully fitted into the slots of her throne chair. She sat quietly, not talking to anyone or interacting in any way, but she had a youthful appeal even though she was several hundred winters old, and her eyes lit up when she saw the prince.

The king, however, looked every bit of his eight hundred winters. Gray hairs streaked through the white hair at his temples, and deep wrinkles grooved the corners of his mouth. But despite his mature look, his eyes were sharp and his body still fit. He held a goblet in one hand, and his forearm was propped on one of the throne's armrests. Black wings draped behind him as he spoke with a noble to his right, but as soon as the hush fell over the room, the king's attention shifted until he was staring directly at me.

The king handed his goblet to a servant, who hurried off, then King Novakin straightened on his throne, his gaze sharpening in my direction.

My knees began to tremble as the reality of why we were here hit me. The prince believed that I could save our dying continent. He'd taken me prisoner because of that, and now everyone was curious to meet who the prince had hidden away in his wing.

Blessed Mother, how have I gotten into this?

"Father." The prince stopped at the stairs leading to the throne and bowed.

I automatically dipped into a deep curtsy. The noble that had been conversing with the king bowed at the prince, then inched down the stairs as the king inclined his head.

"Norivun, who have you brought?"

The sound of the giant ice doors opening behind us pricked my ears, and I turned slightly just as the four males that had been in the outer walkway stepped through them.

The two males in red moved forward just enough to hear us but back enough that they remained discreet. When they stopped at Lord Crimsonale's side, my eyes widened.

The Osaravee archon watched me from the crowd, his expression shrewd.

I whipped back around as the prince said, "This is Ilara Seary, daughter of Mervalee Territory."

I brought my fist to my chest and curtsied again, my entire body dipping while I held onto the prince with my other hand. My knees were shaking so badly now I feared I would fall if I let go.

"Not of noble birth yet beautiful enough to be a princess." King Novakin was smiling when I straightened, and the tight ball that had become my stomach loosened, if only a little. "And what brings you to the Court of Winter, Ilara Seary, daughter of Mervalee Territory?"

My lips parted, but the prince bit out. "Might we have a word in private, Father?"

King Novakin raised an eyebrow, then waved his hand toward the guards at the door. They opened the ice doors with a flourish.

Nothing else was said. All of the nobles filed out of the throne room, as though used to being dismissed with a wave of the king's hand even if they were in the middle of a ball.

Once the room was empty, save for the guards at the door who were far enough away that they probably couldn't hear us, Prince Norivun said, "I believe Ilara is the key to the problem I've been dealing with."

The king sighed. "Ah yes, the *problem*."

I frowned at the king's superfluous tone as the prince replied, "Ilara's affinity has manifested, and she can create *orem*."

The king's features sharpened, and he looked me over a second time. "Impossible. Only the gods can create *orem*."

"Then perhaps she's a goddess," his son replied dryly.

The king's eyes narrowed. "Watch your tongue, Norivun."

The prince's lips thinned. "I know you have your doubts about my concerns, but since Ilara can restore our land's *orem*, such squabbles will ultimately become trivial as she works to replenish what's vanished."

The king drummed his fingers. "How can you be so certain of her magic? I've never heard of such an affinity."

"Because I've witnessed it firsthand."

"You did? Where did such an event occur?"

"She replenished the courtyard outside of the Exorbiant Chamber."

His drumming fingers stopped. "You're jesting."

"I'm not. It's been done. You may see for yourself. I wouldn't be guarding her in my wing if I wasn't sure. She's a very valuable asset. She must be protected."

I turned questioning eyes on the prince. *An asset? A fairy with value?*

Was that truly all he thought I was? A possession? Nothing more? Nothing less?

Blood rushed up my neck, heating my skin, but I kept my lips closed and didn't utter a sound. Maybe I was overreacting.

Or maybe I wasn't.

The prince's fingers curled into my spine as the king laughed, the sound loud and joyful.

"So this is who you've been hiding away." The king's laugh paused. "And all week I've been assuming she was your new courtesan and you were simply bedding her, or are you doing that too?"

My breath sucked in, and the prince's hand curved around my waist more, as though he knew I was about to pull away.

"Far from it," the prince replied. "She'd sooner stab me through the heart than welcome me to her bed." When the king frowned in confusion, Prince Norivun added, "Her brother and parents fell at my hand last season. They were of the dozen that were stirring unrest about the crops."

"Ah, they were some of the fae who wanted to create chaos and strife about the *problem*?" The king shrugged, as though he and the prince discussing my murdered family and private sex life were completely trivial.

Shock rippled through me, and that anger I'd felt when I first met the prince began to simmer.

"I remember that," the king continued. "Such a fuss was

being made, yet I've lived eight hundred winters and have seen how our land ebbs and flows. Yet my son didn't believe me when I told him the panic would pass. It was most tragic indeed." The king gave me a sympathetic smile. "I do apologize. My son's vengeance can be quite wrathful. I'm sure that hasn't been easy for you knowing what he did."

Genuine sympathy filled King Novakin's eyes, and finally finding my voice, I replied, "It has been very difficult, Your Majesty."

The king nodded before addressing the prince again. "Does she possess other affinities?" A strange interest grew in his eyes.

Prince Norivun's lips tightened. "No."

"Just the one? But a very great one if she can truly create *orem*, but to only possess one . . ." The king sighed. "Such a pity. So, she's not like your mother."

My lips parted in confusion. All along the prince had been comparing me to the queen, but now he was acting like I was nothing like her.

Queen Lissandra continued to sit at the king's side, absolutely rigid in her silence.

Smiling again, the king asked, "So how did you come across such a treasure as dear Ilara?"

"I discovered her on my tour of the continent last month. Her garden shone brighter and healthier than any I've ever seen, and the crops were thriving. Hers was the only garden I'd come across in two thousand millees to show such promise, and her village's crops are the healthiest on the continent."

"How interesting." The king pursed his lips. "And what do you propose from here?"

"She needs to train. Similar to Mother, her affinity bloomed late."

"But she's out of the malleable stage?"

"She is."

"Intriguing indeed." The king smiled at me. The gesture was so warm and welcoming and so full of genuine interest and delight that some of my anger diminished even though I was still offended at how easily he'd spoken of my dead family and who I'd bedded. "What are your plans from here? Do you intend to use her to fix the supposed *problem?*"

The prince's hand tightened on my back again. "I do."

The king's smile turned razor sharp again as the queen's fingers gripped her armrest so tightly her knuckles turned white. "Very well. If it appeases you, carry on."

Their discussion continued, yet I stopped listening. All I wanted to do was disappear. Everything about this conversation felt oily and calculated. The prince was speaking of me as though all he cared about was my affinity. The king was speaking of me as though I was another nameless commoner whose only purpose was to serve his kingdom.

And I was stuck here. I'd made a fairy bargain, which meant I had to fulfill it, or I would never be allowed to leave. Even if the prince changed his mind and said I could, the bargain wouldn't allow it, not unless I wanted to suffer the gods' wrath. *Stupid, stupid, stupid.* I never should have made that bargain.

Blood whooshed through my ears, and a deep throbbing sensation born in my gut. *I'm a prisoner. A captive to be used. A pawn in the crown prince's master game plan.*

A flare of lightning coursed through my veins. The prince's

hand abruptly snapped back as though he'd been stung, but he continued talking to his father, and I swore the room had to be spinning. It felt as though it was moving around me, and all I wanted to do was escape. Run. Disappear. But I couldn't, and I was trapped.

And then the throne doors were opening, and nobles were spilling back into the great hall. Prince Norivun was saying something to me, his hand on my back again as his lips brushed my ear. His words turned urgent, but I recoiled. The queen's fingers curled tighter around the armrest of her throne chair until I was certain it would snap. The king began laughing, speaking with the noble again who had returned to his side, the one that he'd banished only moments after I'd appeared.

My breaths came faster. And faster. I needed to leave. I needed to get away from the prince's side. Away from this ugly court.

The prince's grip tightened around my waist. "Ilara. Walk with me outside."

But I kept pulling away as the music started up, and the nobles were dancing again, drinks being guzzled, as their laughter and conversation drifted around the room. The ball had commenced once more.

"No. I need some space." I tore myself from his side. My feet carried me across the room as though the wind was at my back and my dress a giant sail.

"Ilara!" the prince called from behind me.

But I allowed myself to be swallowed by the crowd. Every fairy I passed eyed me with interest and curiosity. Some began whispering. Others tried to engage me, but I traveled by all of them until a male stood in front of me. Broad shoulders, black wings, a pleasant smile.

"Something tells me that you need a drink." Nuwin's lips curved more as he began guiding me away from everyone as the prince's aura pounded into my back.

I dared a glance behind me. Fury filled the prince's face when Nuwin's arm curled around my waist, and then Prince Norivun was striding across the dance floor, his gaze intent on his brother.

"Just get me out of here," I pleaded as I gripped his arm.

Nuwin grinned. "This shall be fun."

CHAPTER 24

True to his promise, the youngest prince whisked me to the side doors that opened to a sprawling lawn of frost-nipped grass, ice flowers, enchanted fountains, and a covered icy topiary maze that had nobles running about it.

Nuwin grabbed two flutes of champagne off a floating tray, and then we were outside, running through the throngs of fae across the frosty landscape until he pulled me into the maze, and we disappeared around one corner.

Breathless, I did my best to keep up, especially when I heard the prince's enraged bellow.

"Nuwin!"

A flutter of giggles and nervous laughter followed from the fae we passed, and within seconds, the maze swallowed us whole. We dipped and turned through ice caves and tunnels. Everything was covered. Nobody flying overhead could see us.

"Where are we going?" I gasped as puffs of mist clouded from my breath.

Somehow, amazingly, Nuwin managed to carry both flutes of

champagne without spilling them, as though he'd done acts exactly like this before.

"There's a hidden exit just up ahead. Nori knows about it, but since there are several hidden exits, he won't know which one we take." He gave me a cheeky smile, as we slid around a corner, right past a couple kissing passionately in the corner. The male had the female's leg hooked around his waist as his other hand plunged into her hair.

She sighed, then moaned when the male trailed his lips down the column of her neck.

"Looks like those two are having fun." Nuwin bumped his elbow against mine and gave me a conspiratorial smile.

I snorted when he waggled his eyebrows.

We darted around another turn, and the young prince stopped at an ice wall.

"Hold this for me, will you, darling?" He handed me the two champagne flutes as a crashing sound came from the maze and another bellow. "Oh my, it sounds like my beloved brother has worked himself into quite a tizzy."

Nuwin bent down and hooked his fingers against something under the ice wall just above the ground, and then the ice melted before us, falling to the side in a wall of water to reveal a door. "This way. Hurry, darling. He'll catch us if we're not quick."

He opened the door and ushered me through. The ice wall formed again on the other side just as he closed the door behind us.

A dark tunnel greeted me. It was so black I couldn't see. "Nuwin?"

His warm hand brushed my waist, drawing me close before he took the champagne flutes. "Follow me."

He led me down the path, his footsteps sure and quick. He moved as nimbly as a snowgum in the Gielis Mountains, as though he too could see in the dark.

"How do you know where we're going?"

He laughed. "I've been playing in these tunnels since I was a boy."

The sound of rushing water reached my ears a second later, and I instinctively inched closer to him as images of plunging into an icy underground river flooded my thoughts, but a second later a warm breeze caressed my cheeks, and we were moving upward.

Light appeared ahead, just a sliver of it around the outline of a door. Nuwin loosened his hold on me and ran his hands near it. The door clicked open, and we stepped into a large room filled with books lining the walls.

"The castle library," he explained. Music strummed through the walls, carrying the same beat as what had been playing in the throne room.

"Are we . . ." I frowned and gestured toward the door. "Did we just pass beneath the throne room?"

"Indeed we did, clever girl. The exits from the maze will drop you off at various locations in the castle. I just happened to pick the one that Nori would least expect since it took us right back to where we'd just fled." He winked and handed me one of the flutes.

My lips parted in a smile at his mischievous expression before bringing the glass to my lips and letting a flood of bubbly liquid tingle my tongue. After I swallowed, I eyed the drink in amazement.

"This is delicious."

"The ball's champagne always is. They flavor it with berries and chocolate to heighten the taste."

I took another drink and then another.

Nuwin chuckled. "Careful there, Ilara Seary. You'll be drunk before you know it if you keep that up."

Ignoring him, I swallowed more. "Maybe drunk is what I want to be. If you'd heard the way your father and brother just spoke of me—" I cut myself off, realizing who I was speaking to. "I'm sorry, my prince. I don't mean to speak ill of them."

But instead of being angry, Nuwin just cocked his head. "He's not as bad as he seems."

"Which one?"

That got a bark of laughter from him. "My brother."

I rolled my eyes. "Then he obviously hasn't murdered half of your family, taken you prisoner, and then treated you as though you were an object to own instead of a living fairy with a beating heart."

Nuwin took a sip from his flute, his expression impossible to read before his lips kicked up. "I can tell he's going to have his hands full with you."

"What's that supposed to mean?"

But instead of replying, Nuwin whisked my empty flute away, then swept me closer to his side. "Shall we return to the ball? I do enjoy dancing with beautiful females."

"I'm not much of a dancer, and I'd rather not be the center of gossip."

"Then we shall drink and eat and watch the dancers if you prefer."

I sighed. Staying in the library and hiding away from the court's prying eyes sounded more appealing, but I couldn't hide forever, and I wouldn't have my first impression to the court be that I was weak and afraid.

Sighing, I nodded toward the door. "Lead the way."

NUWIN LED me back to the throne room, and after we slipped inside, he nabbed me another flute of champagne.

My fingers curled around the cool glass as the tantalizing taste of berries hit my tongue again. I scanned the crowd, searching for the large fairy with talon-tipped wings, but Prince Norivun was nowhere to be seen.

"Do you know where he is?" I took another sip of the drink as a pleasant dizzying feeling swept through me. I lowered my glass. Despite what I'd said to Nuwin earlier, I didn't actually want to be drunk. It would be stupid to allow alcohol to cloud my thoughts on a night such as this.

Nuwin shrugged. "Still in the maze is my best guess. Or, he's exited and is searching in the wrong area of the castle, depending upon which secret door he thought we took. Regardless, he's not here. You should try to enjoy it."

Perhaps Nuwin was right. Music floated through the room, the symphony working toward a crescendo as fae paired in sets of two waltzed across the floor. Laughter and conversation drifted in the air like a melody unto itself. Not surprisingly, the dancing, drinking, and eating continued despite the scene the prince and I had caused earlier.

Forcing my shoulders to relax more, I focused on Nuwin and ignored all prying eyes that had landed on me.

"Does Solisarium often have royal balls?" I asked Nuwin as we traveled along the wall, drawing deeper into the room.

Nuwin's eyebrows rose. "My brother didn't tell you what this ball is for?"

"No, what's it for?"

"It's being held in honor of him reaching a hundred winters. The time has come to select his betrothed."

I nearly snorted champagne through my nose.

Nuwin laughed softly. "I take it he failed to mention any of that?"

"You would be correct."

"Have you not noticed the dozens upon dozens of noble females dressed in their finest?" He swept his arm toward the edge of the room, by the doors that we'd slipped through.

Probably two dozen females waited anxiously by it, peering outside as they primped their hair and whispered among one another behind fluttering fans. More than a few glared at me or sniffed in my direction.

"I just assumed that was the norm for balls."

"It's not. All of those females are hoping to be the next queen, but I doubt they'll even be in the running. Our father is quite particular about who we breed with." The young prince's mouth tightened. "Alas, Nori's been trying to put off this day our entire lives. Our father has stated since we were young boys that he would be choosing our betrotheds."

I frowned. "Why? I thought such archaic practices were no longer followed?"

"I'm afraid it's a tradition that he's resurrected since his own marriage." He nodded toward his parents.

The king was still speaking with the fairy he'd been

engrossed in conversation with earlier, and the queen continued to sit at his side. She looked regal, poised, and so very alone.

"Your parents were an arranged marriage?"

"They were." Nuwin grabbed a small plate of petite meat pies from a tray floating past us and held it out to me. "My mother isn't of noble birth. She never would have been considered for marriage to my father if not for her affinities."

I bit into one of the pies. Flavors rolled over my tongue as I savored the buttery crust and perfectly seasoned hen mixed with gravy. I managed to suppress a moan of delight but barely. I snatched another from the plate before Nuwin could wolf all of them down, then cocked an eyebrow at the prince's younger brother.

"Did your father marry your mother because she has immense magic?"

His lips lifted slyly. "Correct. You made that connection quickly."

I waved a hand. "I've spent enough time with your brother to learn a thing or two. So was their marriage made in the hopes of what, producing powerful heirs?"

"Also correct." His smile grew.

"And who arranged their marriage?"

"My father did."

I laughed softly. "That's absurd. How does one arrange one's own marriage? Isn't that simply proposing?"

"Proposing would imply that the female had a choice. My father was already king by then, and when you're king, you can do as you please—including having a choice of all of the females on the continent. My father sought out the most powerful female he could find and chose her for his bride."

"I take it the marriage wasn't your mother's choice?"

His eyes dimmed. "No, it wasn't."

"So he took your mother as his bride even though she protested?"

"He did."

My frown deepened as I thought of my own parents, of their simple lives. While poor, they'd been content. No, not just content. They'd been *happy*. Even when we didn't have much food on our plates, they were still able to find joy in life. Laughter and love had filled our home. I didn't know how one could find that in a marriage made like a business transaction.

But I would never be able to witness my parents grow old. Their joy had been snuffed out when their lives had been taken too early.

Memories of my parents stirred that slumbering anger in me again. While the prince had not been cruel to me and had even shown me kindness and apologized for their deaths, he'd also taken me for one reason and one reason only—to enslave me to do his bidding.

My fingers curled more tightly around my glass. I brought the flute to my lips as my gaze traveled over the dancers and fae mingling in the room, to the throne that perched atop the ball like a bird peering down from the sky. The king and queen, while sitting beside one another, never spoke, touched, or so much as glanced at one another.

"Is there no love between them? Has no affection ever bloomed?"

A strained look overtook Nuwin's features as his lips thinned. "No, there is no love. Or affection. My mother, she's—" He looked as though he wanted to say more, but then he shook his head. "We should dance. The floor is so crowded none of the observers will see us if we drift toward the center."

I brought a hand to my throat, to the necklace's cool metal and smooth pendant. "I don't want to draw any more attention to myself."

I'd already had too much to drink, but my thoughts were still clear enough to remember the warnings from Daiseeum and the cagey way the prince had acted prior to me entering this room, and I also knew at any moment that clarity could slip. Alcohol was swimming through my veins.

"I think I'm done with this." I deposited my champagne flute on a tray floating by.

Nuwin gave me an appeasing smile. "I know you don't want attention drawn to yourself, but fae are drinking and preoccupied, and my brother isn't here yet. I've bided us enough time to at least enjoy a dance or two. Might as well make the most of it while you're free of him." He bowed with a flourish. "Dance with me, Ilara Seary, daughter of Mervalee Territory."

I sighed. "Oh, all right."

Nuwin swept me away, guiding me through the crowd of onlookers surrounding the dance floor.

As soon as those we'd passed realized that the wingless female the prince had hidden away was back, whispers erupted. Females tittered behind their cupped hands as more and more became aware that I'd returned. The males were just as bad. Some were even leering, as though they truly believed I was a courtesan, and when the prince tired of me, they could be next in line.

I bristled but kept my head held high. Now that everyone in

the room seemed to know of my return, perhaps Nuwin was right. We could at least enjoy ourselves.

We reached the edge of the dance floor, and my heart beat harder as throngs of silks, brocades, and sheer gauzes whipped by our legs as the females twirled about. Half of the dancefloor was filled with voluminous dresses that were so wide they took up three times the space of a single female. Only a handful were dressed in slimmer styles like mine. My gown drifted around me, moving and sliding across my skin like water.

"Ready?" Nuwin's arm curled around my waist, and then we were off.

He glided us effortlessly into the swell of winged bodies with light footsteps. I'd never learned royal dances, and I mumbled an apology when I stumbled across his toes, but Nuwin just pulled me closer until I was flush against his chest, and then he leaned down and whispered, "I'll lead. Just keep your steps light and smile. Everyone's watching."

I hissed in a breath. "I thought you said they wouldn't see me from the middle."

"They won't. Once we get there."

True to his word, he twirled me toward the center of the floor, dancing and spinning us through the crowd of swirling fae. He was an excellent dancer and lifted me just enough that my feet still touched the floor but barely held any weight.

"You're quite strong," I commented when we finally reached the center. Only those of great height or standing on the stairs by the throne could easily see us. "You're practically carrying me."

"Norivun's not the only one with strength." He flashed me a grin and continued to carry me about the room as though I weighed nothing at all.

Music rose and fell in continued hypnotic swells, and I allowed myself to be swept into the rhythm, relying less and less on Nuwin carrying my weight as I learned the footsteps and followed the beat.

Whispers followed me, but I didn't care. The champagne had truly latched onto me, and out here on the floor, nobody was cornering me or trying to engage me in conversation. It was just me and the music.

"You're a natural," Nuwin said softly, his grin speaking volumes as lightheadedness buzzed in my mind.

Swirling sensations roiled within my belly, as though a charge of energy was building with each spin and dip as Nuwin and I moved faster and faster and faster.

Nuwin's lips tugged down. "Your aura is . . ." He cocked his head.

"What was that?"

"I said your aura is—"

"Mind if I cut in?" A noble with curling white hair and a red tunic appeared at Nuwin's side. He was the same male who'd been in the hall before I'd entered the throne room. The youngest prince's hands were still wrapped around my waist as the melody continued, but the noble stayed at our side, moving to the beat.

"What do you want, Michas?"

"I thought it was obvious." The male grinned. "I wish to dance with the lovely lady from Mervalee."

Before Nuwin could protest, the Osaravee noble spun me from the young prince's grip, and then new arms were around me. Strong, commanding, and warm limbs that drew me close.

CHAPTER 25

"And what if I don't want to dance with you?" I said to the male.

His lips curved as his hand trailed down my back. "Shall I take you back to Nuwin? He's looking quite vexed." Despite his offer, the young lord glided us farther away from the prince. "Although I thought you may want to be introduced to some of the court since you're new to Solisarium."

"How do you know I'm new? I could have grown up here and only fled to Mervalee as an adult."

He cocked his head. "I think not." His palm grazed my spine as he spun me in a twirl before pulling me close again. He cupped my hand in his, and the intrigue in his expression grew. "You look lovelier than any female in this room, yet your hands aren't soft. Not like the other court females."

Since his tone held no derision, I merely shrugged. "Callouses form when one's required to work to survive."

"You work?"

"I do." Even if trying to restore *orem* wasn't anywhere near as taxing as laboring in the fields, I was being paid for it, therefore, it counted as work. Besides, I had already been granted more rulibs than I could count, and I was also receiving free room and board. A giggle threatened to hit me. Mother, that was funny. To think I was being paid in not only rulibs but also in feathered beds and petite mince pies.

"Is something funny?"

I managed to muffle my laugh. "I was just thinking about my latest profession."

"Which is?" His eyes darkened as his gaze raked over my frame. My cleavage swelled from the dress, and his hand lay dangerously close to my backside.

I scoffed. "It's not what you're thinking."

"Such a shame."

"For you maybe."

He chuckled. "Indeed. So tell me, Ilara Seary, daughter of Mervalee Territory, if you are not a courtesan, what is your profession? And how did you end up here, hidden away by the prince?"

I smiled coyly, then cursed all of the champagne I'd consumed. While I wasn't drunk, the alcohol had loosened my tongue and was making me do bold things. *Stupid* things, like flirt with this male, so I pressed my lips together. This male was asking a lot of questions, as though he was on a mission to learn as much as he could about me. And I might be new to the court, but I'd already learned that innocent curiosity wasn't what drove fae here.

So I merely replied, "I suppose you shall have to keep wondering as I don't intend to tell you."

The noble laughed, his head tilting back before he glided us through two pairs of dancing fae. "Regardless of where you come from, Lady Seary, it's a pleasure to meet you. I'm Lord Michas Crimsonale, heir to Highsteer Castle and son of Osaravee Territory. I'm very pleased to make your acquaintance."

I stiffened in his arms as the music's tempo increased. "Your father is Lord Crimsonale, the male who sits on the king's council?"

"He is."

Of course. No wonder he was seeking information about me. His father had probably instructed him to do so. "And the other male, the one with the trim beard that you were standing with, is he your brother?"

"That's correct. Sirus is ten winters my junior."

A ball of anxiety formed in my stomach. "Your father seems very interested in me."

"He does? Why do you suppose that is?"

I studied his expression, looking for any traces of deceit but found none. Blessed Mother, I couldn't tell what was a game and what was genuine with him. If only Cailis were here. Her truth affinity would decipher immediately if Michas was lying. But my sister wasn't at my side, so I decided to keep my answer honest yet vague. "He followed us to Harrivee Territory the other day."

Michas's eyes turned to saucers. "Why would he do such a thing?"

"You truly don't know?"

"On my honor, my lady, I don't."

I sighed. Truly, I had no idea if he was being honest. "Your father heard that the prince had taken a wingless female captive, and he sought me out. It was after I met your father that I was invited to this ball. And now, how ironic, that the first fairy I'm dancing with outside of the royal family is another Crimsonale."

Michas laughed. "All right, all right. You got me. I'm intrigued by you, but my father didn't send me over here on an ulterior motive. I came of my own accord. I truly wanted to dance with you because you're new, and Prince Norivun and I . . ." He shrugged. "We have a bit of a history, and I knew he would be irritated if I spent time with you. There, you've caught me, and I've spilled all. Do you still wish to dance with me?"

I studied his expression and desperately wished again that Cailis was with me. But seeing as she wasn't, I knew I'd have to settle with trusting my gut, which was currently telling me that Michas was a troublemaker but perhaps not a deceitful fairy.

I shrugged as I tugged my hand free. "Honestly? I think I've had enough dancing. My head is beginning to swim."

"Of course, allow me." Michas glided us off the dance floor, and I caught sight of Nuwin on the opposite side of the room, worry rolling across his features as he began making his way toward us, but the throne room was large, and other fae kept stopping him to engage him in conversation.

I couldn't help but wonder if Michas had intentionally chosen an exit as far from Nuwin as possible. The young Crimsonale led me through the throng of onlookers. One female's gaze was piercing when I passed. She was tall, reed-thin, and had a pointy chin. Her eyes narrowed when she beheld me.

Shuddering, I nearly jumped when Michas whispered into my ear, "And that would be Lady Taberitha Wormiful, the archon of Kroravee Territory."

"She looks like she wants to eat me."

"She might. She's been known to devour young ladies of the court."

He chuckled as I hurried on, but despite the distance I put between me and Lady Wormiful, I still felt her eyes digging into my back as though an ice pick severed my spine.

Once through the crowd, the Osaravee noble didn't stop. Michas led me to another set of doors, behind the throne that led to a balcony. The queen watched us when we passed. She still sat alone, speaking to no one.

"Does the queen often sit by herself without socializing?" I asked.

Michas shrugged. "Usually. She's never been loquacious."

My brows pinched. Loquacious or not, her expression said there was more to it than that. A sadness clung to her, almost like a veil of desperation, and I was reminded of how she looked in that brief glimpse I'd gotten of her when the prince had flown me past her tower, when he'd uttered the peculiar words, *She lives in peace.*

She didn't look peaceful, though. She looked anxious and lonely.

Mulling that over, I followed the Osaravee noble outside. Crisp, cold air greeted me when we stepped onto the balcony. Goosebumps immediately broke out across my skin, and I shivered, rubbing my arms.

"How ridiculous of me. You're freezing." Michas slipped his coat off and placed it around my shoulders before I could protest. Heat from the clothing soaked into my chilled skin as his scent flooded me. He smelled of juniper and a hint of cinnamon—not bad but not overly interesting either.

I pulled his coat closer, thankful for the warmth.

He offered a crooked smile. "I figured the fresh air would do you good, and the cold out here will keep some of the pestering nobles away."

I inhaled the cool breeze. "Thank you."

Michas leaned his forearms against the railing, which overlooked the edge of the maze peeking out from around the castle's corner. Since he wasn't crowding me and truly seemed interested in my well-being, I faced him more.

"Can I ask you something?" I quirked an eyebrow.

"Anything."

"What's happening in the court right now? Why have fae gone missing?"

Michas cleared his throat. "Where did you hear that?"

"Is it true?"

He interlocked his fingers and looked down. After a long moment, he finally said, "The continent is starving. Did you know that too?"

My heart beat harder. "Yes."

His eyebrows rose. "I'm surprised. The prince seems intent on keeping it hushed. Fae have died for voicing their concerns."

"Don't you mean they've been murdered?" My insides clenched. I knew all too well what he spoke of.

"I suppose that's the less dignified way of saying it."

"Or just the truth."

He inclined his head. "True. In that case, if we're to speak freely, I suppose it shouldn't come as a surprise to you when I say that some are whispering that we shouldn't live on this continent at all, that it was never a natural place for us to inhabit despite our realm's magic, and if we're going to survive, we'll need to move. Perhaps that's the reason fae are disappearing, because commoners are starting to say that too, and the prince doesn't want those beliefs to spread."

"You're saying that the crown prince is the reason several commoners have disappeared during the past weeks? But he was gone. He wasn't even in the castle."

"But was he?" Michas raised his eyebrows. "The prince can mistphase easily and frequently. His immense magic allows him to do so. He's one of the few fae who could mistphase multiple times per day and not need to recharge his magic with rest and nutrition."

My lips parted. For one, to think of the Solis fae not living on the northern continent was absurd, and two, at what Michas was implying—that the prince had been sneaking in and out of the castle all of the time that I'd been locked in the Exorbiant Chamber, unbeknownst to me and his staff, and that during those returns, he'd been murdering more fae to prevent increased dissent from growing...

"He wouldn't do that," I whispered.

Michas laughed. "Wouldn't he? How well do you know our prince, Ilara?"

Shaking, I wrapped my arms around myself. Granted, I hadn't liked how the king and Prince Norivun had been speaking of me when Norivun introduced me to his father, but the sides I'd seen of the crown prince during the past week . . . They weren't that of a cold, heartless murderer.

But isn't that exactly what he did to Mother, Father, and Tormesh? Murder them in cold blood?

That small voice of reason broke through my thoughts. My shivers increased.

"Why would anyone think that we could move?" I finally

said. "The Solis fae have resided on the northern continent for thousands of winters. If we didn't live here, where would we go?" I pictured the Glassen Barrier Islands and the Lochen fae who lived there and on the thousands of islands south of it. But our kind couldn't live in the water, and those islands weren't big enough to accommodate all of us, not unless we invaded their small continent thousands of millees away.

Michas straightened and leaned a hip against the railing. "Some say we should reside on the Nolus continent." He crossed his arms and watched me carefully, and for the first time, I really looked at him.

He wasn't overly tall, but he was broad and heavily muscled. Thick, wide wings were tucked into his back. They weren't tall like the prince's were, but they appeared heavy. Like all Solis fae, he had silver hair and blue eyes, but the curls in his hair were less common. His face was pleasant enough. Straight nose. Firm lips. Round eyes. He was rather attractive, actually.

Shaking myself from my trivial thoughts, I realigned myself to our conversation. "The Nolus continent, are you serious?"

"I am. Some are saying we should go south, over the Elixias Mountains to live on the Nolus continent where the climate is warm, and magic isn't needed to sustain our food sources. My father has been pushing for support in the council."

"But that's not our land."

"It may not be, but who's to say it shouldn't be?" Again, that carefully assessing expression overtook his face.

An icy feeling slid through my veins at what he was implying. "But the Nolus fae live there."

"They do."

"They wouldn't welcome us."

"No, they probably would not."

The chilling feeling in me grew. "It sounds like you're speaking of war, of taking the land by force. Is that what you're saying, Michas?"

He shrugged and gave a lopsided smile before turning his attention back to the maze. Below, a few fae ran over the frosty cobblestones and laughed, chasing each other before dipping back into the icy topiary. "I suppose I'm simply answering your question."

"Does the king know of this talk?"

"Of course, he does. He keeps telling my father such a move is preposterous."

I sighed inwardly, feeling relief that the king opposed such actions. Leaning against the railing more, I asked, "Has there been support for an invasion from others?"

I sincerely hoped there hadn't been. Such talk wasn't just ridiculous—it was idiotic, and to even contemplate it was worrisome. We'd lived in harmony with the Nolus fae for hundreds, no *thousands* of winters, despite our bordering land. And that was because we honored that border. We kept to ourselves. They kept to theirs. It was an unspoken tradition among our kind. The different species of fae stayed on their continents for the most part, too prideful to venture to other parts of the realm, as though doing so would imply their continent wasn't superior.

Some fae, however, lived elsewhere, but I could only recall ever meeting one Nolus fairy in all of my life. It had been in Firlim's harvest market, and that fairy had been living in the north for most of his adult life.

"There's been support of . . . concern," Michas finally replied evasively. He drifted closer and pulled his jacket around me more, his hands hovering just over my breasts. His expression shifted as his gaze stayed on my cleavage, and the heat around him grew.

I suppressed an eyeroll. So *that* was where my time with him was going.

But I was glad for the excuse to leave. I needed to think, because what Michas had declared told me exactly why the prince had taken me. He wanted to use my magic to restore the *orem* not just to keep us from starving but to prevent a war.

"I'm going back inside." I made a move to push away from the balcony's railing, but Michas stepped into my path.

"I'm sorry if I've made you uncomfortable. Please, stay. We don't need to speak of political strife."

I crossed my arms. "The political talk isn't why I'm leaving."

He held his palms up, his stance non-threatening. "I'm sorry. I'll keep my distance." He took a step back. "But please stay. There are to be fireworks soon. The view from here will be unparalleled."

His tone held no aggression, yet I eyed him with suspicion. "Why are you interested in me and wanting to keep me with you?"

He smiled, the look so charming that I once again felt he was being honest. "The prince has taken an interest in you, which of course, intrigues me. I personally have found our conversation stimulating. Your brashness and honesty are rare. And truthfully, Ilara, you're an absolutely beautiful female. Any male would endeavor to keep your attention. So, will you stay?" He drifted closer to my side, not touching me again, but he was close enough that it wasn't entirely proper. "You're truly breathtaking. I would love for you to accompany—"

An avalanche of power suddenly crashed into me, sucking the breath from my chest as the crown prince appeared in the doorway, his hair tousled and his body flexing with power. His aura pounded from him in waves as he stood in the balcony's doorway with Nuwin just behind him.

"See, brother. We've found her, and she's just fine," Nuwin said, clapping the crown prince on the back.

But the prince's gaze landed on where Michas stood, and a savage expression rippled across his features. "Step away from her. Now."

The Osaravee lord's lips peeled back. "I've done nothing wrong, my prince. She's here of her own choosing."

"I said, *Step away from her.*"

Michas muttered a sound of irritation, then dipped his head toward me. "Good night to you, Lady Seary. It was a pleasure to make your acquaintance." With that, he stalked past the prince and Nuwin and returned to the throne room.

Nuwin made to follow him, but Prince Norivun extended a wing, stopping him. "I'm not through with you, brother."

Nuwin gave a lopsided smile. "I'm sure you're not."

"Did you think it was a game? You dare to take her from my side on tonight of all nights?"

The younger prince's expression turned sheepish. "She needed a break from you, brother. I simply provided her an escape. I was trying to be a gentlefae."

Norivun lowered his wing and closed the space between them until they stood toe to toe. "You know what she is to me, yet you still play your games?" he said it so quietly that I almost didn't hear him.

What I was to him? I cocked my head, wondering what he meant by that comment.

Nuwin gave his brother an appeasing smile and patted his shoulder. "It was just some harmless fun, Nori. All's well. And look, Michas even kept her warm." Nuwin gestured to the jacket I wore.

The prince cursed as the aura around him strengthened. Bowing, Nuwin gave me a wink before leaving the balcony and closing the door behind him.

Alone on the balcony with the crown prince, I stiffened as he prowled closer to me. The air seemed to thin with each step that he took until it felt as though I couldn't catch my breath. All the while, I kept thinking about what Michas had claimed—that Norivun had mistphased back to the castle repeatedly during his time away to murder more fae.

Vivid blue irises swirled with power as the prince's nostrils flared. "Did Michas hurt you?"

"No, not at all." I pulled the noble's jacket tighter around me. "We talked and danced, and he said he wanted to get to know me more. That's all."

"But he was nearly . . . touching you."

"So?"

The crown prince's eyes narrowed further. "Why are you wearing his jacket?"

"Not that it's any of your business, but I was cold, and he offered it."

His frown deepened, and then in a swift move, Michas's jacket was off my shoulders and fluttering to the ground. Cold air assaulted me, but before I could gasp, the prince unbuttoned his own jacket and slid it around my shoulders. Warmth as hot as a roaring fire settled over my skin, and the prince's tantalizing scent of snow and cedar came next.

My heart pounded as his top settled around me. "What did you do that for?"

"I don't like seeing his clothes on you."

"Why?"

"Because."

"Because *why*?"

"Does it matter?"

I straightened and knew if I didn't ask now, I would always wonder. "Can I ask you something, and do you promise to be honest?"

His expression turned guarded. "What do you want to ask me?"

"Did you mistphase repeatedly back to the castle during the month I was locked within the Exorbiant Chamber to handle commoners who'd come to the castle with their concerns of the dying crops?"

His lips parted as genuine confusion swam across his features. "No, of course not."

"Not once?"

"Not once."

"Then why did Michas accuse you of such?"

A low growl rumbled in his chest. "Because Michas Crimsonale is a conniving bastard who would sooner see me gutted than be heir to the throne."

My eyes widened.

The prince shook his head. "Michas and I have a bit of a history. He cuts down my integrity every chance he gets."

"So, you're not lying? You never came back to the castle, not even once, in the month you were gone?"

His eyes softened. "No, Ilara. I'm not lying to you. I never returned in that time."

Some of the swirling worry in my gut subsided. But Blessed Mother, Prince Norivun seemed honest too. Either that or my gut instincts were completely off. Rubbing my temples, I shook my head. I didn't know what to believe or who was lying, but perhaps it truly was as the prince claimed—that Michas worked to undermine the crown prince every chance he got. I supposed it was fitting and went hand in hand with what I'd experienced tonight.

Crossing my arms, I changed the subject. "You know, it was quite offensive how you and the king spoke of me."

"You're angry with me." He raked a hand through his hair. "I thought you were, and I know I spoke aloofly and how it must have seemed to you, but . . ." He tore a hand through his hair again. "Please believe me when I say that things are not as they seem."

"If they're not as they seem, then how are they?"

Warring emotions played across his features. "It's important that my father doesn't know what you are to me. It's important that I act a certain way around you when he's near."

"What does that even mean?"

He closed the distance between us. "You ask too many questions."

My entire body locked up when his head lowered. He placed a hand on either side of me, each palm gripping the balcony behind me, and the strength of his aura pounded through me, imprisoning me within its power.

He leaned down, and his nose brushed against my neck. A

searing fire coated my skin when he whispered, "How about I tell you something else? I don't like it when you run from me, and I don't like it when I find you in another male's company, especially when you're wearing his clothes."

My insides fluttered. Blessed Mother, my entire body felt as though it was coming alive. His lips were nearly pressing to my throat.

"That's very . . . possessive sounding."

He growled low in his chest. "You have no idea."

And strangely, I had a feeling I didn't. It suddenly felt as though I didn't understand anything. Not him. Not this court. Not even my own feelings. Because I wanted him to kiss me. Touch me. Hold me. That in itself verified that I'd lost my mind, because he was still the male who'd destroyed everything I held dear. So how could I want those things?

He shifted closer and brushed against me. My nipples peaked at the contact, and a satisfied purr came from his throat.

His mouth was moving closer to mine. Closer. *Closer*, with every shallow breath I took.

He inhaled slowly, as though savoring something, and then his lips pressed to mine.

My gasp was trapped in his mouth, but his lips were moving, slowly at first but then with demanding purpose.

A moan escaped me, and my entire body zinged in awareness. My arms wrapped around his neck. I was kissing him in return as his hands gripped my hips and wrenched me closer.

Blessed Mother.

Heat flooded my core as the prince ravaged my mouth. He tasted of sin and snow, spice and fire, and I'd never tasted anything so sweet, so *addictive.*

I moaned as my fingers tangled through his hair as he hoisted me up on the balcony. He spread my thighs, my gown lifting as his hard body stepped between my legs.

His rigid length found my entrance immediately, even though my underthings and his pants still prevented true contact. But it was enough for me to feel all of him. He pressed his cock right against my most intimate area. And *Mother Below*, he was so stiff. So thick.

My core flooded with moisture—already I was primed for him. I wanted him and was willing to acquiesce to whatever he demanded.

I moaned and rubbed against him, needing more. *More.*

His hand traveled up my back to cup my neck. I instinctively arched into him.

"Fuck, Ilara," he breathed.

He deepened his kiss while his other hand roamed everywhere . . . over my spine, along my thigh, up my breast. He briefly cupped my heated flesh as he tweaked my nipple through the thin gown.

I cried out in his mouth.

Breaking the kiss, his lips traveled across my jaw and down my throat while his hands held me, owning me.

With each path his lips and hands traveled, his aura grew denser, more potent, and then the air was kissing my skin, sliding over my scorched flesh, stroking me in the most tantalizing ways, and Mother, *I was on fire*. I had no idea his affinity could do that.

He dragged his mouth back to mine and then hooked my leg around his waist. His cock was right at my entrance again. All it would take was the swipe of my underthings to the side and the

loosening of his pants, and that thick girth would be plunging inside me.

"My, oh my, brother. You certainly didn't waste any time."

Nuwin's snickering comment had the glassy fog shattering all around me. I gasped, pulling away from the crown prince just as a terrifying snarl ripped from his throat.

Prince Norivun released my leg and shielded my body with his in the same beat. "Get the fuck out of here, Nuwin."

"Trust me, I wish I could, but I'm afraid the time has come. Father is asking for you."

Norivun seethed. "Not now. Not yet."

His furious response was enough to clear my head, to cut through my lust, and . . .

What in the realm am I doing?

I hastily pushed against him and slid off the balcony, straightening my attire and hoping my hair wasn't a mess, but the prince refused to release his grip on me.

His cock pressed into my abdomen, and he was still very much ready. He continued scowling at his brother, but Nuwin only raised his hands in apology.

"Father's asking. I figured it would be better if I found you versus him."

Norivun's wings extended slightly, shielding me completely from view as I straightened my gown more.

Mother Below, I'd nearly fucked the crown prince—the very male who'd *murdered my family.*

My cheeks burned in humiliation.

"Ilara?" The prince looked down at me again. My mind was such a jumbling mess. "Lara," he said so quietly that I almost didn't hear him. "I have to—"

"Here he is. I knew he was still out here." Michas appeared behind Nuwin, and his eyes widened when he saw how closely the prince and I stood. "Ock, did we interrupt something?"

"No," Nuwin said quickly, *too* quickly. Michas retrieved his jacket from the ground as Nuwin forced a bright smile. "The crown prince was just about to head inside. Weren't you, brother?"

The prince stiffened.

"Shall I escort Lady Seary?" Michas offered.

"*No,*" the prince growled, and his aura pounded out of him.

"You intend to have her at your side while . . ." Michas let his words hang, his eyebrows rising.

I gave both the prince and his brother a confused look as I continued to relentlessly chastise myself for what I'd done.

"What's happening?" I finally asked.

Michas grinned. "The king is going to announce Prince Norivun's potential betrotheds. Didn't you hear? Tonight is the beginning of the Rising Queen Trial."

CHAPTER 26

The *Rising Queen Trial*? What?

I brought a hand to my forehead. No, I hadn't known. Or . . . maybe I had. I briefly remembered Finnley and Birnee talking last month about an upcoming trial in the capital. Perhaps this had been what they'd been speaking of.

"Time to go, Nori," Nuwin said under his breath, his words soft and full of apology.

The prince gave me one last look, a look full of heat and savage longing, before he snarled and ripped himself away from me.

Numbly, I followed, and Nuwin stayed at my side as the prince prowled back into the throne room.

But Prince Norivun kept glancing over his shoulder, kept eyeing me, then his brother, then Michas, as a permanent mask of fury painted itself on his features.

At least I had the foresight to return the crown prince's jacket right before he came into everyone's view, but my mind was still swimming, and my body was still throbbing by what had just happened.

And what in the realms *had* happened? As much as I didn't want to admit it, I'd just kissed the prince. Worse, I'd wanted to do much more than that and probably would have if we hadn't been interrupted.

And now he was going to meet his betrothed?

A nauseating feeling swept through me, and I barely had the wherewithal to put one foot in front of the other without tripping. Thankfully Nuwin seemed to understand my state of mind because he kept a firm grip on me and prevented me from falling.

Inside the castle, the dancing and music had stopped, and the center of the room had been cleared.

All of the attending fae formed a U-shape around the throne, the great crowd expanding all of the way to the back of the room. Lined up at the front of the group were three females.

My breath caught as I surveyed their opulent gowns, jeweled necks, and flawless makeup. Behind them stood nobles, who I guessed were their parents.

"Ah, he's finally decided to join us," the king called.

A tittering of laughter rose from the crowd as King Novakin beckoned Prince Norivun forward. Another sickening feeling swept through me when I beheld the three females again. He was to marry one of them?

My stomach clenched, and sweat lined my palms. Gods, what was wrong with me? What did I care who the prince married?

Another pulse of the prince's aura shot out of him as his scowl deepened.

"I'm sorry, brother," Nuwin whispered. "I know it's not what you wanted."

"It doesn't matter what I want." The prince nudged closer to his brother. "But by gods, Nuwin, if you pull another stunt like you did earlier and take her somewhere I can't protect her, I'll have your head."

For the first time since meeting the prince's brother, Nuwin didn't smile cheekily or reply with a facetious quip. He nodded gravely. "I won't. On my honor."

Nuwin moved closer to my side as the crown prince glanced briefly at me. His gaze was weighted as fire and ice seemed to clash within his soul.

Without another word, he proceeded to the throne as the three sets of parents proudly displayed their daughters. The young females all stepped forward, smiling and curtsying prettily.

A male fairy stood in front of them and bowed deeply. "Your Majesty, I have scoured the continent these past five winters, and I have returned with the most blessed females of our realm. I present them to you now."

Dozens of the capital's females, the ones who'd been dressed so finely and had looked so hopeful, all gave sniveling and envious looks toward the three. Nuwin had been right. None of them were in the running.

"Thank you, Sir Featherton," the king replied. "Proceed."

Prince Norivun grew even more rigid as Sir Featherton swept an arm in a flourishing motion, and the three sets of parents and their daughters stepped forward.

All of the females had beautiful black wings—wings I would never have.

"And their affinities?" the king asked.

"Lady Meegana Ockson, daughter of Harrivee Territory, has been blessed with three," Sir Featherton replied.

The female in the yellow gown held her chin high as Sir Featherton gushed, "She has an elemental affinity—water—a shapeshifting affinity, and she also possesses a sensory affinity—sound."

"What does she shift into?" the king asked shrewdly.

"A colantha, Your Majesty," Sir Featherton replied, bowing deeply.

A murmur erupted among the crowd at hearing she could transform into a large jungle cat, and the king nodded approvingly.

"Very nice." The king glanced at the next. "And what about her?"

The female's father and mother ushered the second female forward. A purple gown covered her head to toe, but she moved her lithe figure with purpose and swagger. Her silver hair was pinned back with clips, which amplified her delicate features and rosebud mouth. The female looked innocent and fragile, but a sharp gleam coated her eyes as she sized up the two females beside her. I recognized that look all too well. It was a look Vorl would have before he did something hideous to me.

Sir Featherton waved toward her dramatically. "Lady Georgyanna Endalaver, daughter of Kroravee Territory, has been blessed with *four* affinities, Your Majesty."

A huge eruption of whispers followed that statement. The king sat up straighter in his seat as the queen made a sound in her throat. A sharp look from the king had her quietening before he addressed Sir Featherton. "Four? Are you sure?"

"Indeed," Sir Featherton replied. "Lady Georgyanna's elemental affinity is fire, and she also possesses an electric affinity, a constructo affinity, and an emotional affinity—manipulation."

"This has been tested?" the king asked.

Sir Featherton bowed again. "Yes, Your Majesty. All three have been thoroughly tested before I brought them here."

The king tapped his chin. "A colantha shapeshifter is quite rare, which could make up for only having three affinities. But to have four . . ." He tapped his chin again and assessed the last female. "And her?"

The female's parents shuffled nervously as Sir Featherton replied, "Lady Beatrice Leafton, daughter of Prinavee Territory. Blessed with three affinities. An elemental affinity—earth, a sensory affinity of sight, and her strongest affinity, which is telekinesis."

An eruption of whispers broke out over that. Psychic affinities were also rare, especially telekinesis.

"Only three, but very powerful." The king leaned back in his chair, frowning. "I had hoped to find a female with more affinities, but I suppose we must make do with what we have."

A scattering of laughter rose from the crowd, but the females' parents all wore affronted expressions while the queen continued to sit rigidly. I squeezed Nuwin's arm. He placed his hand over mine, his expression resigned.

As if sensing the parents' displeasure, the king smiled widely. "Welcome to the Court of Winter, daughters of the Solis continent. All of you are worthy mates for my son."

The females released collective sighs of relief as their parents' discontented demeanors turned prideful.

Sir Featherton bowed smugly. "Indeed, Your Majesty."

❄ 307 ❄

The king cast a side-eye my way, but then his attention drifted to my wingless back, and his interest withered as he returned to the three before him.

As though knowing the Trial had begun to become the prince's betrothed, the three females all eyed Norivun. They wore masks of curiosity, interest, and even possession. The one in the purple—Lady Georgyanna Endalaver—practically looked like a colantha herself, even though that wasn't her affinity, but she kept casting feral glances at the other two females, as though sizing up her competition.

"How many affinities does the crown prince have?" I tried to ask Nuwin lightly, but that throbbing sensation had grown in my stomach again. I felt hot. Itchy. And seeing these females look at the crown prince as though they wanted to mate with him right here and now . . . It felt like fire flooded my veins.

"Six," Nuwin replied.

My head snapped back. *Six?* I sputtered, then coughed lightly to hide my surprise. Six affinities. I'd never heard of anyone that powerful in all of my life.

"And your mother?"

"Five," Nuwin replied.

I glanced at the queen, who seemed so harmless and docile. To think that the female possessed that kind of power.

"And the king?"

"Only two, hence, why he sought out my mother."

As if sensing that we'd been talking about him, Prince Norivun cast a side-eye my way. His eyes were bright. Raw.

My heart beat harder and harder until blood thundered through my ears. Why was he looking at me like that? And why was I suddenly wishing that these three females would vanish?

"I need some air," I said to Nuwin, discreetly removing myself from his side.

"Ilara," Nuwin called, reaching for me. "Wait!"

But I'd already slipped past him and headed toward the doors that led to the ice topiary maze.

Nobody paid attention to me as I wove through the crowd. It seemed that the court's fickle interest in me had already passed, given the arrival of the three new females.

I slid by everyone as that throbbing sensation grew in me more and more. *Air. I needed air.*

I burst through the doors, barely having the wherewithal to ensure they closed behind me, and then I was running across the cobblestones toward the maze as the first firework appeared above me. The celebration was beginning. The prince was to marry. And all I could picture were those three beautiful females with unrivaled power all vying for the prince's hand.

He was to marry one of them.

And I was to be his slave. His slave to prevent a war.

Air. I need air. I can't breathe.

I sucked in breath after breath, but no matter what I did, the fire inside me grew until it felt like I was burning alive.

Another firework burst above me and then another. Voices carried to me, and I realized the throne room doors had spilled open, and the attendants were coming out to enjoy the show as they commenced the beginning of the Trial that would determine the prince's fiancée and eventually the next queen to the Court of Winter.

I quickly moved behind an ice sculpture so nobody would see me, then pushed away from the sculpture and took off around the maze. Nuwin called for me again, but I didn't stop.

The laughter and conversation carried on behind me as more and more fireworks exploded above while the crowd jeered and roared their approval.

Run. Just run.

I careened around a corner and was about to start searching for the prince's private wing when a dark figure emerged in my path.

I skidded to a stop, my feet sliding across the slick cobblestones, and I nearly collided with the stranger when strong hands enclosed me. Familiar hands. And then a scent hit me. A scent that I would know anywhere.

Cloves and tobacco.

Terror slid through my veins as I gazed up at my village's archon. Vorl smirked, his dark expression highlighted by another burst of fireworks.

I tried to pull back, tried to make sense of how he could be here and now. This couldn't be happening. I must be dreaming.

"Let me go!" I proclaimed, as memories of the seasons of abuse that I'd suffered under this male's hands reared within me.

"I think not." His hand shot up, gripping me by the throat before he pinned me to the maze's wall.

I clawed at him, trying to free myself as that throbbing sensation grew and grew inside me until it felt as though something were about to be born, unleashed, or awoken, but I *couldn't breathe.* I had no air.

No air.

Vorl winced when my nails raked down his skin, but I didn't cut him deep enough for him to let me go.

"I wondered what he did with you," Vorl hissed as his mouth met my ear. He pushed his large body against mine as his wings extended, blocking his activities from anyone who might happen to walk by. His erection speared my abdomen, his excitement at what he was doing evident.

"Wa . . . why . . . here?" I choked out. Thrashing, I clawed at him more as he lifted me, dangling me above the ground.

"Why am I in the capital, or why am I here pursuing you?" With his free hand, he scratched his chin, his cruel mask telling me he was relishing his show of power. "I'm in the capital because a courier arrived in our village earlier this week, stating that the crown prince requested Cailis's presence at the Court of Winter. Naturally, as our village's archon, I felt it was my duty to accompany her to ensure she had safe passage. And what can I say. I've missed you, sweet Ilara. I wanted to see you for myself."

He pushed into me again, and his tongue shot out, tasting my skin.

I wanted to gag in disgust, but I couldn't breathe, and my thoughts turned with rapid fire to my sister. I hadn't seen her.

"Where . . . Cailis?" That burning sensation grew even more in me until it felt as though a volcano was about to erupt from my core, but it was just on the precipice. There, but not within reach.

"She's probably in her chambers, waiting until the morning to seek you out as she was directed by the castle staff when we arrived. They said you were busy this evening but would be free in the morn." His eyes narrowed, taking on a predatory gleam. "Imagine my surprise when I saw you tonight, parading alongside the crown prince as though you're something special. And I see that you commissioned a fairy who actually has strong enough magic to glamour your hair."

He leaned in closer until his hot breath wafted over my skin. "Do you really think that will hide that you're defective? Doesn't your wingless back already say that? Or is that how you won him? Have you whored yourself to him as you pretended to be something you're not? Is that why he's so enraptured with you?" Vorl's hand tightened more around my throat. "And to think you never gave me that sweet cunt between your legs. But did you give it to him?"

His hand locked down harder. So incredibly painfully, much tighter than he ever had before.

A gurgling sensation came from my throat, and then nothing at all. My windpipe was crushing. Closing completely. I was going to die. I knew it. I couldn't fight him. I never had been able to.

Stars danced on the edge of my vision as I pictured Cailis waiting somewhere within the castle, then I pictured my parents and brother.

This was how my end was to be. Hidden by a maze at the Court of Winter, while everyone else celebrated the next era of succession.

"Answer me!" Vorl slammed my head against the ice wall, and I blacked out for the briefest moment, but then his grip loosened just enough for me to suck in a whisper of air.

"Let. Go!" I choked on the words and clawed relentlessly at his hands, but his face darkened with rage, and his grip remained.

"I think not." He wrapped his other hand around my throat, and in that moment, I knew his intention.

He was going to kill me.

He was going to murder me.

I would never see Cailis again.

The sheer terror that evoked brought a new round of panic into me. I clawed frantically. Hit. Kicked. Thrashed. I took every ounce of fight left in me as I tried to tear from his limbs and break free.

And just when my vision threatened to swim black again, a crack opened within me. A giant fissure. It pried my chest in two as a barrel of power shot out of me.

Vorl roared in pain just as footsteps came running from around the maze's corner.

"Ilara!" Nuwin called.

I fell to the ground as Vorl flew off me. Erupting magic poured from me as fire and wind flew in a tornadoing spiral around my frame, and then I was stumbling to a stand as the prince's illusion magic cracked all around me.

A cataclysmic explosion of power engulfed my body. And then the prince was there. The king. The court. They were all watching as my village's archon staggered to his feet.

Vorl pointed at me accusingly, his face twisted in pain. "She tried to kill me! She's a murderer!"

But when Vorl tried to cast an illusion over my throat, my magic ripped through it, and that was when I felt the prince's power rise.

"You dared to touch her? To hurt her again?" the prince roared as a snarl of absolute fury split his lips. And then he was at my side, traveling to me on a gust of air.

"Lara," he whispered. His gaze traveled over my face, down my throat, oscillating between fury and fear.

"I'm okay," I managed to croak.

Gasps and cries came from the court as the fireworks continued. Explosions felt as though they came from everywhere.

"I'm sorry," the prince whispered. His face twisted in pain

before that mind-numbing rage coated it again. "I should have protected you."

Power still spiraled around me as shocked whispers and shouts came from the crowd. I was out of control. I didn't know what was happening, but fire and wind still swirled around me, bathing me in light and air that the prince seemed immune to. Or maybe it was purposefully cushioning him. I didn't know.

"Nuwin, hold her," the prince said, his expression savage as he handed me off to his brother.

Nuwin supported my weight as the prince flew to Vorl on the same beat. Rage contorted the crown prince's features as he grabbed Vorl by his shirt and lifted him up. Prince Norivun's affinity rose with a vengeance as a look of sheer terror covered my archon's face.

"You dared hurt her?" The deadly calmness of Norivun's words sent shivers down my spine, and the quietness of his question was more terrifying than any anger that could pour from his lips. "She's *mine*, and you touched her?"

"I didn't! I would never—"

The prince slammed his head into Vorl, nearly knocking the archon out, and then his affinity was like death on wings. Vorl let out a torturous bellow as an answering throb of power came from my gut when Vorl's head lolled back. The archon's body seized. His eyes rolled white.

Something wispy rose from his body. Translucent and sheer.

Vorl's body slackened in the prince's grip as that shimmering shadow rose higher and higher.

Dying.

The archon was dying.

Prince Norivun was sucking his soul, his face cold, the deadly intent in his expression clear.

"No," I whispered. My affinity shot out of me and latched onto that floating shadow, as though I'd somehow commanded it to do so. Vorl's soul stopped. It hovered mid-air, and my conscience tugged between death and life.

I could let him go.

I could let the prince finish what he'd started.

But despite all that Vorl had done to me, despite all of his tormenting, bullying, and vindictive rage, *this* wasn't the answer. Punishment, yes, but not death. There had been too much death.

"No, my prince," I croaked quietly as my throat ached.

The prince whipped toward me, just as my magic fully wrapped around Vorl's soul. Phantom hands enclosed his departing spirit as an instinct awakened within me. It was the same sensation I'd sensed in High Liss when the prince had killed the shapeshifter and then when the guard had nearly died at my arrival to the castle.

This. This was what I could do. My affinity didn't create *orem*. It created life. The prince was slightly wrong about my power. Only the gods could create natural *orem*, but my life-giving affinity was able to replenish our land's natural *orem* while also giving life to plants and souls that were being taken to the divine realms. My affinity was the opposite of the prince's momentous power.

I grabbed Vorl's spirit and wrenched it from the air before slamming it back into the archon.

Vorl's eyes opened wide as his mouth gaped in a sudden inhale. Shocked screams and muffled cries came from the crowd as the prince's eyes widened in shock.

I staggered under the depth of magic that had just been pulled from me, but Nuwin supported me, holding me up.

The prince dropped Vorl as though he'd been burned. He stared at his hands, disbelief lining his features as the crowd erupted in a flurry of shouts and hissed comments.

"What is she?"

"What did she do?"

Their comments drifted toward me, but I barely heard them.

I swayed away from the maze, toward Vorl as he sat on the ground, breathing but unconscious. When I reached his side, the prince shifted closer to me.

"Ilara?" he said quietly, a tremor to his tone.

But then the magnitude of what I'd done stole all of the energy from me. It felt as though a veil descended over my eyes, and then the ground was rushing up to greet me.

A scream came from the crowd as a crescendo of fireworks exploded in the court's finale.

The last thing I remembered was someone catching me before my head cracked onto the ice.

And then I remembered nothing at all.

CHAPTER 27

I awoke to the feel of soft hands dabbing a cool cloth over my face. Sweet scents of juniper blossoms tickled my nose as a strum of immense magic pulsed around me.

"She's awakening." Daiseeum's sweet voice cut through the fog in my mind.

"Thank the Mother! Ilara? Can you hear me? I'm here." My sister's frantic words grew stronger and sharper with every breath she took.

"Cailis?" I croaked.

Another hand patted mine, then a male said, "She shall be all right. It's not as serious as you'd feared, my prince."

I briefly recognized Murl, the castle healer, and then warm hands were closing over mine as my sister and Daiseeum let go.

Strong, hard, unyielding hands. Those hands could only belong to one fairy.

I opened my eyes to see Prince Norivun hovering above me as he held my hands in his own.

"Blessed Mother," he breathed. His expression looked haggard, his hair tousled, his eyes bloodshot.

I glanced over his shoulder. I was in the Exorbiant Chamber, and Cailis stood to the side of my bed, her features twisting, but an intense rush of relief filled me at seeing her again. Nuwin was also in my room, along with the prince's four guards.

"What happened?" I brought a hand to my forehead as I struggled to remember how I ended up here and why all of them were looking at me as though I were at death's door.

And then it came crashing back.

Fireworks.

Vorl.

Being choked.

Air and Fire.

Creating *life*.

My breath sucked in. "What did I do?"

"What you did is fully manifest." Murl still stood to the side of my bed, wearing a stern expression. "Your affinities collided and were born at once. I've been told you had one affinity manifest in the previous weeks, but it seems there were others that wanted to be born."

My eyes widened more. "*Affinities*? I have more than one?"

"You have at least four, possibly more," the prince replied. "You have an air element, fire element, the ability to create *orem*, and the ability to—" His brow furrowed.

"Return a soul," I whispered. A vivid memory slammed to the front of my mind. The prince had enacted his affinity on Vorl. If not for me, the archon would be dead. I'd wielded enough power to counteract the prince's strongest affinity. *Blessed Mother indeed.* "What happened to Vorl?"

The prince's gaze dipped to my throat, to where bruises no doubt lay unless Murl had healed them. His lip curled as his aura pounded out of him. "He's been detained for assaulting a lady of the court."

I straightened more as the soft covers swirled around me. "But I'm not a lady."

"You are now."

I frowned. "What?"

The four guards all ruffled their wings from behind the prince. Nish scowled.

The crown prince watched me closely. "The king has officially appointed you as a lady of the court."

Ice slid through my veins. "Why would he do that?"

"Because you're to join the Rising Queen Trial." Nuwin smiled, looking quite pleased. "Only a lady can become a queen."

"*What?*"

The prince winced. "I shall try not to be offended by your reaction."

"But I don't actually have four affinities. I think my affinity that replenishes the *orem* is actually the same affinity that pulls a soul back into a body. I believe what it does is create life, in our land and in fae. So if it's true that I have affinities for two elements, then I only have *three* affinities total. Surely, that doesn't make me a contender in the Trial."

The prince's scowl deepened as Nish sniggered. Haxil cut his fellow guard a sharp glare.

"Three affinities is still enough to have you in the Trial," the prince said stiffly.

"But why would the king want that?" I pressed. Cailis murmured her agreement. I could only imagine what my sister was thinking as the Death Master—the murderer of our family—held my hands.

"My father saw your powers manifest." Prince Norivun lifted a lock of my hair, and with a jolt, I realized it was black again. "My illusion will no longer cover you, not unless you allow it. You're too strong, and he saw that. So as of now, Lady Ilara Seary, daughter of Mervalee Territory, you've been made a lady of the court and have officially been entered into the Trial to become the next queen."

"But then I might have to . . . marry you."

His face slackened, his expression impossible to read. "Would that be so bad?"

Cailis hissed, her eyes burning as they locked with hatred onto the prince.

Tears threatened to overwhelm me at all that had happened, but then I remembered our kiss, the electric attraction between us, but he'd *killed my family*.

I glanced at Cailis. Her hatred for the prince was nearly palpable, exactly as I had felt only a month ago.

I snatched my hands away from the crown prince. I couldn't marry him. Not even if I'd seen other sides to him, sides that weren't entirely evil. Because how could I possibly marry the male who'd killed my parents and brother?

The prince's eyes shuttered, and his hands clenched into fists as that swirling throbbing began in my gut again. *Blessed Mother*. With a start, I realized that feeling in my stomach was my magic.

Taking deep breaths, I tried to calm it, but anger stirred in me. "I can't marry you. You murdered my family."

Prince Norivun's mouth opened, then closed. He remained silent, but an answering pulse of his aura stroked mine.

Nuwin let out a low whistle as the prince's guards all took a step closer to my bed. And that was when it hit me, why the four were here.

My power now rivaled the prince's. I'd *stopped* the prince from enacting his soul-sucking rage on Vorl, and they now saw me as a potential *threat* to their prince.

I inched back, pressing my spine into the bed's headboard. "What if I don't want to marry you? What if I refuse to enter the Trial that could make me the next queen?"

Prince Norivun's jaw muscle ticked. "You cannot. You've been commanded by the king of the Solis continent to partake."

"But what about replenishing our continent's *orem*? I thought that was my purpose?"

"It's now *one* of your purposes but not the only one. You'll start training with your tutor this week while continuing to travel to fields with me each day as planned. We'll work to replenish our continent's *orem*, but that's not all you'll do. You'll also be entering the Trial. Your days will be busy and tiring, but the king has commanded it."

I clenched the sheets in my hands, balling them into fists. "But we made a bargain. You're sealed by magic. You promised that if I replaced the land's *orem* that I could return home."

"I did."

"But you're saying now that I have to enter this Trial as well."

His expression remained impossible to read, yet his eyes burned like sapphires. "I'm afraid the two are mutually exclusive."

"So I'm to be a slave to this court. It doesn't matter if I save our land?"

"You'll not be a slave. You may one day be queen. And while

I cannot stop you from returning to your home after you replenish our continent's *orem*—you're correct that the bargain protects you in that aspect—I cannot promise you that you won't be a married female when you do so."

"Married to you," I whispered as shock crept through me.

He nodded, and for a moment, a look of wildness shone in his eyes. The prince wanted that. For whatever reason, he wanted *me*.

But for the life of me, I didn't know if I felt that in return for him. Too much had been done. Too many lives had been taken at his hand, which meant I needed to find a way out of this Trial.

BOOK TWO IN FAE OF SNOW & ICE

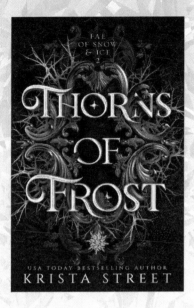

Being entered into the Rising Queen Trial is equivalent to death. If I win, I'll marry my enemy. If I lose, I'll marry another fae of the king's choosing. Either way, my freedom is lost unless I find a way to escape.

Intent on fleeing, I train my new affinities and learn what's needed to survive while pretending to vie for the throne. With my sister at my side, I know we'll find a way to prevent my enslavement to the Court of Winter.

But the crown prince has other ideas. As Prince Norivun's interest in me grows, I'm determined to avoid his allure, until he reveals sides of himself he'd kept hidden—sides that make me want to succumb to the innate need burning inside me.

Now that his secrets are laid bare, devastating consequences loom for me and him. Consequences that not even the powerful prince could have foreseen.

THANK YOU

Thank you for reading *Court of Winter* book one in the *Fae of Snow &
Ice* series.

If you would like to know what Norivun was thinking when he first met
Ilara, and you live in the USA or Canada, sign up for Krista's new
release text alerts, and you'll receive a FREE digital copy of Chapter 3
from *Court of Winter*, told from Norivun's point of view.

**Simply text the word NORI to 888-403-4316 on your
mobile phone.**

Message and data rates may apply, you'll only receive a text when Krista
releases a new book, and you can opt out at any time. Or, if you live
outside of North America, visit Krista's website to learn more.

www.kristastreet.com/noribonus

To learn more about Krista's other books and series, visit her website.
Links to all of her books, along with links to her social media platforms,
are available on every page.

Made in the USA
Middletown, DE
30 January 2024

48844012R00203